BOOKS BY ALVIN JOHNSON

NOVELS

SHORT STORIES

AUTOBIOGRAPHY

NONFICTION

A TOUCH OF COLOR

A TOUCH OF COLOR

AND

OTHER TALES

BY

ALVIN JOHNSON

ATHENEUM

NEW YORK
1963

TO MY DAUGHTERS

CONTENTS

A TOUCH OF COLOR

A
TOUCH
OF
COLOR

SHE STOOD on the station platform waiting for the train
to move on. At last it was gone. Before her was a
pleasant valley with a checkerboard of fields, corn knee
high, wheat and oats almost as high. A playful south
wind made lovely patterns in the wheat and oat fields.
At first a strong gust made a whole field show light
green. Then the gust split into a dozen air streams, each
patterning itself in the fields in light green. The gusts of
wind were heavy with the fragrance of flowers. Oh yes,
that grove of basswood. Around Chicago the basswood
had not been so fragrant.

"So this is Nebraska, Douglas Bluff," said Helena
Wilson to herself. "The pioneers called it God's country.

It looks like that."

She turned to look at the town. The railway station placed at the edge of the town presented a view of its whole anatomy.

There on one side was a little river. It had been crooked, no doubt, with bright clean water. It had been straightened, and Helena knew she would find it dirty for she knew progress. She just surmised it now.

Facing the river was a row of business places needing space, not style: the lumber yard, the flour mill, the slaughterhouse, ice company, coal yard, and the dumps for foundered wagons and shattered machinery.

On the town side was First Street, with little shops: the carpenter's, the upholsterer's, the printer's, Old Moe's Clothes Shop—it was incredible how many little concerns could find a place on this Nebraska street.

Second Street had all the big stores, on the river side. On the other side were the combination of shop and living quarters of the lawyers, doctors, bank clerks and other hard-working professionals. The third house from the west was the one she had leased by mail. It looked wonderful in the morning light. It was set back a fair distance from the street, a little gabled house with a balcony, its front entirely covered by climbing roses, now beginning to show scarlet pink bloom. Surely she would be happy there.

But she wanted to continue her survey of the town, which had been well Baedekered by her friend Josie in the Chicago shop. There was Third Street, the home of *the* people, the banker, the county judge, the proprietors of the big grocery store and the big hardware store, the big livestock buyer, the big corn and wheat buyer, and a number of retired capitalists who had bought up homesteads at five dollars an acre and sold them for thirty dollars.

Fourth Street was the home of aspirants to the order

of *the* people. Some were edging in. They had incomes, not yet very large. The houses were spacious, most of them clapboard painted white, with wide porches and pleasant balconies. Some of the houses were of stucco, timbered in the Nebraska Queen Anne pattern, with special emphasis on rectangles.

Fifth Street was one of small houses, occupied by artisans, clerks, school teachers and farmers who had retired on little. Above the street was a grassy slope and at its very top, overlooking the field checkerboard on the other side of the hill, was the most enormous house in town, red brick with a dozen turrets, round and square, topped with tall peaks or with little domes. The house dated back to the time a contractor paved First and Second Streets with brick and found he had an enormous supply of brick left over, which he could have for nothing, and a fine crew of workers the town could still keep on its payroll. Political reformers had raised a row about it, and the contractor had sold the house and moved to California. The house was now occupied by a pair of real aristocrats, a lawyer who had been aide-de-camp of Robert E. Lee, and his wife, a New Orleans lady who had inherited the profits from generations of slave owners and slave dealers. They called the house the Mansion. But the lower sort in town called it the Graft House.

Her survey of the town finished, Helena Wilson set out to visit the house she had rented by mail. On her way, she thought, she might find a printer's shop and have her sign set up in a card to be tacked on the door of her house. She was sure she would find a printer on First Street. And she had not passed five buildings when she found a sign: Bill Brown, Printer.

Bill was a stout, easy-built man, with a friendly, humorous face.

"What can I do for you, young lady?"

"I want you to print me a sign I can put up on my door."

"Sure." He handed her a scratch pad. She wrote.

He read aloud, "Helena Wilson, B.Sc. Dress Designer."

"Well," he said, " 'Helena.' You spell it with an a or an e? Most girls here spell it with e."

"I spell it with a," she said with finality.

"And will you tell me what those letters B.Sc. mean?"

"Bachelor of Science."

"You a bachelor? Gee whiz! I took you for a pretty young woman."

"Thank you. Bachelor of Science is just a college degree."

"I swan. You a college girl? Well." He read again. "Dress designer. A fancy word for dressmaker?"

"No. I may make dresses, but I may design them for others to make."

"Oh, I see. You are a fashion expert."

"No. Of course I know the fashions, and take account of them when I'm designing."

The printer rubbed his eyebrows. "All right. You wait a few minutes and I'll have your card."

In an incredibly short time he was back with a neat little card: Helena Wilson, B.Sc., Dress Designer.

"I heard you have rented the Rose Cottage on Second Street. The door frame is soft pine; you can put on your sign with thumb tacks. You'll need four but you better take six, if you drop one or two. And you owe me a quarter."

A quarter? In Chicago a printer would not touch his press for less than two dollars and a half. This was Nebraska. She liked it.

She liked it still better as she came up to her Rose Cottage. Besides a dozen full-blown roses the front exhibited a thousand buds. She'd have to push rose stems back, to make a place for her sign.

She unlocked the door and stepped in. Of course there was the musty smell of an unoccupied house. But she opened the doors and windows and the south wind, laden with basswood perfume, drove the musty smell out.

She surveyed the house. A pleasant parlor with dining room shut off by sliding doors. A neat capacious kitchen. Upstairs two pleasant bedrooms and a bathroom. And everything immaculately clean.

Had anyone in the East ever found so satisfactory a house to move into? But this was Nebraska, and she liked Nebraska still more.

The rear porch was encumbered with crates and boxes, Helena's furniture, household equipment and books. She stood looking at the rather formidable pile. A fourteen-year-old boy appeared around the corner of the house.

"Lady, can I help you get your things into the house?"

"That will be wonderful."

"I'll run home and get a hammer and chisel."

He was gone, but in five minutes he was back with the tools. Helena had never seen anyone work so fast. In two hours the furniture was in its place, the books in the book cases, the tableware on the table, the kitchenware where it belonged.

"You're a magician," she said. "What is your name?"

"I'm Billy Banks."

"Well Billy, what do I owe you?"

"Nothing. I like to help people."

"That's fine, and I'm very grateful to you. But I saw a nice ice cream palace down the street. I want you to take this dollar and treat your girl."

"I haven't got a girl."

"Every boy has a girl if he has a dollar."

He laughed. "That's so. I might take Sally Williams. She's a nice girl, awfully shy. She's in my high school class." He pocketed the silver dollar.

"That's just right."

"She thinks she's homely, but sometimes I don't think so."

"You know when they first take diamonds out of the mine they look like ordinary pebbles, not worth anything. The diamond cutter gets hold of the pebble, works on it a while and it comes out a dazzling jewel, worth many thousands of dollars. Often fourteen-year-old girls are like that diamond pebble."

"That's Sally," Billy said with conviction.

The next morning Billy brought Sally to Helena's door. "Maybe you could make a dress for Sally. My dad runs the clothing store, and he says he will pay for it if it doesn't come too high." He hurried away.

Yes, Sally was an uncut diamond, but a diamond. She had a fine white brow, too much concealed by her hair, both too long and too short. She had good brown eyes but lost their value by avoiding straightforward looks. Her nose and chin were good and her mouth would have been good it she hadn't developed the habit of pressing her lips together, producing lines that disfigured all the lower part of her face. As she was well grown she had been put into a dress designed for an eighteen-year-old, if anybody. She stooped habitually, to the distress of any dress.

"Sally," said Helena, "we are going to do an experiment. We're going to see what you are like when you have on a dress designed to show you your true self."

Sally made a movement nearly like a shudder. "I'm sorry, Miss Wilson, I don't think we can do anything. I didn't want to come. Bill just took me by the neck and pulled me here. You can't make me a dress without a big lot of money, and I haven't got any money, and I don't want to take money from Bill's father. My dad is a carpenter and he's been out of work for four months. He's a good dad. He'd give me money if he could. He can't."

"My dear Sally, you don't understand. There isn't any question of money here. I wouldn't take a cent from you. It's important for me to know can I dress fourteen-year-old girls so they will look like themselves? If you say so, I'll give you some money to let me try out my idea on you."

"Oh no!" cried Sally. Helena noted that she had already doffed much of her homeliness.

"You are fortunate that you are growing tall," said Helena. "Men don't care nowadays for 'my little sweetheart,' 'my little wife.' They like women tall enough to look them in the eyes, on a level." Immediately Sally began to straighten up.

"One thing you must do for me," Helena continued. "You must avoid stooping, when it's not absolutely necessary. I can't do a proper back of a dress if the wearer keeps stooping like an old woman." Sally's back straightened up immediately.

Helena took measurements, plenty of them. She wouldn't tell Sally what the color or the pattern of the cloth would be. Sally was to come back and try the dress on.

She came back in five days The dress was put on: "Can I wear such colors?" Sally asked herself, but knew she could. Was that herself she saw in the cheval glass, that lovely distinguished young lady? She couldn't believe it.

"What do you see in the glass?" Helena asked.

Sally stammered, "I . . . I . . ."

"You see a good girl. A modest girl. A true and faithful girl. A pretty girl."

"No," said Sally catching her breath.

"Yes. A pretty girl. And Sally, when you go to the high school I want you to remember, it is a pretty girl who is walking on your feet. You will do better in every class, if you remember that."

Sally couldn't think of a word to say, but Helena understood.

"Sally, you must go home. I'll wrap up your old dress, for you to put back in your closet, for the Salvation Army. Come again in October and we'll have another experiment on fall and winter clothes."

The next morning Billy turned up. "Say, lady, you cut the diamond all right. Everybody says, Sally is the prettiest girl in the summer school. And she's going to go steady with me. I ain't worth it, but I did bring her to you."

"Billy, you are worth it and so is Sally. Go steady: it's a long time before you could get married and maybe you won't get married. But it's a wonderful thing for boys and girls to go steady. They grow up into the kind of men and women that make this country."

He folded his arms, as if to embrace himself. "Say, Miss Wilson. My dad runs the biggest dress shop in town. He says Sally couldn't buy such a dress for twenty-five dollars. Says that when a snooty woman comes in and can't be satisfied with the dresses he has he'll send her to you."

Helena wanted to laugh. What she had done for Sally she had done, she thought, out of human kindness, but now it looked as if it were good business too.

Maybe, she thought, really good business is like that.

There couldn't be any customers yet, she thought. Why not ride out through the lovely Nebraska country? She went to the livery stable and hired a friendly horse, which seemed to have known her long and would enjoy going over hill and valley with her.

She had ridden out ten or twelve miles and was returning. As she neared the town she saw racing toward her a fine red pig and an owner chasing him. As the pig came up, Helena leaned over and gave it a little cut with her riding whip. The pig turned and ran toward his breathless master, but coming to some tall weeds by the fence dived into them and reappeared on the other side.

"That's where that devil of a pig got through," said the man, trying to recover his breath. He found an old post and thrust it through the tunnel the pig had made under the barbwire fence.

"That's what you can expect of Duroc Jerseys," said Helena. "They're awfully smart. Look at your neighbor's pig pen: Chester Whites. They don't make any trouble."

"For Pete's sake! A young woman who knows Duroc Jerseys and Chester Whites!"

"Yes, and she knows those Chester Whites make bigger hogs than your Duroc Jerseys. She knows, too, that your Duroc Jerseys make more pork out of a bushel of corn than your neighbor's Chester Whites."

"By George! That's what I say, but my neighbor says I can't prove it."

"You don't have to prove it. The Illinois College of Agriculture has worked out that problem scientifically."

"I never heard of that. But say! Aren't you the dressmaker who has come to town this week? And you know about hogs?"

"Next time you are in town come in and have a cup of tea with me, in the Rose Cottage. I'll show you how I come to know about Duroc Jerseys."

"My, I'm coming to town this afternoon."

"You know where the Rose Cottage is. Maybe we'd better know each other's names. I'm Helena Wilson."

"I'm Tom Hart. But I'm just a dirt farmer."

"You mean the kind of farmer that grows the crops that feed us all. The Chinese consider him the most honorable figure in society. And the Chinese are wise people."

At four Tom Hart dropped in. It shocked him that Helena didn't take cream and sugar in her tea. She explained that the Chinese and Japanese have been drinking tea for five thousand years but have never put cream or sugar in it. He tried straight tea, and it was pretty good, he admitted.

"You are going to tell me how you came to know Duroc Jerseys and Chester Whites."

She went to her bookcase and picked out a volume. "Here, Harris *On the Pig.*"

"Gosh! A whole book about pigs?"

"Oh, I have six other books on pigs. But Harris wrote for farmers; these other authors have written for professors and students. Harris is a little old-fashioned and has some ideas that have gone by the board. It's still the best book for a practical man like you. Let me lend it to you."

"I'm not a reader. I don't think I could follow it."

"Of course you could. Take it along, and bring it back when you've read it."

The next day was a Saturday, and Helena decided to spend the morning putting her books in order. But it was a day just warm enough for one to feel that this must have been the temperature of Eden. Instead of working, Helena sat in her most comfortable chair, looking out of the window at her climbing roses. There were hundreds of roses in full bloom, where there had been barely a dozen the day before. The soft breeze was heavily scented with rose and basswood perfume.

"I hope Nebraska doesn't have many days like this. How can one make a living, when living is so delicious?"

Her doorbell rang. She opened the door to admit a girl of perhaps eighteen or nineteen. A girl of good stature, who was obviously apologetic for being so tall. She walked with steps half length and rounded her shoulders to a debutante slouch. Her face could have been pretty, but subduing her eyes to debutante modesty and a simpering mishandling of what could have been a pretty mouth robbed her of the charm that was really hers.

"I'm Mildred Hart," she lisped, and giggled for no visible reason. "My brother Tom says you know all about pigs, and so you'd know how to make a dress for me. He thinks I'm awfully fat." More giggling.

"Oh, you're the sister of the young man I met yesterday, Tom Hart. You have a witty brother. What he told me was that you are a pretty girl with a fine figure I'd enjoy dressing up." Tom hadn't mentioned Mildred. But where was the harm in a little friendly invention?

Mildred giggled again. "That's like Tom. An awful flatterer and an awful tease. I need a new summer dress, badly. And Tom says, you could make me one in a jiffy. I've brought a sample of the cloth. Isn't that a pretty pattern?"

Helena looked at the sample. Sweet sixteen, again, sixteen ridden to exhaustion.

"My dear," she said, "I can't design a dress for you in that material. It is debutante material, but you are a young woman in the full flush of maturity."

The girl was angry. "I don't go to a dressmaker to have her tell me what kind of pattern I may wear."

"You shouldn't. But you haven't come to a dressmaker, but to a dress designer. Dress designing is an art. No artist will paint your picture as you want it, but as he sees you, with clearer eyes than you use in seeing yourself."

"I know what I want. And the boys like me in the kind of dresses I choose."

"Yes, the boys nibble. But do they bite?"

Mildred blushed. For anger. This interloper, throwing up to her the inefficacy of her technique? For the nibbling that fell short of biting had been her grief for at least three years.

"Listen, my dear," said Helena. "I don't think we can do business. You want what you want, and you can get it from any seamstress. I am restrained by my art from doing anything I don't consider right. But let us have a cup of tea. That is one thing we can have in common."

Mildred was still snarling over "Do they bite?"

Mildred had no liking for tea. But why not? Maybe she could get back at this insolent outsider.

"You call yourself a dress designer," she said as she sipped her tea. "What is the difference between a dress designer and a dressmaker?"

"A dress designer is an artist with an artist's responsibility. A dressmaker has only the responsibility of keeping the stitches true.

"A dress designer has just one object, to dress a woman to make her appear just what she is. The dress designer's work is a failure unless the woman she dresses is more nearly herself than she had been before.

"Every person in the world is unique. There are millions of people in the world, but in all the millions there is not one who is a duplicate of you. Your uniqueness is a marvel. And the dress designer is nothing unless she can discover that uniqueness and bring it out."

"But suppose I am a little piggy, as my brother sometimes says. Would you design a little piggy dress for me?"

"Yes; but not till I understood the little piggy, with all its honesty and charm."

"Well, suppose you show me a sample of the dress you think I ought to wear."

"All right. Here is one."

"You want to make me look like a schoolma'am."

"Not a bad figure to look like, if you want to look like somebody else. But we can design a dress that makes you look like yourself, yourself stripped of all the imitations of other persons one picks up unconsciously."

"Maybe," said Mildred. "It won't hurt to try. If I don't like the dress I can give it to our hired girl."

However deeply Mildred had resented Helena's suggestions as to how she should carry her figure and order the expression of her face, she followed the suggestions when she put on the new dress. What she saw in the mirror was no longer the shop-worn debutante, but the tall, graceful figure of a girl in the first bloom of womanhood. Her eyes were frank and grave, her lips seriously composed but ready to flash out in a smile. Could that charming young lady be herself, Mildred?

"Well, I guess it will do," she said.

"Yes," said Helena, a bit nettled by Mildred's ungracious acceptance of her art. "It *will* do. And be on your guard. They will bite."

Mildred frowned. But she glanced at her image in the glass and smiled.

The girls of Mildred's set had no reservations. Two of them came to the Rose Cottage the next day. Mildred had warned them, Helena was very hoity toity and would brush aside any preferences they had for color or pattern. They expressed no preferences. And in a few days they walked away in new dresses that seemed to them something that raised them toward the level of *the* people.

More girls came. Helena was swift with her needle, but her customers were inundating her. She had to have help. And she found it through Billy Banks, who dropped in from time to time, to boast of the remarkable progress Sally was making in her studies. Billy told her of a little seamstress working in his father's store, mending the defects in dresses the salesmen couldn't explain away. There wasn't much of such work, and the seamstress was starving. Billy's father thought Helena could use her.

Of course she could. Soon she had the seamstress installed in one of her bedrooms, sewing away for dear life and loving the job.

Not only girls but young matrons were coming in for dresses. But neither girls nor matrons came from *the* people, the Pathfinder Park set.

Pathfinder Park, Helena soon learned, was the exclusive possession of *the* people, who generously opened it to everybody for the May and October festivals. It was a tract of gently sloping land, backed by a steep hillside forested with walnut and burr oak. General Fremont had camped in the shade of the trees, on his way west, to find a path through the mountain country to the Pacific Northwest. On the traditional spot of Fremont's camp a group of prosperous citizens had built a casino, with billiard rooms in the basement, a large hall for dances, and many rooms equipped with card tables where men played poker and ladies played royal whist, introduced by Mrs. Winslow who had learned from the French gentry of New Orleans that royal whist was the game that solaced the declining years of Talleyrand.

The Pathfinder Park was dominated by the Winslows, proprietors of the Mansion, "the Graft House on the Hill." Hugh Winslow, the former aide-de-camp of Robert E. Lee, was a lawyer who had made himself extremely popular in a community otherwise dominated by veterans of the Federal armies. Hugh Winslow had modeled his demeanor and his principles of life on Robert E. Lee, a fine general indeed, but highly valued as the finest gentleman America had ever produced. The courtesy with which Hugh Winslow treated friend and opponent alike set a standard for the whole community.

Still loyal to the South, Hugh Winslow accepted the

victory of the North with good grace. America had remained a united nation, for which he was thankful. No man would think of recalling Winslow's career as a rebel officer. Sometimes an overheated abolitionist lady would inundate him with a diatribe on the inhuman behavior of the rebel forces. "Why don't you answer her?" someone might ask.

"A gentleman never contradicts a lady," he would say. And this principle entered into the code of the community.

The principle was of great value to his wife. At every meeting of *the* people, Henrietta Winslow fought the Civil War over, to a different conclusion. As she saw it, the South had won the war. But Mr. Lincoln had drafted a ruck of worthless foreigners, Germans and Scandinavians, to supply forces for that low tanner, Grant. These foreigners fought like butchers, and finally the Southern gentlemen had to give up.

She knew what those beasts were like. She had been in New Orleans when it was occupied by Federal troops under Beast Butler, who had actually issued an order that the soldiers should treat the finest ladies as women of the town.

There were two veterans among *the* people who had served under Butler in the occupation. They knew what the order actually was, and what the provocation that led to it. But they could not contradict a lady.

Henrietta Winslow was most eloquent on the Negro problem. It had been a great mistake to free the Negroes, slaves by nature and God's will. A New Orleans scholar had proved that the Negro is not of the human race. Just as the ass was not of the race of the horse. Cross horse and ass, the offspring is a mule, infertile. Cross white and black, the offspring might be fertile, for the time. Cross them again, the quadroon, the octaroon would be fertile. But beyond the octaroon the sterility of the hybrid showed itself.

"My dear," said Hugh Winslow, "what you have said is a wonderful illustration of the working of the popular mind on points of law. In many states by act of legislature and in other states by judicial decision, any person with less than one-sixteenth of Negro blood is white. If a person of one-sixteenth Negro blood marries a white she or he can't have Negro children, but they can have white children ad lib."

"Yes, and they may be black as the ace of spades," said Henrietta triumphantly. She had had the last word.

Twice a year Henrietta Winslow led a group of matrons and young girls to New Orleans to have dresses designed by a charming French modiste and executed by Negro seamstresses—"the best labor force in the world if you keep them in their place."

There could be no chance for Helena Wilson to break into the trade of *the* people. But she had more than she could do without it.

She was succeeding. But she had been too certain of success to find it very thrilling. Indeed, she was getting a bit tired of measuring maids and matrons for dresses and racking her mind for patterns and colors to give distinction to a woman who appeared, at least at first, to be totally devoid of distinction. And the fragrance of the fields drew her powerfully. It was the time when oats and wheat were in bloom, inconspicuously, but forming patterns with new shades of color under the caressing breeze.

Returning after a ten-mile ride she saw something unusual in a field of oats. In the center of the field there was a spot of ripe oats, as it appeared. She knew that the plant breeders were trying to develop a strain of oats that ripened early. It would be useful in the far north. Could this be the strain? There was no fence, and she rode down at the edge of the field. Leaving her horse to browse unlawfully on the oats, she walked out to the ripe spot.

Chinch bugs! Millions of them. They had killed the oats in the central spot and were now working around the edges. Every green oat stalk was blackened with thousands of insects sucking the sap.

She returned to her horse and rode back to the highway. A lone horseman was approaching. He nodded.

"I beg pardon for interrupting your thoughts," she said. "But do you know the farmer who owns this oats field?"

"Yes, I do."

"He's on the point of losing his whole crop. You see that dry spot? Chinch bugs."

He looked incredulous. "I've read of chinch bugs. I never heard of them in this country. I wouldn't know them if I saw them."

"You'd know them if you smelled them."

"How so?"

"Come down with me into the field. You'll find out."

He turned his horse and they rode side by side along the field. He bounced off his horse, landing lightly as a bird on his feet. What a figure of a horseman, she thought. Yes, she knew who he was.

They walked through the oats to the dry spot.

"Now do you smell them?"

"I smell something I shouldn't say in the presence of a lady."

"You smell bed bugs. That's the smell of the chinch bug. See what they're doing to those green stems."

"For Heaven's sake! But what can he do about it?"

"He can set fire to the dead oats, the fire will kill the chinch bugs around the edges, and the rest of his crop will be saved."

The man turned toward the nearby farm house and shouted, "Bill Stone!" Helena had never heard so loud a voice.

A thin voice from the house responded. "Hey!"

"You're losing your crop of oats. Come here. Bring some matches."

Bill Stone ran up through the oats.

"Look at those chinch bugs. Millions of them. Burn 'em out or you lose your crop."

"But I don't want to burn up my oats."

"Just this dry stuff that's dead anyway. The lady says it will scorch the bugs around the edges."

"Maybe."

"Maybe! You deserve to lose your crop. You're losing some of it every minute."

"Well," Bill Stone drew a match from the box.

"Not here," said Helena. "Fire it against the wind. It won't run far in the green oats."

Against the wind or with it, the fire roared over the dead oats and singed the green stems that had been black with chinch bugs. Millions of insects had perished. No doubt a few had escaped, but not enough to do serious damage.

"I've lost three acres of crop," Bill Stone said mournfully. "On my best land."

"You're wonderful," said Helena's new acquaintance. "A lady who knows ten times as much about farming as yokels like you and me comes along and saves most of your crop. Seventeen acres of it. And all the thanks you give her is to mourn over what you had lost anyway."

"That's all right," said Helena. "When I lose something I don't comfort myself by thinking it could be worse. If I break my arm I won't be rejoicing because it wasn't my neck."

"That's right, lady," said Bill Stone. "But I do appreciate what you've done for me."

The visitors returned to their horses and rode along side by side, saying nothing. It gave Helena a chance to size up her companion. He was a very large man, over six feet tall, but so well proportioned, with his broad shoulders and great chest, that you wouldn't think of him as a tall man. He had a strong neck, like a column, she thought, and a well-sculptured head. The most striking feature was his eyes, large, beautifully blue, with the quality that made you feel light from them was shining on your face when he looked at you.

Joel Arbuthnot was surely his name. Helena's friend in the Chicago shop had described him.

"Here's your Rose Cottage," he said. "Suppose I take the horses down to the livery stable."

"And come back for a cup of tea."

"In ten minutes."

Helena dismounted and held out the strap of her bridle. Joel caught it and rode on.

He was back in less than ten minutes. His luminous eyes surveyed the room. Helena felt that his eyes were illuminating the walls, her table and desk, the books irregularly set in the book cases.

"It's a charming custom you bring in from the East," he said. "For a lady to invite a man to tea without even asking him for his name."

"Oh, I know your name, Joel Arbuthnot. And I know enough about you to make you an old acquaintance. Your cousin Millicent worked in the same shop with me in Chicago. It was through her I came to know all about this town and you."

"Milly is a romancer. But tell me what she told you about me. I'll score it as true or false."

"All right. You are the only son of the biggest farmer in this county."

"True."

"Your father hopes you'll sow your wild oats and settle down to running the farm."

"Partly true. I haven't got the oats in the ground yet, and once they are started, people tell me, they take a lot of time to make a crop."

"Your mother wanted you to go to college, and there were four colleges that invited you to register with them."

"They saw in me an addition to football manpower. It never occurred to any of them to inquire whether I had a head. A strong back was sufficient for college success."

"Milly says you have all kinds of talents, but out of a sense of fairness you don't exercise any of them."

"Was that a nice thing for a cousin to say about a man? But let it stand as true."

"And she says you are the biggest fish in the county matrimonial pool. Every girl has her hook out, well baited. But you move around among the lines like a lordly pike who has no stomach for hooks."

Joel laughed. "But did she predict what a brand-new hook might do?"

Of course he would say that. Helena felt as if a shade of color was threatening her cheeks, and she felt annoyed with herself.

"The most fruitful place for a brand-new hook is deep in the bureau drawer."

"Maybe. But Milly has written me reams and reams about you. What do you say to our trying the true and false game?"

"All right."

"You were born in a village on the banks of the Ohio River."

"True. My earliest memory is of a neat little cottage on a bluff, looking across the river to Old Kentucky, 'where the meadow grass is blue.' I wanted to see blue grass and I teased my mother into getting a river boatman to take us across. The grass wasn't blue, but lovely green, and you could run around in it with bare feet and not get stiff stems between your toes."

"Your mother was a dressmaker, very popular in the village. But when your father died she removed to Cincinnati, where she could make a better living, and find better schools for you."

"We were very happy there."

"But when you graduated from high school your mother removed to Urbana and had you register in the University. She wanted to raise you out of the slavery of dressmaking."

"Oh no! My mother did not consider dressmaking slavery. To her it was an art, a fine art. She had trained me in her art and had taught me her philosophy. She hoped that I would always remain true to the art. But she believed that every artist should be at home in the world of ideas. Otherwise his art might grow stiff and stale."

"All right. That's why you went to the University. But at the end of the first semester you went over to the Agricultural College."

"Yes. I had bad luck in the University. There were good teachers in the University, but it was my lot to have only teachers bored with their work and discontented with their lives. My fellow students were bored too and cared for nothing but passing marks.

"I visited a friend at the Agricultural College. How different! Every teacher was on his toes. Maybe his rhetoric was not perfect, but the energy with which he used it was wonderful. The students too were on their toes. They were all taking part in experiments, not model experiments as in the University laboratories, but real experiments, to breed a wheat resistant to rust, a rye resistant to frost, to graft native shrubs with scions from the East, or Europe, or China. The student felt that he was putting his hand to help Nature's process of creation. Nature could make an improved variety of plants in a million years; the student could help Nature to develop the variety in ten years."

"And then you went to Chicago, got an ordinary job in the finishing plant of a dressmaking concern, and in no time at all were picked out by the boss to be assistant manager of the shop. And soon you were manager in complete control of the fifty girls working there. Of whom my cousin Milly was one.

"You were a great success. Milly says there was a terrible turnover before you took charge. Ten girls quit every month. Under you, labor turnover disappeared. No girl left except to be married or buried."

"Mostly true, but exaggerated."

"But you got discontented and tried to get Milly to come with you out here. Milly wouldn't leave Chicago; everybody would say she was a failure if she came home. You decided to come alone. Your boss was desolate. He would have raised your salary, given you a fancy title. What you needed, he said, was to get married, and he put it up to a junior partner. But you quit."

"I resented that. When a man gets bored to death with his job, people don't say he needs to get married. Hasn't a woman the same right to get bored? Must they sling the marriage question at her?"

"I hope I haven't offended you. I was just saying what Milly wrote to me."

"You didn't offend me. But what you said reawakened the feeling I had when my boss introduced the junior partner."

Joel rose. "We've covered ground enough to make us old friends. And let me tell you, if anybody had talked the way you can talk about agricultural experimenting when I was a boy, I'd be breeding plants now."

"When does one cease being a boy?"

"Never, if I could sit at your feet."

She laughed. "A rather big shadow for my feet."

"If you're going to let me call again, you'll have to push that brand-new hook a little farther back in your bureau drawer."

"Come again when you feel like it. I have tea every afternoon at four. But your cup is still full."

"Next time I'll drink it first thing, before I'm too interested to think of it."

He was gone. The light of his gorgeous blue eyes seemed to linger in the room.

"Am I just a goose?" she asked herself.

Helena's work was mushrooming. She had taken on another seamstress and was importing a third from another town. Upstairs two sewing machines were already humming.

Her teas, too, were booming. There were a half dozen young men who had asked for the privilege of dropping in. Joel was usually first, but in a few minutes he would groan, "Another bloke."

"I never see you alone," he complained. "How can you educate me in a mob?"

"I educate you?"

"Yes. Don't I know you think I shouldn't be fooling around doing nothing? And don't I know you feel sure you could make something out of me?"

"Listen, I'm a dress designer. I can make something out of the looks, and also the sense of living, of girls and women. But a man—"

"Oh, by the way, I've brought you a present." He handed her a little casket. She stripped off the paper. An ornate little case one might get at the jeweler's.

"You see," he said, "I've been worried about that brand-new hook. It will rust in your bureau drawer. I've put cotton wool in this case to protect it."

"It would rust worse hanging in the water."

"But how long would it hang there?"

She felt herself blushing again. Only faintly, but under Joel's luminous eyes.

"Damn it, here comes another bloke—three of them. The day is spoiled. I'll open the door, but I'd rather lock it."

They were three young blades who carried themselves as acceptable anywhere, Charlie Sutherland, James Wilkinson and Harry Hendricks. How they made their living Helena did not know, nor did she care. Her curiosity about life was wide ranging, but it stopped short of an interest in men's business.

"I have something very serious to bring up," said Charlie with mock gravity. "The social structure of this town is being knocked topsy turvy.

"You know Mrs. Caleb Smith. She has a hired girl Olga, not a year out of Sweden. Well, Miss Wilson, you've been dressing Olga up. When you meet her on the street or in church you ask yourself, 'Where did this distinguished beauty come from?' She moves around in a crowd as if she were as good as anyone."

"She is," said Helena. "In her working hours Olga is Mrs. Smith's hired girl, but in her free time she is herself, a very beautiful and charming young woman."

"Mrs. Smith says, after meeting Olga in church she can't say, 'Bring in the coffee, and make it snappy.' She has to say, 'Miss Olga, will you please bring in the coffee?' "

"That's fine," said Helena energetically.

"Boys, let me tell you something, something you can see for yourselves. In Helena Wilson we see for the first time in our lives an honest-to-God democrat. You can't listen to her without thinking, By George, the Declaration of Independence is not a bunch of words. It's the truth. And I feel abashed when I think how far I have to go to get up to her."

Helena blushed. There was no concealing the fact that Joel's praise affected her deeply.

"Excuse me, Miss Wilson. Sometimes I talk too much. I can't help it. And so, good afternoon. I'll see you again tomorrow if the tea holds out."

Helena scolded herself severely. She had let her feelings run away with her common sense. All those allusions to the brand-new hook were simply Joel's wit. That little case for her hook. She pulled off the cover and drew out the cotton. A ring! A beautiful diamond. She came near fainting.

She would give it back to him, next time he came. He was a gorgeous figure, but he was not for her. Joel's father was the richest farmer in the county, worth a quarter of a million, people said. Helena had never met him, nor Joel's mother. Joel had never had her invited to his home for dinner. That was sufficient proof that her repute didn't count with Joel's family.

They would of course be looking for a daughter-in-law. She would have to come from one of the elite families, or perhaps be an heiress from Lincoln or Omaha. A mere dress designer? How silly could she be?

The next day she heard a timid rapping on her door, a bit early for tea time. She opened the door. Tom Hart, the Duroc Jersey man she hadn't seen in six weeks. He had his left arm in a sling, and what appeared to be the late stage of a black eye.

"Why, Mr. Hart! I thought you had cut me off your calling list. But you've been in an accident."

"No, a fight. The other man fought and I took it. Didn't you read about it in the paper?"

"I'm sorry to say, I've not been reading the *Argus.* I subscribe for an Omaha paper which brings me more news that I can digest."

"Did you ever hear of Emory Hartwell?"

"No. Tell me about him."

"Emory's an old-timer who lives in a hut at the foot of First Street. He's a little crazy, but not enough, the doctors say, to put him in the asylum. His only joy in life is knocking men down.

"I was having a glass of beer at the bar. Emory slipped in through the door. I didn't see him or hear him. Suddenly I got an awful whack on the temple that just put me to sleep. I fell over a stool and broke my arm. Emory pulled me by the legs to the corner and hit me over my left eye. 'I should have taken it out," he said to the saloonkeeper."

"What! Your eye?"

"Yes. You see, Emory grew up in the Southwest. In the old days the boys in the camps did a good deal of what they called 'wrastling.' It wasn't wrestling as we know it here. No holds were barred, and the man who got the other fellow down had a right to gouge out an eye—usually a left eye. Emory has a litle box with five eyes. They look like little dried prunes.

"Those wrestlers let their right thumb nail grow about an inch too long, as a gouging tool. Emory's got that kind of thumb nail now, but the only time he used it in Nebraska he got two years in the pen. He hates this country of softies. But he swears he's going to get one more eye before he dies. Joel Arbuthnot's."

"Joel's eye!"

"Yes, you may have noticed, Joel has rather unusual eyes. You see them once and somehow they stick in your mind. They've been sticking in Emory's mind for years. You might say, he's crazy about them."

Helena felt faint. "Does the county let such a beast run around, at large?"

"What can the county do? It can't put a man in jail for what he's dreaming, planning. It can only deal with overt acts. They put him in jail for two months for knocking me down. Emory liked that. He says he gets better grub in jail than he can fix for himself in his shack. The penitentiary, he says, is different. There the grub is poor. He'd rather not go to the penitentiary, but Joel's eye would be worth it."

Helena clutched the arms of her chair.

"What holds Emory back," Tom continued, "isn't the fear of the penitentiary but something stronger. Joel carries a gun, day and night. And he is the best pistol shot in the state. He takes the top prize at every pistol meet. He's so quick with the pistol they say he can shoot the wing off a butterfly he wants to catch alive. And he has given out, if Emory comes near him he'll shoot, not to wing Emory and put him in the hospital, but to put him underground. Emory doesn't like that. He says the grub underground is mighty poor. Too many worms in it."

Tom laughed over the grim joke. Helena did not even smile. Women have no sense of humor, Tom said to himself.

There was a knocking at the door. Tom opened it, to admit three of the "blokes." It was a relief.

"Joel's gone off to Omaha with five carloads of steers," Charlie Sutherland reported. "Now we other blokes can get in a word edgewise, Miss Wilson."

What the blokes wanted to talk about was local politics, something Helena knew nothing about and cared less. Should they run Mr. Winslow for Congress? Perhaps it was too early to elect a former rebel soldier, it might stir up the old war bitterness. Or it might help to reconcile the South to the Northern victory. About it and about; the sum of the discussion was zero, but it was a relief to Helena.

She had a bad night. Her mother had a maxim: "If you come to an obstacle you can't surmount, go around it and put it out of your mind." She couldn't put Emory and his lust for Joel's eye out of her mind. She might for moments keep her mind on something else but Emory would be back in her mind again.

It's of no use to put the cat out, she philosophized, if you can't close the door.

In her childhood she had read with horror the story of an Indian scheming to get a woman's beautiful hair as a scalp for his tepee pole. That was long ago and far away. Here and now, in her own small circle of acquaintance, a man was moving about with a lust more hideous than the Indian's.

She could not endure the thought of a morning with customers in a hurry to get dresses. She would ride into the country. If anything could quiet her spirits, the sweet monotony of the checkerboard of fields could do it.

It was a sultry morning, with not a breath of air stirring. The owner of the livery stable warned her. There would be a thunder shower before she knew. Better look for shelter.

For several miles the road wound among little grassy hills, apparently not fertile enough to be reduced to farm land. Wild roses besprinkled the whole landscape, pink, red, white, with yellow centers, and a look of the sweetest, most innocent confidence in the blue sky overhead. And everywhere the compass plant, an ungainly weed with leaves the size of a man's hand with the fingers spread out. Not all the leaves obeyed the traditional rule of ranging themselves to point north and south, but enough of them to have directed a bewildered pioneer traveler.

She came to an escarpment where she could look down on a pleasant valley, checkerboarded with fields and houses that looked new, well spaced over the valley, perhaps twenty-five or thirty of them. Near the center was a small white schoolhouse with a flag drooping on its white painted flagstaff.

On a stubble field Helena saw seven litle whirlwinds parading in single file, apparently bowing to one another from time to time. A comical spectacle, if anything in inanimate nature can be comic. Helena laughed and felt somehow a bit abashed for laughing at nothing but whirling stubble.

But a big drop of water on her hand put an end to her speculations on comic nature. There was a rumbling of thunder in the distance. She touched her horse's flank with her whip and galloped down to the settlement. She hitched her horse in the empty woodshed by the nearest house and was knocking on the house door when the first rain came, "in bucketfuls" as the pioneers liked to say. The house felt staunch, though it trembled under the storm roaring over the valley. It had grown dark, and the farmer lit a lantern and opened the door.

He was fairly tall, sturdy and well built. His eyes were very light blue and had a look of gentle appeal, as if he had always wanted to do the right thing but might have missed it. The wife could have been pretty. She appeared to want desperately to make the worst of things. She wore a soiled gingham dress and carried herself in such a way that her young breasts hung down like an old hag's. Her face, which could have been pretty, was disfigured by the downward lines of discontent.

"I think I've seen you at the church," Helena said. The truth was, she had never been near the church. But she had to make conversation.

"Naw, I used to go to church in town. But now all them women are dressed up like ladies. There's a woman come to town from the East who dressed them up fit to kill. I ain't got nothin' to wear but my old wedding gown. It's blue, but it's gone yellow under the armpits. No, I don't go to church."

"Josie's gonna have a new dress, soon as I sell my hogs," said the farmer. "We seen a mighty nice dress in the clothing store window. Josie likes it. Costs thirty dollars, but we can afford it when I sell my hogs."

"I don't want that dress," said Josie. "Since that woman came to town and makes dresses to order you can't wear a ready-made dress. Makes you look like Old Mother Hubbard."

"Then why don't you go and have a dress made to your order?"

"It would cost like fun. That woman wouldn't want to make a dress for a farmer's wife. And if she did she'd want all the money there is."

"Listen, Josephine," Helena said. "You've never asked me my name. I'm Helena Wilson, the dress designer who came in from the East that you are talking about."

"Says you."

"Says I. Now I want your husband to bring you in to me tomorrow morning, at the Rose Cottage. I'll design you a dress that will suit you. Tomorrow is Tuesday: you'll come on Friday and try it on and on Sunday you'll go to church in it."

Josie seemed to be shrinking into a ball of flesh.

"But what will it cost?"

"Twenty dollars if you can afford it. And I can wait for the money till your husband sells his hogs."

"You don't have to wait," said the husband. "If it's only twenty dollars I got that now."

The rain was over. Helena bade Josephine good-bye and went out to recover her horse. The husband followed her.

"Say, Miss Wilson, make it good, and if it costs more I'll pay it when I sell my hogs. She's a good girl but feels awful about her old clo'es."

They came next day to the Rose Cottage. Josephine

had become fairly tamed over night. She balked at having to stand up straight for measurements. But she soon became docile.

And on Friday, when she came to be dressed up, she wasn't the same person. As she looked at herself in the glass in her new clothes she fell into a fit of crying. Helena put her arm around her and kissed her.

"Listen, my dear, as I had your measurements I've made a little work dress for you—I call it a laboratory dress. It's for you to wear in the kitchen."

It was of linen, striped white and blue, with a blue ribbon to close the throat.

Josephine looked at herself in the mirror.

"My God," she said, "I can't go around among my pots and pans looking so swell as this."

"Listen, Josephine, this is a laboratory dress. A kitchen is a laboratory, a most interesting laboratory where you can do wonderful things.

"I saw you have a fine patch of cabbages. All you do with cabbage is to boil it, and your husband doesn't like it, and neither do you. You make cole slaw, and your husband eats it, but you get tired of making it. That's all you've been making of cabbage.

"The Romans called cabbage the queen of all vegetables, because you can make a hundred tasty dishes out of it. You make two. But make a laboratory out of your kitchen and you'll make twenty."

The next morning Josephine's husband came in.

"My wife feels I've got to have a new suit too. You said you could wait till I sell my hogs. But I don't know what is right. Will you go to the clothing store with me and pick out a suit?"

"I'm not an expert on men's clothing," Helena said. "But I'll go with you."

The clothing merchant was very obsequious to Helena. He brought out one suit after another. No—No—

No, said Helena. But here was one, a tweed, that looked right for this blue-eyed young farmer.

"Let's see it on him."

Yes, it was right. "By George, I look as if I amount to something." He did look like that.

The next Monday Joel reappeared for tea. To Helena life again seemed complete. Not quite, for the "blokes" were there. But Joel stood up among them like a giant tree among brambles.

"Time for you to be back," said Charlie Sutherland. "Miss Wilson has been pushing her revolution. She dressed up a farmer's wife like the banker's lady and dressed up the farmer too. And now all the farmers' wives, and the farmers too, want to be dressed up."

"That's only the beginning," said Joel. "The first man I met when I got back was Helena's friend the farmer. Did you know, Helena, that farm belongs to me and your friend is my tenant?"

"I didn't," said Helena.

"Well, he told me. Helena had ordered his wife to make a laboratory out of the kitchen. I went out there and agreed on this little change and that. But I said, you can't have a laboratory without running water. They have a good force pump, but that won't do. I had to agree to build another wing, with a water tank insulated against frost upstairs. That would give them a real bathroom, cold water but plenty of it for the laboratory too. Lots of digging for putting in pipes, but Helena's friend, the farmer, is dying to dig."

"And what a devil of trouble that is going to make," said Charlie. "Maybe Joel can afford it, but other landlords can't. Now all the tenant farmers will want running water and inside bathrooms and toilets. The washtub and the privy had been good enough for them."

"Well, boys, you've heard Helena talking about farming as a way of life. Not a miserable European peasant way of life, but an American way of life, with the farmer standing up like the man he is and his wife sorry for her poor sister who married a banker and has no real life. Helena is always right, and we landlords have to learn how to be American landlords, and care more for happy tenants than for cash rents."

Charlie rose and the other "blokes" felt it was time for them to go. In a few minutes Helena and Joel were alone.

They sat by an open window looking out at Helena's little flower garden. Neither could think of anything to say.

"Look at that pestilential rabbit," said Helena. "He is biting off one of my lilies. He can't eat it. There he is biting off another."

A sharp report at her right. The rabbit lay dead. Joel's pistol, but she hadn't seen him draw it nor did she see what he did with it afterward. All a matter of seconds.

A load seemed to drop off Helena's mind. With an instant pistol like that Joel and his eye were safe. She could dismiss the thought of Emory.

"Before you went away, Joel, you presented me with a lovely casket, supposed to be empty. But I found in it a priceless piece of your property. I have to return it."

"Won't you let findings be keepings?"

"Not yet, Joel. Why do we communicate in symbols? Why can't we use plain English?"

"We can. Will you marry me, Helena?"

"I'd be the happiest woman in the world if I could just say yes. I can't say it now.

"You see, Joel, I have to consider the facts. You are the only son of a powerful man, all his hope. You are the apple of your mother's eye. They have thought much of your future, and they naturally feel, the mate you choose is half of your future. They know many esti-

mable young ladies, have known them from childhood,
know their families and all their kin. I come in from the
East and make something of a success of my art, or
profession. Nothing is known of me except what I tell,
and I do not know enough about myself to tell much.
I did not know my father, for he died when I was a little
child. I knew my mother and grandmother, but other
kin I did not know.

"If you married me now your parents would think
of me as an adventuress who came in from the East to
steal the jewel of their lives."

"I don't think so, Helena. When they come to know
you their judgment will be the same as mine."

"I hope so. But until they come to know me we are
friends, the best of friends."

"All right. I must leave you now. I am too much
moved to keep the distance you desire."

Spring was coming on apace. Helena had no time for
excursions into the country, or even for long conversa-
tional teas. For spring would bring the social event of
the year, the May Day festival at Pathfinder Park. Every
woman and girl had to have a new dress for the occasion.

Helena was responsible for the adornment of the
middle-class women and girls, also for those who were
edging into the middle class. She had no responsibility
for the elite. The women of the elite were already with
Mrs. Winslow in New Orleans, where the modiste,
newly returned from her annual visit to Paris, was dressing them up as befitted their social position.

New fashions had sprung up in Paris and had
promptly leapt the Atlantic. This did not greatly disturb
Helena. For she knew every fashion leaves a bridge from
its predecessor. Helena could keep near the bridge and
say, "fashionable, but not extreme." Women in Eastern

cities might like to go as far as permissible in blatancy of style, but the small Western towns were still dominated by country-mouse modesty. Helena could remain true to her principles of dress, dignity and grace with an ingredient of sprightliness well modulated to the character of her client.

May Day was perfect in weather. The Nebraska breeze had never been softer, the Nebraska sunshine had never been whiter. Pathfinder Park was a carpet of fresh green, set off with the gold of forsythia bushes, a new and much admired introduction from the East. Most spring flowers were yet to come, but the tables were decorated with vases of pasque flowers, not designed by nature for a cut flower but displaying marvelous shades of pink in their drooping petals. But the real floral displays were the women in their new dresses moving in groups on the lawn.

Helena had the theory that the bright light of Nebraska demanded strong colors, and she had used strong colors, with moderation. The elite, who grouped themselves apart, pronounced the colors garish; but they were not. The sun did not make much of their own colors, designed for the soft light of the Seine.

The prevailing mood of the festival was one of gaiety and joy of the spring. But the elite were not so happy as in earlier years. An essential vitamin of the elite spirit is the envious admiration of the non-elite. Formerly the non-elite, in their haphazard new dresses from the clothing stores, had surveyed with longing admiration the New Orleans dresses of the elite. This year the looks of envy and admiration were missing. As it seemed to the elite, these ordinary women and girls thought they were as well dressed, and more becomingly. Elite ears caught a pert saying that was circulating in the crowd: "Mrs. Winslow is trying to prove that New Orleans isn't so hot after all."

How vulgar! But it is easier to reject vulgar dispraise with your mind than with your spirit.

Helena was not at the party. She had felt that some of the elite might take the occasion to snub her. So she sat at home and indulged herself in her favorite novel. It was so absorbing she almost forgot that her art was on trial at the festival.

There was a knock on the door. Joel, in high spirits:

"You should have been there to see how your dresses made a royal show. Those clients of yours carried themselves like highborn ladies in fiction. That Swedish hired girl made a sensation. The boys fell over themselves trying to get introduced to her. And I couldn't help thinking, why will a man be spending his time wooing a knockkneed simpering banker's daughter when there is such an exquisite beauty in town?"

"And why should a man be spending his time wooing a mere dressmaker?"

"Because through some defect in my eyes, perhaps, the dressmaker is overwhelmingly beautiful to me. And besides, she has brains enough for both of us, when we are married."

"When troubles cease." Helena had a vague presentiment of troubles coming.

And they were indeed coming. Two days later copies of the *Chicago Interocean* were circulating in the town with an article on the society page describing the May Day party. It had been known to the hosts of the party that a Chicago reporter was in town. Indeed, they had invited him to the party, hoping for an inch of space. But a whole article!

Their own town, Douglas Bluff, was declared by the reporter to be the style capital of the prairie states. Nowhere else could you see such a galaxy of beautiful women and girls dressed in so wide a variety of color and pattern, all with the same consummate good taste.

The dresses had all been designed, the reporter had been told, by a miracle worker, Miss Helena Wilson, formerly of Chicago, where her work was widely known and highly esteemed.

"What was most striking in Miss Wilson's work, as exhibited in the Douglas Bluff May Day Festival, was its authentic Americanism. Her color schemes were designed to greet the strong American light; her patterns were designed to bring out the lines of grace and dignity of the American woman. America was at last emancipating herself from the French dress designer, who naturally formed his conceptions on his French models, of shorter stature and softer lines, bodies we may ungenerously describe as a bit pudgy. American imitations have indeed tried to adapt the French design to the very different American figure. But adaptations lack vitality, integrity.

"As if to remind us of the late era of imitation of France there was a small group of women dressed in the conventional Franco-American style, dim colors, vaguely uncertain figures, an uneasy sense of being out of character. They served however to underscore the beauty of true American design."

There were in town only five subscribers to the *Interocean,* but the copies circulated widely, bringing satisfaction to many and wrath to some. Mrs. Winslow refused to read the article. "I don't have to read the scribblings of a vulgar and ignorant reporter. Of course, he was given a good fat fee by the Creature." This was the only name she had for Helena Wilson. It was a refinement of her father's word, Critter. In farm language a critter is any member of the cow family. In town a critter is a runty heifer that jumps fences and makes trouble, but more commonly an obnoxious woman.

Helena read the article with deep misgivings.

The next day Helena went to the bank to cash a

check. The armchair in the lobby was occupied by a sharp-faced woman, apparently middle-aged, with brown eyes angrily fixed on a window where a cashier was working over a mass of papers, checks, pinned to dozens of explanatory sheets.

"That must be Mrs. Winslow," Helena thought.

The woman had heard the cashier's "Good morning, Miss Wilson."

"The Creature!" Mrs. Winslow glared steadily at her. Helena returned the look with calm eyes which dropped to scan Mrs. Winslow's dress, to the lady's fierce indignation. For she was wearing a dress exhibiting the fashion of two years gone by. She was saving her good new dresses.

"Brazen hussy," Mrs. Winslow said to herself. "Common seamstress posing as dress designer." An idea occurred to her suddenly. She knew Helena had been born in an Ohio River county. The population there was said to be frightfully mixed, a lot of Negroes passing for whites. That was it! The Creature was a Negro. That explained her brazen gaze, the hoity-toity way she carried her shoulders, her impudent claim to professional standing. Mrs. Winslow had known in New Orleans dozens of Negroes who could pass for white. She knew the breed.

As her carriage mounted the hill Mrs. Winslow's surmise transformed itself into conviction. Certainly the Creature was a Negro. She recalled now that she had somewhere a clipping from the *Picayune,* an article on "Passing," the accepted term for the intrusion of Negroes of fair complexion into white communities. She found the clipping. Yes, it paid special attention to the Ohio River counties.

It offered a compelling historical account of the River counties. When settlers came in from the East they found the region infested with a virulent form of malaria, which turned a man into a shaking skeleton and killed a woman. If the settlers brought wives along with them, they were soon widowers. Sick men could not live as bachelors. And so the settlers crossed the river into Kentucky and bought Negro girls immune to malaria to serve as housekeepers and mistresses. The girls proved very fertile, and soon the region was swarming with little mulattoes. The children grew up, new settlers found it cheaper to marry mulattoes than to buy slave girls. Next a generation of quadroons, then one of octaroons and Negroes that could pass for white. Thus Negro blood spread through the community.

After the War many emancipated slaves crossed the river. They were very unwelcome to the Negro whites, who, if they could manage it, moved to cities like Cincinnati, to lose their identity in the city mob. From there they moved to Northern communities, where nobody suspected them of having Negro blood. Some married into the best Northern families, who might meet with the painful experience of a coal black baby born to two apparently pure white parents.

"There's no doubt about it," Mrs. Winslow said to herself, "the Creature was born in a village on the Ohio. Her family moved to Cincinnati. Then to Urbana, Illinois. A typical case."

Helena's shop was marking time. The girls who had been so eager to start on their fall dresses did not appear. Helena would have had no work for her seamstresses if a half-dozen farmers' wives had not come in to be dressed up. Helena made them dresses, threw in a kitchen dress and a cookbook and lectured them on the necessity of turning the kitchen into a laboratory.

A group of girls had gathered to discuss this terrible news about Helena Wilson. A Negro? Did Helena know that her secret was now known to everybody? Somebody ought to tell her.

"I'll tell her," said Mildred Hart, who had never entirely forgiven Helena for brushing aside her preferences for colors and designs. How biggety Helena had been. Now Mildred thought she had the explanation.

Mildred made a show of deep interest in the autumn styles, but soon came to the point.

"You know, Mrs. Winslow is terribly sore about that article. And she says you inspired it. She says the reporter spent his nights in your house."

Helena laughed. "She might have asked the three seamstresses who do spend their nights in my house where on earth I could have found room for a guest. The fact is I never met that reporter. I'm sorry about the article. It was unfair, and bound to make trouble."

"And she says she has found out that you are a Negro."

"I a Negro?" Helena laughed again. "See how dark my complexion is. And you will have noticed, my hair is kinky."

There was nothing more to say, Mildred thought. Helena meant to brazen it out. A Negro would.

In the afternoon Tom Hart, Mildred's brother, appeared for tea.

"You have heard that vixen up on the hill is circulating lies about you."

"Yes, I've just heard it from your sister Mildred."

"That woman—she ought to be tarred and feathered and ridden on a rail out of the county. I don't know what Joel will do when he comes back from Omaha. He'll want to shoot her."

"I hope not. Do people believe Mrs. Winslow's yarn?"

"The men don't. A lot of us were in the Union Army. She's been telling the most awful lies about us for years. If you believed her, Sherman's army robbed every man and raped every woman on the march through Georgia. I was there and know there was never an army with orders to lay enemy country waste that treated the civil population with the decency of Sherman's army."

"If nobody believes her what harm can she do?"

"I said the men know she is just a common liar. They wouldn't believe her under oath. But women are different. They are apt to believe anything bad about a woman. Maybe I shouldn't say that."

"You should, for it's more or less true." She recalled her talk with Mildred. That girl believed those slanders, she now was convinced.

"You ought to sue her for libel."

"It would do no good. I know of a case in Illinois where the court decided it was not libelous to call a man a Negro, because under the law a Negro is just as good as any other man."

"She says you were born in an Ohio River county where practically everybody has Negro blood. But you could send down there and get the records of marriage and births in your family."

"I wouldn't find any records. Before we moved to Urbana my mother and I visited the village where I was born. We looked up the records, hoping to find items that would help us to find the remote kin of my father. All there was in the church record was 'Married the 17th of September of this year James Wilson and Rebecca Jones. May God give them increase.' There were no records at all of earlier years. If any had been kept they had been destroyed when the old church burned down."

She continued, "And so you see, I have no proof that I have no Negro blood. And Mrs. Winslow has no proof that I have. And so people will have to believe what they want to believe."

Tom rose to go. "It's a damn outrage. But I want you to know, nobody could make me believe that you have Negro blood."

"Thank you. But I want you to say something more.

I want you to say if I did have Negro blood it would make no difference between us."

"Sure. You are the finest woman in the county. Whatever blood you have."

Helena had kept a brave face. But inside she was not so robust. Her world, she felt, had fallen in pieces.

It was true, she could not prove that she had no Negro blood. People would have to believe what they would, and it was true, women were prone to believe the worst.

Among them Joel's mother. She was no doubt too intelligent to give full credence to the poisonous Mrs. Winslow, but even slight credence would be an insurmountable obstacle to Helena's hopes. Joel's mother would demand that her son's wife must be beyond suspicion.

Had she a right to be so sorry for herself? There were thousands of women, as true and able as she was, with a trace of Negro blood that did not show, who had "passed" successfully for whites. They were all living in fear of an explosion of gossip that might bespatter them with the mire of race prejudice.

Perhaps it was just that some white persons who were falsely charged with Negro blood should be put through the same ordeal as vicarious sacrifices to atone for the cruelty of their kind.

Still, she had not been a party to the shameful persecution of persons with Negro blood. She had stood out against it in the one instance that came within her range of action.

In the Chicago finishing shop there was one girl, a skillful and faithful worker, who fell under the suspicion of her fellow workers. Some gossip had filtered in from outside. A committee of the employees was formed, and approached her table.

"We can't work with Negro girls," the chairman had declared.

"All right. You don't have to work with Estella, if that is what you mean. Please go to your table and gather up your belongings. I will call up the cashier and ask him to pay you for a full week's work."

"Does that mean I'm fired?"

"It does." Helena turned to look for the other members of the committee, but they were on their way back to their tables.

An hour later the chairman returned to Helena's table. She had been crying.

"Do I have to go? If I don't say anything more against Estella?"

"You would still try to freeze her out. You would encourage the other girls to do the same. She would be miserable. Now, Estella is a good girl, as good as any of you. She is supposed to have Negro blood. That is just as good blood as any. And any girl who makes it hard for her will be fired."

"I could take her to lunch, and be nice to her."

"If you can I'll be glad to have you stay."

There never was any more trouble about Estella. The girls took her into their fellowship and found her charming.

Joel had returned. It was too early in the morning to call on Helena. Joel walked swiftly to the livery stable and mounted his horse. He would ride out and have breakfast with Tom Hart.

Tom was warmly cordial but seemed embarrassed. After several attempts to start an account of something indifferent, he blurted out:

"Joel, while you were away Hell broke loose here."

"Hell broke loose? What do you mean?"

"You know that article about the May festival. It made Mrs. Winslow crazy mad."

"She's crazy anyway."

"She's been circulating the statement that Helena bribed the reporter and entertained him in her house overnight."

"The old bitch!"

"And she's been circulating a story that Helena is a Negro, one of those mixed bloods that can pass for white in the North, where people don't know Negroes."

Joel sprang up and walked up and down the room, working hard to get his anger under control.

"She ought to be shot. She's a born liar; nobody pays any attention to what she says. She can't hurt Helena."

"That's what I would have said. But I'm not so sure. The Vixen claims she has proof. And there are some people, mostly among the womenfolk, who think there may be something in it."

"I've got to see Helena." He looked at his watch. "Hell, it's only eight. I'll ride around a while. I've got to cool off. Breakfast? No, thank you. I can't eat."

Helena greeted Joel eagerly. Her face was pale and her eyelids heavy, as of insomnia and weeping. Joel seized her hand and held it firmly.

"Helena, I've heard about those slanders set loose by the lying Vixen up on the hill. They don't trouble you, do they?"

"Joel, they wouldn't have troubled me as I was when I first came here. If the Vixen had accused me of having Negro blood, I would not have cared, because to me Negro blood is as good as any blood. But you came into my life. I did not realize how deep you are in my life until the late events threatened loss of you."

"Loss of me? Do you think I care what kind of blood you have? It's all good blood that helped to make Helena."

"I knew you would feel that, Joel. But I have to think of your mother. You are her life, her hope. She might have come around to accepting me, as matters stood last week. She could not accept a daughter-in-law with Negro blood.

"She is wise enough to discount the animus of the Vixen. She probably realizes that the Vixen has no proof whatever of her assertions. But she knows, too, I can't prove that I do not have Negro blood. If I have it, it infiltrated my heredity seven or eight generations ago. Who can know his heredity through seven or eight generations? You may be able to trace a direct line through as many generations, but your ancestors married out and brought in other genealogical trees. Scores of them that you can never track down.

"Almost everybody has heard of the 'throwback.' A person with Negro blood so thinned by white unions that there appears to be no trace of it may yet give birth to an apparently full-blooded Negro. Scientists accept the possibility of a throwback, although not one instance of a true throwback has ever been seen by any scientist. Mathematicians have computed that a true throwback from the seventh generation can happen once in seven trillion births.

"One in several trillion is very close to zero. But in the popular mind it looms as a reality.

"Your mother almost certainly has absorbed this delusion of the popular mind. She no doubt would have the deadly fear, if you marry me, that her grandchild may be coal black."

"If my mother is such a fool I shall pay no attention to her wishes. I'll marry you whatever she feels about it."

"Joel, I can't bear the idea of years of bitter conflict with your mother over you. Sometime, somehow we are bound to be united, but I can't see how, just now. But please, Joel, go away now. I am bursting with tears; I have to let them flow. Day after tomorrow I'll be myself again."

Joel rose. "May I kiss you?"

"Yes. But then go quickly."

The next morning Helena hardly had energy to rise and dress. She was tired, infinitely tired. She wanted to sleep but could not.

Her doorbell rang. A customer, oh Lord! She opened the door to admit an elderly lady.

"Do you design dresses for old ladies?"

Helena studied the woman's face. Sharp features, and a veiled expression. Intelligent, or perhaps struggling for intelligence.

"You're not an old woman. Perhaps fifty-five."

"I'm fifty-seven."

"And you dress as if you were sixty-seven. That is an honorable age, but there is no good reason for anticipating it."

The woman shrugged her shoulders. It was clear to Helena, the woman had not the slightest interest in clothes. Who was she?

The woman clasped and unclasped her hands. A familiar gesture. Helena knew now who she was. Joel's mother. Luella Arbuthnot.

"Mrs. Arbuthnot, some day I may design a dress for you. Not today. You haven't any interest whatever in clothes. You came here to talk about your son Joel."

"Joel never told me you are a mind reader."

"Neither you nor I care to beat around the bush. So let us have what is in your mind."

"For years I've wanted Joel to get married. I want a grandchild. I need one, to make me feel life goes on. There were several girls I'd have been glad to call daughter-in-law. They are nice girls, of good families

I have known all my life. They were educated, not very much educated, perhaps, compared to you. Joel played around with them to please me, but not one of them could hold his interest. Then you came to the village. He says he fell in love with you the first day, somewhere out in an oats field, and he has been getting deeper and deeper. He says the water is not only over his head but he is walking on the bottom."

Helena smiled. "Joel's language is quite graphic."

"I confess, I wasn't for you. You had come in from the East, and I didn't know anything about you or your folks. But you were having an awfully good influence on Joel. He never could make up his mind what he wanted to do. His father wanted him to take over the management of our land—it's a big lot of land. But Joel couldn't get interested in farming. Now he wants to be an agriculturist. He has taken a twenty-acre field and has planted all sorts of things on it. He says he's going to cross wheat and make fine new varieties he will name for you and me. He has turned one of our biggest rooms into a laboratory, and every week he runs down to the Experiment Station, to look at apparatus and find out how to work it. He hasn't told you about it. He says you'll be surprised when you marry him."

Oh Joel! What a man she had lost. For it was clear, this gentle lady had come to declare the match impossible.

"But now those awful things have come out and I can't feel the same about Joel's choice."

"Those awful things are two," Helena said. "The first is that I inspired, perhaps paid for, the article on your May Day festival. That is a plain lie. I never saw the reporter, I didn't even know there was a Chicago reporter in town. The first I knew of the article was when someone showed me a clipping of it. If I had known such an article was being written I'd have hunted down the reporter and begged him not to write any article on the Festival. It could do only harm."

"That settles the first question for me," said Mrs. Arbuthnot. "I've always known Mrs. Winslow is an out-and-out liar. But was she lying when she said you have Negro blood?"

"She was lying when she said she has proof of it. There is no such proof."

"But I can believe you. Do you know, for certain, that you do not have Negro blood?"

"No. It was not known to my mother or my grand-mother that Negro blood might have infiltrated the family heredity. They were truth-speaking women, and they would have told me. But I do not know, and they did not know what might have happened, say, a hundred and fifty years before."

"Then you may have Negro blood, and if Joel mar-ried you your child might be a throwback. A coal black Negro."

"Yes. But the mathematical biologists have calculated the chances. After five generations there could be one throwback to fifty million births. After seven genera-tions—and if there is Negro infiltration in my blood it is not nearer than seven generations—there may be one throwback to three trillion births."

"But still, there is a chance."

"Yes, and to a mother a chance is a chance, however small. Mind-reading again, you are going to ask me to promise not to marry Joel. I can't do that, but I will promise not to marry him until you ask me. Is that enough?"

"Yes. Probably you despise me, for letting myself be ruled by so small a chance."

"No. There is no place for mathematics in mother love. But now we are agreed on the main issue, let us have some tea and talk a little while." She continued,

"That problem of the throwback is interesting.

"People in general think of the throwback as part of the Negro problem. But throwbacks can happen anywhere. Everybody has ancestors of unsavory reputation —pirates, highwaymen, burglars, thieves. A baby may be born who is a replica of one of these. Captain Kidd left heirs to his blood, legitimate or illegitimate. So did Torquemada. The blood of the mother of Bloody Queen Mary infiltrated much of the gentry, quite possibly the Arbuthnot family.

"Now why should you be so afraid Joel might have a throwback to a Negro and not be worried over the danger of a throwback to some low criminal? The criminal was white, and you assume the white man is superior, the black man inferior.

"There is not a scientist in the world whose work commands respect who would dare to assert that the Negro is by nature inferior to the white. In spite of the handicaps we impose on the Negro, he is able to show that he can be as good a mathematician, scientist, artist, writer as the white. America's greatest statesman, Alexander Hamilton, is believed to have had Negro blood. The greatest story teller in history, Alexander Dumas, was a mulatto.

"It is our conscience that makes us insist that the Negro is an inferior man. If he is not, our holding him in slavery down to the Civil War is a horrible gangrene on our national conscience. The discrimination we still practice is another gangrene. If we are to have ease of mind we have to make the Negro an inferior.

"For the sake of your conscience, my friend, you have to make me an inferior woman, to justify what you are doing to me."

"No! I consider you superior to any woman I've ever known. I may some time ask you to marry Joel, but not now."

"The impossible sometimes happens; the possible rarely."

"I'll quote that to Joel. He's always quoting sayings of yours I can't always understand. He says there is a whole philosophy in them. But I must leave you now. We'll be friends, won't we?"

"Yes, surely."

Helena expected Joel in the morning, but he did not appear. Perhaps he was angered by her promise to his mother. What difference did the promise make? With it or without it she could not marry Joel without his mother's consent.

The door opened and Mrs. Arbuthnot came in and without greeting sank into an armchair. She was very pale and her hair hung in tangles as if it had not been combed.

"Joel shot——" Mrs. Arbuthnot was struggling for the name.

Helena clutched the edge of the table to steady herself. Joel shot Mrs. Winslow! When he left her he was evidently trying to control the furious rage he felt toward Mrs. Winslow. Shot her! All Helena's world turned to ashes. The penitentiary for life, or worse.

"I can't remember his name. Emerson or something like that."

Emory! Helena dropped to her knees. "Thank God! Thank God!"

"Why, Helena! What are you thanking God for? Poor Joel is up at the courthouse under arrest and his father is there arranging bail for him. He'll be tried and maybe sent to the penitentiary."

"I thought it was someone else. That Emory was a beast. A horrible beast. Oh, Mrs. Arbuthnot, what a relief! Now I won't have those horrible nightmares. Joel's eye is safe."

"Joel's eye? Why, Helena, are you being hysterical?"

"Didn't you know that beast was watching and waiting night and day for a chance to get Joel down and gouge out his left eye?"

"Gouge out his eye? What had Joel done to him?"

"Nothing. Emory had lived in the camps of the Southwest, where men wrestled and the victor gouged out the beaten man's eye. He has five dried eyes in his shack down by the river. He's told lots of people that he would have Joel's eye before he died."

"Why?"

"Because he'd got his heart set on that eye. Just as an Indian prince may have his heart set on a jewel and may kill any member of his family who stands in the way of his getting it."

"Joel never told me about that."

"He wouldn't. But you may have noticed, he always carried a pistol."

"I'm upset. Will you pour me a glass of ice water? Pour a little on my head. There. I was going to faint and I have a lot to say.

"I went down to ask Mr. Winslow to take Joel's case. They say he is the best lawyer in town. He said it wouldn't do for him to plead before a jury. The elections are coming on and the politicians are fighting the Civil War over again. Everybody knows Mr. Winslow was a Confederate officer. But that is not the worst that is against him. The county is up in arms against the Winslows, for Mrs. Winslow's slandering you, Helena."

"The county up in arms for me?" asked Helena in astonishment.

"Mr. Winslow says you are the most popular person the county has ever known. He says the charge against Joel isn't murder, but manslaughter."

"Beast slaughter."

"He says Joel can't get more than five years for that and probably won't get more than a year."

"Joel in the penitentiary! And for a great public service. A panther at large couldn't be more dangerous than Emory—and Joel would be highly honored for shooting it."

"Mr. Winslow says there is one way out. If Joel marries you he can't be convicted. There will be farmers on every jury, and no farmer will send Helena Wilson's husband to the penitentiary."

"But there will be twelve jurors."

"Yes, and some may be for convicting. But a jury has to be unanimous. Mr. Winslow says, if even one juror holds out the jury will be dismissed and the case put before another jury, which will also have farmers on it. And if that jury fails to agree, as it will, the case will be nolle prossed, whatever that means, and Joel will be free.

"Mr. Winslow seemed to think Joel and I wouldn't know you and set out to argue that it would be a good match. He said he knew there was not a shred of evidence for those slanders and that you are one of the finest women in the state. And he said Joel is a man no woman would refuse."

Helena smiled. "Mr. Winslow understands human nature."

"But now, Helena, what are you going to do?"

"Are you asking me to marry Joel?"

"Yes."

"My answer is, as soon as possible."

"You're my daughter already. Kiss me."

The door opened and Joel stepped in, catching the two women kissing.

"Well!" he exclaimed. "Do I actually see this, or is it an hallucination?"

"Helena and I have decided that you are to marry her soon."

Joel put a great arm around each woman. "Soon? When this trial is over?"

"No. We don't want to wait," his mother said.

"But is it right for a man to marry when he may have to go to prison, perhaps for years?" he said. "Isn't that making her a kind of widow?"

"If I must wait I'd rather wait as widow than as fiancee."

"In a week, then."

"No," said Helena. "There are no obstacles now; there may be in a week. There may be a court order, commanding you to cease and desist from marrying. We have a golden opportunity now. There is a Greek maxim, When you meet Lady Opportunity, grab her by the forelock; she has no back hair. I'm for tomorrow."

And tomorrow it was.

Helena had never met William Arbuthnot before the wedding. He was a farm-empire builder who managed without assistance his own huge farm and his many tenant farms. He was seldom seen in town, except at the bank or in the stockyards. He was said to be a man of very few words, words which always meant business.

Now at the wedding supper Helena could see just what kind of father-in-law she had. She was seated at his right and could survey his great head, clothed in graying hair and a blunt pointed beard, sparsely graying, and great eyebrows, all black. Under his eyebrows were blue eyes, large like Joel's but sunny rather than luminous. He was as tall as Joel and had the same broad shoulders, huge chest and mighty arms, too long for even his large body.

He turned toward Helena. "Now at last I have a chance to get acquainted with my expensive daughter-in-law."

"Expensive? Did you ever hear of a less expensive wedding? A dollar and a half for the license. The minister wouldn't take a fee. This wedding supper, money couldn't buy it, but it was skill that made it, not money."

"I was thinking of what you did to Joel while he was courting you. You made him turn one of my farmhouses into a nice city cottage, with running water and a bathroom. You made him turn the kitchen into a laboratory, and dressed up the farmer's wife for Sundays and for the kitchen you put her into something like a nurse's uniform, only prettier."

"She'll be the better cook for that."

"She is. I dropped in to see what you and Joel were doing to my property, and she invited me to lunch. Our Metropolitan Hotel here on Second Street couldn't possibly match that lunch. But now all my tenants want me to make cottages out of the farmhouses, and the wives want their kitchens to be laboratories. They say you will make them laboratory uniforms."

"I will. Where's the harm in that?"

"You know I have twenty-seven tenant farms, every farmer insisting now on a nice cottage to live in. That isn't all. My fellow landlords are mad as hops. They say I'm encouraging their tenants to demand the moon. They threaten to sell out."

"For you to buy up."

Mr. Arbuthnot sat back and laughed, a curiously melodious laugh for so huge a chest.

"That's right. But I would never have expected a dressmaker—pardon me, a dress designer—to see the point so quickly. The long and the short of it is this. You have brought into this county the idea of an American way of life for the tenant farmer. And that means an American way of life for the landlord. He can't just sit back and collect his rent. He's got to plan and scheme to make his tenants brag of him as a man who cares more for farming and farm life than for money."

"Poor fellow!" said Helena, smiling into his eyes. They were twinkling.

"Now look at it," he said. "Twenty-six more farmhouses to be turned into cottages. A lot of them to be replaced, for now I've looked into them, a lot of my farmhouses can't be made fit to live in. That will cost a mint of money."

"Before you squander all your money on your tenants, build a house, a little house for Joel and me, somewhere on this farm."

"Isn't this house big enough for two couples?"

"It is. But you know the Chinese character that means discord. It is a picture of two women under one roof."

"Are you going to quarrel with your mother-in-law?"

"No. But you know, every woman sometimes wakes up in the morning in a very sour humor. If there is another woman in the house, she thinks, 'What did that woman mean by what she said at table, last evening? She meant so and so; it was just like her. I'll go and tell her the truth about herself.' Now, that kind of truth is bitter and its savor sticks on the palate a long time.

"Now, if she has to walk two hundred yards to get to the other woman, the 'truth' oozes out and what she says is 'Our Dorothy Perkins roses are beginning to bloom,' or 'The oriole is hanging its nest on the highest branch of our elm tree.' "

"I guess you're right. You and Joel pick out a site and draw your plans. I'll begin to build next Monday."

Helena liked her father-in-law, intensely. He was always making out that he disapproved of anything she admired and approved of anything she detested. It was an extraordinary way of establishing an intimate understanding. The expression of his sunny eyes told plainly what he really thought.

One evening at supper he put on a very grave face and began, "My dear, there is a sound rule that you should never present bad news at supper. It ruins the night. Reserve it for breakfast, when there is a whole day to digest it. But I breakfast at 5:30 and have to go off immediately to harass my tenants. You are still asleep when I go. And so I have to tell you the terrible news now. You are losing a friend. Losing her forever."

"A friend? Who?"

"Mrs. Winslow. She has gone back to New Orleans with the most cordial injunction to all Nebraskans to go to Hell."

"Oh dear!" Helena laughed.

"You aren't very patriotic, and you stayed out here fussing about the plans of your house when all good citizens were joining in a monster parade. Parading for Grant, who would be elected anyway if nobody made a speech for him and if everybody stayed at home attending to his business. But the politicians have to make a big show as if the election of Grant were in doubt. The bloody shirt is flapping all over Nebraska.

"After the parade a mob of high school boys and other naughty youngsters went up on the hill to parade around the Mansion. As they marched they sang, of course, 'We will hang Jeff Davis on a sour apple tree' and 'For beneath the Tanner's torch you will see the loyal North rout the copperheads and rebels once again.'

"And one boy would yell, 'Who has Negro blood?' And they'd all yell, 'Mrs. Winslow.' And the first boy yelled, 'Where did she get it?' And the other answered, 'From her plantations. She drinks Negro blood for milk.'

"The boy who yelled the questions was standing right under the upstairs bay window. Mrs. Winslow grabbed a pitcher of ice water and poured it on his head. He yelled, 'It wasn't ice water you poured in New Orleans. Hurrah for Beast Butler.' And all the boys marched around, yelling, 'Hurrah for Beast Butler.'

"Mrs. Winslow ran to the servants' quarters and ordered the gardener to get on a horse and ride to the city hall and demand protection. The chief of police said all the force—that is just one man in an old Civil War uniform—was assigned to the parade. Were the boys breaking windows or doing other property damage? No? Well then, Mrs. Winslow had better pay no attention to them. Boys would be boys.

"When Mr. Winslow came home he found his wife, two maids and the gardener packing trunks. They had six trunks packed and roped. They had another six before morning. At eight in the morning Mrs. Winslow boarded the train for Omaha, where she would change to a train for St. Louis and New Orleans."

Mr. Arbuthnot dropped his mock gravity. "I'm very sorry for Mr. Winslow. He is a fine lawyer and a fine man. Soon he'd have been in our Supreme Court, and if the Democrats ever get in, he might have a chance at the Supreme Court in Washington. Now he'll have to open an office in New Orleans where there are too many lawyers and too little law."

The day of the trial had come. Joel had gone down to the courthouse in the early morning. He had been summoned for nine o'clock, but he wanted to be early. Helena and Luella were breakfasting with Mr. Arbuthnot. Breakfasting and eating nothing but crumbs of toast. Mr. Arbuthnot devoured his chop and asked for another.

"It will be lots of fun. Pity we can't be there but the prosecuting attorney would kick us out for influencing the jury. They picked the jury yesterday. A majority are farmers. Everybody knows a farmer wouldn't convict Helena's husband. It's just going to be a monkey show.

"I'll take you down when the jury is about ready to come back to the court room. The jury will want to shake hands with the woman who weighed more with them than the laws of Nebraska."

His speech and his manner were very reassuring. But

it is impossible wholly to reassure women whose hearts are under the hammer.

The judge appeared early in the court room. He was uneasy. He was always uneasy in the court room, for he had had no legal training and he was always in fear that the lawyers might pull the wool over his eyes.

In that county no man who had legal training could be elected judge. It was the opinion of the community that law and justice are not on speaking terms. And the community was for justice. A pleasant, honest business-man was the community ideal of a judge. Such was Judge MacLean. He had spent many hours since his election in leafing through Blackstone, Kent's *Commentaries,* the Nebraska Statutes, and the Reports of the State Supreme Court. And the more he read the more confused he became.

He called the Court to order and read a florid address on law and justice, prepared by one of the lawyers. His pronunciation was far from perfect, but nobody paid any attention to the address. Then he read the indictment and the charge, neither making any impression. What the court room was waiting for was the drama of reality.

The prosecuting attorney made a speech nobody listened to and called the first witness. He was a slight and worried fellow who was in charge of the soda fountain in the drugstore where the tragedy took place. He had a name but the court room called him simply the soda jerk.

It had been a very hot day, the jerk testified, and Joel Arbuthnot had come in for a drink of soda— No, it was lemonade. Nobody else was there. The door had opened noiselessly. The jerk had not seen anyone come in. Joel had turned around suddenly and said in a loud voice, "Emory, come one step nearer and you are dead." Emory flew at him like a cat, Joel shot and Emory fell in a heap on the floor. His feet kicked a little, one of his arms reached out, his head moved a little and then he was still.

"Mr. Defense Attorney," said the judge. "Do you wish to cross-examine the witness?"

"No. For once a witness is telling the truth."

The jury laughed. The prosecuting attorney frowned.

"Next witness." It was the Chief of Police.

"You were on the spot soon after the tragedy?"

"Yes, Joel Arbuthnot came to my office and said he had killed a man in the drugstore. Of course I went up to see how it was."

"Your Honor," said the prosecuting attorney, "you've got to order the words, 'Joel Arbuthnot came to my office,' struck out and warn the jury to disregard them. It prejudices the case of the State."

"Why, Hell," said the judge. "I beg pardon, but how did the Chief of Police learn of the killing? Objection overruled."

"Mr. Chief of Police, you examined the body, did you find any lethal weapons on it?"

"What kind of weapons?"

"Lethal. Deadly. Pistols or knives."

"No. Nothing."

"Did he have even a jack knife?"

"No. The only thing he had in his pocket was a nail scissors. He was always trimming his long thumb nail, to keep it ready for gouging eyes."

"Your Honor, you have to strike out what he says about the nail scissors. It is irrelevant, and prejudicial to the State's case."

"Well," said the judge, "it seemed interesting to me and to throw some light. But I'll instruct the jury not to make too much of it. Mr. Defense Attorney, do you want to cross-examine the witness?"

"No. Again we have a witness speaking the truth."

The third witness was a surgeon who had examined the body.

He testified that the bullet had entered the body above the left clavicle. It had cut through a lung and severed the aorta. It had cut through the right auricle and ventricle and had lodged in the right femur.

"Mr. Defense Attorney, do you wish to cross-examine the witness?"

"The jury don't know what aorta or clavicle and auricle and ventricle are. Was the corpus shot through the heart?"

"Yes."

"That's sufficient."

"We'll hear witnesses for the defense," said the judge. Tom Hart stepped forward and was sworn.

"Were you present at the tragedy?" the prosecuting attorney demanded.

"No, but I know what Emory was after. He knocked me in the head, blacked my eye when I was down and said, 'Too bad, if only you were Joel. I'd get his eye. I'll get it before I die.' "

"Your Honor," cried the prosecuting attorney, "this witness has said nothing relevant to the case. His evidence must be struck out."

"Why, Hell," said Tom, "ain't it relevant that Emory had been watching day and night, for years, to gouge out one of Joel's eyes?"

"Your Honor, I demand that you order this witness arrested for contempt of court. He has persisted, after my protest, in bringing in irrelevancies to prejudice the case of the State."

"Well," said the judge, "I don't see the contempt. But, Tom, you've talked enough. Don't let us hear anything more."

"Has the Defense any other witnesses?" asked the Judge.

"No, your Honor."

"The prosecution will sum up."

The prosecuting attorney began his speech with sweet reasonableness. The deceased Emory had indeed made an unprovoked attack on Joel, meaning to do him bodily injury. Joel had the constitutional right of self-defense.

"But the Nebraska courts scrutinize closely the plea of self-defense. They had the example of our sister state, Texas. There, at first, when a man found an enemy drawing a pistol on him, he shot, if he reached his trigger first. That was self-defense, and he went scot free. Next, a plea was offered, 'He reached for his gun. I shot him.' Self-defense. But the next stage was, 'I thought he was going to reach for his gun, and I shot him.' Self-defense again, even if the man had no gun. But with such a plea accepted any man could shoot a rival in love or business and go free.

"The State of Nebraska will have none of the privilege of free killing. A man has a right to defend himself when attacked, but are there not other possible defenses besides killing? Joel is a big strong man. Vigorous, young. His victim was a small man, far along in his sixties, physically nothing. One blow of Joel's fist would have flattened him out. Or if it was necessary to shoot, Joel could have shot him in the shoulder or the leg, to disable him. There was no necessity to kill Emory. At least Joel should have tried other ways of defending himself.

"In the circumstances the State does not charge murder. It does charge manslaughter. And a term in prison of five years or even of one would be salutary. It would discourage killing in self-defense when there are other means of self-defense.

"The State rests."

The attorney for the defense rose.

"You've heard what you can do in self-defense. If a man jumps at you with an inch of extra thumbnail to gouge out your eye, just slap him and say, 'Quit it.' He may decide your eye is too hard to get, and decide to go after another fellow's eye. Your eye or mine, maybe.

"My honorable opponent says Joel could have stopped the attacker with a shot in shoulder or leg. You can't stop a man with a small calibre pistol. Joel had a 32. It makes a small hole that only aggravates the attacker.

"I want to tell you a little story. There was an officer of one of the societies for kindness to animals, out walking in Wyoming. As he was going through the sage brush he met a mountain lion. The animal didn't look friendly, but the man said, 'Nice kitty, nice kitty.' Oh, no, he wouldn't shoot it. Why, the poor thing couldn't have weighed sixty pounds, and he was a big fellow, weighing, I judge, two hundred and forty." He fixed his eyes on the prosecuting attorney, who was of about that weight. The jurors fixed their eyes there too, and grinned.

"Well, the mountain lion flew at him. He got it by the throat and was choking it a little to calm it, but the animal's hind leg claws were tearing out his victuals—excuse me, I meant vitals."

The court room roared with laughter. When quiet was restored the defense attorney said,

"That's the kind of self-defense the prosecuting attorney believes in.

"The defense rests."

The jury retired to their room. They were in high spirits. "That defense attorney is as good as a variety show."

The foreman read the charge to the jury. "Well boys, what are we going to do? Acquit or convict?"

"Acquit," said one. "Acquit, acquit," became a chorus. But one man, Harrison Smith, said, "I don't agree." He was a "reader" and considered himself an authority on politics and law.

"Don't let's go too fast, boys," he said. "There is something in what the prosecutor says. We don't want self-defense to grow into a charter for miscellaneous killing. I would be happy if Joel could be sentenced for a week, or a month. It would put a brake on self-defense killings."

The eleven other jurors argued with him and soon began to get angry. Harrison Smith held out stubbornly. He was standing for a principle, he said. The principle, "Thou shalt not kill."

At last the foreman of the jury rapped for silence.

"Boys, we can't agree with Harrison Smith, but we've got to admire him. He stands for principle, if the skies tumble in. They won't do that, but his career will.

"He's planning to run for the legislature. He'd make a good legislator. But when the farmers learn that he held out for tearing her new husband away from Helena Wilson and sticking him in the penitentiary there won't be a vote for him in the county. He can't be elected dog catcher. And I don't know how his business will go. I think he'd better go back to the Missouri bresh, where he came from, and go in for raising goats."

Harrison Smith said nothing, but was visibly disturbed.

"Now look here, Harrison," said the foreman, "it's really six of one and half a dozen of the other, to you. Let's draw straws. If you get the short one you vote with us. If you get the long one you'll hang the jury. We'll report that we can't agree."

"All right."

The foreman got two straws, pinched them to equal length. Harrison saw the fraud, but drew just the same and announced that he had the short straw and would vote for acquittal.

As the jury filed in, two women came into the court room. The first to see them cried, "Helena Wilson Arbuthnot!" The whole room rose and applauded.

Joel was making his way to them through the pressure of handshakes. The foreman of the jury reached Helena first.

"Say, Mrs. Helena, I worked hard for you. Don't I get a kiss for that?"

Helena offered her lips. In old-fashioned novels, she said to herself, women took great pleasure in bewhiskered kisses. A rugged race, in those days.

The new house was rising swiftly, as if by magic. The site was a little peninsula between two deep gullies running parallel down to the creek that curved its way through the Arbuthnot farm. The peninsula ran approximately east and west, its point peering at the sunrise through clumps of red elm trees, clusters of a dozen gracefully curved stems, looking when in leaf like giant ferns. By good luck the elms had escaped the depredations of the small boys of the neighborhood who regarded "slippery elm" bark as a necessity to chew in school hours when the teacher wasn't looking.

The north gully bank was set with box elders, known in the East as ash-leaved maples. Helena meant to replace them with evergreens, rising rank above rank from the bottom of the gully. Full grown they would strain the biting snow out of the blizzard that could be expected every year. The neighbors said evergreens wouldn't grow in Nebraska, the proof being that there were no native evergreens short of Long Pine out among the sandhills. Helena knew why. Every year since glacial times, prairie fire had swept over the grassy plains of central Nebraska. If any evergreen had ever put its head above the grass the prairie fire would have singed it to death. Some box elders had survived the fires. The box elder is a weed tree you can't kill. There were cottonwoods and willows by the creeks and some elms, red and white, on banks where erosion held back the growth of inflammable grass. Now, with the prairie fire extinguished, Helena was sure she could grow a fine grove of Minnesota pine.

The site was a good three hundred yards from the old Arbuthnot house as Helena had specified. Joel had paved the path with bright pebbles from the creek bed, pebbles so smoothly rounded one could walk on them in bare feet. Already the path was being firmed by Luella's and Helena's feet. Mornings and afternoons they had to look at the new construction and note its progress.

"When the house is finished," Luella said, "how will you find time to keep up your dress designing in town? Joel needs your help on his agricultural experiments. He says the Indians are right. It takes a woman's hand to make plants grow."

"I've thought that all out," said Helena. "I want to work with Joel, but I don't want my dress designing shop in the Rose Cottage to die out. I've been training my seamstresses to take over. The one I took on first will be a first-class dress designer when she overcomes her excessive modesty. I've had her design a dozen dresses and she did it well. A lady of the Pathfinder Park set came in for a dress and I had Gracie do it. She made a design bolder than I would have made, and better. And the other two seamstresses are crazy about designing. They will make it.

"Maybe I shouldn't compare my modest art of designing with the great arts, but in some way they are alike. The arts, both great and small, can be transmitted.

"Do you suppose that all those square miles of painting that are credited to Rubens were done by his own hand? He had talented assistants and an assistant could do the hounds at the feet of Artemis as well as the Master could. People go all the way to St. Petersburg to see what they consider the best work of Rubens. He never lived in St. Petersburg long enough to cover all those enormous wall spaces with his own hand. Some of the best of them, it is surmised, are entirely the work of a disciple, who could out-Rubens Rubens himself."

Events were pushing forward the transfer of the art of dress designing, for Helena was "expecting." Nebraska was still the land

"Where children are blessings, and he who has most,
Has heirs to his freedom and riches to boast."

But when a man met a woman whose slender body was being molded by the hand of God as a vase to hold the priceless bud of human life with its infinite possibilities, he did not let his glance drop below the woman's face. And even so it was the rule for the woman to avoid the looks of men, even of a father-in-law. Helena kept herself to the upstairs sun parlor of her new house. The gravel path was trodden only by the feet of Luella, who came to visit early in the morning and late in the morning, in the afternoon and the evening too, if there was moonlight.

Luella was filled with anxiety. She recalled the ordeal she had suffered when Joel was a-borning. It looked to her as if Helena was carrying just as big a baby, and Helena was smaller than she. But there was not the least sign of anxiety on Helena's face. It was as calm and beautiful as the face of a marble Aphrodite.

The crisis came. Helena insisted that Luella should not come into the house until it was over. The nurse and the doctor would take care of her. She might groan or even howl and she did not want Luella to hear her.

The birth proceeded slowly, and as the second day wore on Luella felt another hour of anxiety would kill her. But at last the baby bounded into the world with a great cry. The nurse carried it out of the room to show it to Joel.

He came tiptoeing in. Helena's face was pale, but her eyes were bright.

"You don't have to whisper, Joel. I'm all right. All through the ages women have been able to get right up and take care of their babies. I could, but I don't need to. Go and bring Mother. Don't tell her anything about the baby but that his name is Richard, after her father."

"I'd rather have had the baby a girl like you."

"It might have been a strapping big girl, taking after you, or a little skinny boy, taking after me. We'd better be content."

The three hundred yards between the houses seemed a mile to Joel. But in five minutes he led Luella into Helena's room. Helena drew the sheet over young Richard.

"Nobody shall criticize my baby the first hour of his life."

"Daughter, he's your baby but my grandchild. I don't care if he is black as the ace of spades. He's my grandchild and I have a right to see him and hold him in my arms."

Helena drew back the sheet. Oh, what a pink baby! Pink from head to his downcurling little toes. Pink except for a thin covering of yellow hair on his head, a big head elongated by birth molding but still a beautiful head. What wide shoulders, what a big round chest, and arms and legs too long even for such a body.

Luella bent down over him. The baby opened his big blue eyes and seemed to give Luella an incredulous look. She must have been a strange sight, for a baby is not born with a sense of perspective. What Richard saw was a curving plane with all objects in sight flattened on it. He closed his eyes.

Luella picked him up and pressed him against her breast. He opened his eyes again. The corners of his mouth twitched.

"He smiled at me," Luella cried. "Joel did that when he was half an hour old. My Joel come back to me as a baby. My Joel!" she returned the baby to his mother's side and dropped on her knees.

"Thank you, God! *Thank you! Thank you!*"

"Because he's white," said Helena.

"No! Because he's safe. Because we have my Joel over again. I wish he had at least a touch of color. I'd prove to you that color foolishness is burned out of me, down to the soles of my feet."

"Kiss me, Mother. And now, Joel will show you the little apartment we've fitted up for you, so that when you are tired, or it's stormy, or Richard is sick, you won't have to plod back to the other house."

Luella smiled faintly, "Two women under one roof."

"Two women under one roof is an abstraction," Helena said. "You and I, with Joel and Richard between us, are realities. That is something quite different."

THE
FARM
BY
THE
LAKE

"GOOD FENCES make good neighbors" according to
Robert Frost. He was thinking of Vermont fences built
of fieldstone and designed to last until the next geologic
upheaval raises Vermont to Himalayan heights or sinks
it deep under the ocean. On the Nebraska prairie good
fences are more needed, for there is much more livestock to invade a neighbor's field and destroy his crops.
There is no fieldstone on the prairie for fencing. A good
prairie fence is of barbwire stretched taut as a rod and
securely stapled to sound oak posts. It will not last forever like Robert Frost's stone fence. Fifteen years make
up the probable life of the posts. But they can be replaced gradually, as rot destroys their footing.

Karl Hedeman had built good fences. Where the line had to cross a small stream he set posts, usually with big knots on the thick end, very deep and slanted with the stream. But the prairie had a hazard not known to Robert Frost, the flash-flood, or as it was known on the prairie, the cloud burst. An innocent little stream, gurgling over its bed of many-colored gravel, might suddenly become a river twenty feet deep and fifty yards wide.

The flood might pass over the fence with no damage except the clothing of the wires with rubbish that would rust them if it weren't promptly pulled off. But the flood that initiates this story brought along a huge up-rooted oak, with short, broken branches and roots, which caught in Karl's fence. The force of the flood spun the oak trunk like a great bobbin, pulling the wires from their posts and winding them in a tangled spool Karl and his son Bertil would have to work on for days. When the flood subsided there were great gaps in the fence on both sides of the stream, opening the Hedeman pasture to the farm of a good but violent-tempered neighbor, Clara Gustavsen, who would never accept the forces of nature as an excuse.

Bertil had driven the cows in from the pasture for the milking. To his grave concern the bull was missing. He had gone visiting, Bertil was sure, to the Gustavsens'. He was not a vicious bull, but he had a habit of walking off the premises any person who in his opinion didn't belong there. A few days earlier a townsman who had come into the Hedeman pasture to shoot quail came in great indignation to the house, his shirt and trousers lacerated beyond repair.

"Your gentleman cow chased me, meant to kill me, and I got stuck in your damn barbwire fence."

In that refined age "bull" was a four-letter word never voiced in the hearing of women. One said "gentleman cow," or simply "animal" with a special intonation. Karl Hedeman was of earlier traditions and called a bull a bull, to the distress of refined hearers.

Karl and Bertil regarded quail hunters as the lowest form of life. Their farm was a quail sanctuary and when they heard gunshots in their wood lot they would go out and chase the hunters off. For once the bull had done the job, and they loved him for it.

Bulls had no terrors for Bertil, a robust young man of twelve. A boy quick on his feet can outrun a bull, except when the beast is charging. Then the boy can do an about turn while the bull charges on. If a bull pretended to tangle with Bertil, the boy ran up to the bull's flank and hit him on a horn with a stout stick, hit him at the base of the horn where the nerves are concentrated. The bull would twist his neck and make a horrible face. Such a blow, Karl Hedeman said, gave a pain like a bull-sized toothache. After one taste of the stick the bull had great respect for Bertil.

It would be milking time at Clara Gustavsen's and the Hedeman bull would be turning up in the cow yard. Bertil ran to the breach in the fence, through the sticky silt and up the bank. Suddenly the air was torn with the shrillest shrieks Bertil had ever heard. He ran up to see Clara Gustavsen flying, with the bull walking her off the premises. The bull meant no harm but Clara thought he was charging to gore her. She was running for dear life with a splashing bucket of milk in one hand, the other holding above her huge white knee all the skirts she had, red and blue, yellow and striped, all flopping in the wind. Bertil ran up to the bull, who stopped to twist his neck and make a face in anticipation of a blow on the horn. Bertil caught him by the nose ring.

Clara kept running and shrieking, the last of the milk in the pail splashing her skirts. Bertil had never seen anything so funny as her many-colored skirts flopping around her over-buxom knee. He laughed with the un-restrained laughter of boyhood.

She stopped running, and turned toward him in great rage.

"You wicked boy! Laughing at a poor woman run-ning for her life, with that fiend of an animal of yours trying to kill her. I'll give you something to laugh about." She approached with hand stretched out to slap him.

"I'll have to let the 'animal' go," he said.

"No, no! Take him away! But I'll come and talk with your father in the morning. He will whip you. Wicked boy."

Clara spoke broken English, interspersed with Swed-ish words. One could reproduce her speech, but the reader wouldn't understand it. Besides, a part of her speech was rural Swedish sing-song, the principle of which consists in placing the accented syllable an octave higher or lower than the rest of the word.

The next morning Karl Hedeman and Bertil were at the grindstone, getting the ax in shape for the fall wood-cutting. Clara appeared, flanked by Axel her husband. Clara's face was contorted with rage. She hadn't cooled off since Bertil left her yard with the bull.

"Hedeman, let me tell you about that nice boy of yours. Your gentleman cow was after me, to kill me. I was running for my life, and your nice boy laughed at me. He must be whipped."

Karl Hedeman stroked his beard. "My son said he didn't laugh till he got the bull by the nose ring. Maybe he was laughing at the bull. It does look funny, to see that big black bull twisting his neck and making a face, when a twelve-year-old boy goes after him."

Instantly Clara's rage shifted to Karl Hedeman.

"Axel!" she cried. "Did you hear those words?" (The "words" in question were the unsayable word bull,

heard more than once.) "He insulted me. At him, Axel!
At him!"

Poor Axel swung his fists menacingly and came one
step toward Karl Hedeman, who came one step toward
Axel. His father, Bertil could see, was amused: Axel
attack him!

Axel considered himself a small, weak man and Hedeman a big strong one. Axel was really bigger and
stronger than Hedeman. But all the lines of his body
and personality curved downward. Hedeman's lines
curved upward.

"At him, Axel!"

Axel came forward one more step. Terror seized him,
he turned right and fled over the garden, deep mud from
the rains. Hedeman followed him at the double quick
of an old soldier, something more terrifying than straight
running, for it can go on indefinitely. In the middle of
the garden Axel's wooden shoes stuck fast in the mud.
Axel ran on in his stocking feet. Hedeman stopped. No
need to pursue poor Axel farther. Clara was pursuing
him, all her rage newly concentrated on Axel.

Karl Hedeman returned to the grindstone.

"Bertil," he said, "I don't blame you for laughing.
When things are so funny you have to laugh. But you
don't need to laugh aloud. Laughing aloud is just like a
hen cackling when she has laid an egg. It doesn't do
her any good. Ducks lay bigger eggs, but don't quack
about them.

"Haven't I had a lot just now to laugh about? What
will happen to Axel when Clara gets hold of him? But
I laugh inside me. Learn to do that. It will save you
trouble."

The next morning Karl and Bertil were again at the
grindstone, putting the scythes in shape. Clara appeared,
all honeyed smiles.

"Poigie"—her affectionate name for Bertil—just the Swedish word for boy—"my gentleman cow has run off to the Reservation. Axel won't go after him. There are many gentlemen cows on the Reservation, and Axel is afraid of them. You are not afraid. You are so brave."

Gross flattery; but Bertil was not repelled. He was very young.

"My gentleman cow had plenty of company at home. But he had to go and look for other company. Just like other gentlemen." She shot a mischievous glance at Karl, which Bertil resented.

"Bertil," Karl said, "you'll have to do it. That's what comes of getting yourself the reputation of a toreador."

The Reservation was a stretch of prairie the size of a county that had been set apart for the Winnebago and Omaha Indians. It was rolling grass land except for a small wooded tract near a large stream. There the Indians had set up there tepees, leaving the prairie near the settlement utterly vacant. There was a farm every half mile abutting on the Reservation. Every farmer along the Reservation line kept many more cows than he could graze on his own land. He had plenty of free grass on the Reservation, thanks to the high respect Indians had for bulls, a respect like most forms of respect grounded in ignorance. Indians have never been cattle breeders and therefore know exactly as much about cows and bulls as white city folk know. They do not know that the bull is as a rule a fairly friendly animal, sometimes with a rather primitive sense of humor.

So the Winnebago Indians totally misinterpreted the behavior of a bull who visited the tepee settlement of the Indians. Chief Little Thunder came out to drive away the bull, who quietly took the Chief by the waist between his two horns and tossed him up to the top of his tepee. The bull didn't gore him. But the Chief and the whole tribe misunderstood bulls thereafter. The farmers had a hundred square miles of good grass, undisputed by its rightful owners.

In Bertil's twelve-year-old maturity he knew bulls. He knew that he could outrun and sidestep any bull. Sometimes he would flaunt a red handkerchief before a bull's eyes. The bull never responded in wrath, as the bull of fiction does. Bertil did not know until years later that a bull can't see red at all. There is a defect in the structure of his eye that makes a red object appear a dirty dun. But ever since the time of the Minoans, inventors of the bull fight, people have talked about a "red rag to a bull."

Bertil did not relish the chore of going down on the Reservation to find Clara's bull. He would have to walk two or three miles to find the bull, and the sky threatened a thunderstorm. The prairie looked vast, with its tangle of low grassy hills. The farmers' herds would be grazing in obscure valleys where they could find the rare blue joint grass, as sweet as sugar cane. Fortunately the prairie was not such a tangle of hills as it appeared. There would be long ridges one could follow and survey the valleys on both sides. In a two- or three-mile walk one could catch sight of a dozen herds of cattle.

Bertil wasn't disappointed in failing to find Clara's bull in the first herd, or the second or the third. Such is the perversity of the grazing beast, it is continually going farther even to fare worse. But finally Bertil came to a herd in which two bulls were pawing up the sod and bellowing at each other. Yes, one was Clara's bull.

Bertil went down the valley. Clara's bull knew him and tried to hide among the cows. But Bertil went into the herd after him, brandishing his stick. The bull twisted his neck in anticipation of a blow on one of his horns. The boy caught him by the nose ring, snapped on a rope and set out for home. Two miles to go, and the thunderstorm was coming on. Soon the bull and Bertil were splashing their way through a heavy downpour.

The sky was bright again when Bertil led the bull through Clara's yard and tied him up securely in his stall. Then Clara descended upon Bertil with all her heavy charm. She had been so worried about him when the storm came on. But she knew Bertil wasn't afraid of lightning. Or of gentlemen cows. Or anything. He would be a brave soldier like his father.

Gross flattery again; but when one is twelve, one takes kindly to flattery from whatever source.

Clara and Axel had come from Sweden in one of those beneficent rate wars among immigrant shipping companies, when one could go from Stockholm to Nebraska for twenty-five dollars. That was about all the capital Clara and Axel had. They descended upon a remotely related Swedish family on a farm ten miles from Hedeman's. The relatives, finding that Clara and Axel had only three dollars between them, advised them to appeal to Hedeman, who had a passion for planting immigrants on farms.

There was a forty-acre farm adjoining Hedeman's which had been deserted by its owner years before. The house was giving up to the weather, and so was the barn. The field, twenty acres of fertile land, was blanketed with the dead weeds of three seasons.

The farm, properly worked, could make a living for a farmer. It was to be had for $500, $100 in cash and $400 on a two-year mortgage. Hedeman always kept a modest hoard of money, gold eagles, in the base of the kitchen clock. He gave the necessary hundred to Clara and Axel, and advised them to buy the place in Clara's name. Mortgages tended to drift into the hands of loan sharks, who made harsh exactions at the time of renewal, threatening foreclosure. A loan shark in that country did not dare to plunder a woman mortgagor. There had been loan sharks who tried it and got tarred and feathered and ridden out of the county on rails.

And so the little farm was owned by Clara. Hedeman had tried to make it clear that this was only a legality; that the farm belonged to both of them. Clara could never see that. The farm was hers. Axel was her hired man, subject to her orders.

Out of neighborliness Hedeman reshingled the house and patched the plaster. He cleaned out the well and put in a pump. He ran a furrow around the field and burned off the blanket of dead weeds. Then he enlisted two neighbors to help him get the field plowed and planted to corn. He found a team, second rate but cheap, for Axel and loaned him farm machinery. He bought Clara a good milch cow, a farrowing sow and a dozen hens.

The farm would soon supply all the food Clara and Axel needed. If the season proved good the field would produce a thousand bushels of corn, worth $250; but in the fall Clara could buy a carload of cattle driven back from summer grazing in the west, and fattening them, could make $500 out of the $250 worth of corn. Then Clara could begin to pay off her debts.

The season was a good one. Axel produced the thousand bushels of corn and had to work down to Christmas husking it, with the cold wind and light snows to keep him miserable. Clara bought the range cattle and fattened them and came out $600 ahead. Now, Hedeman suggested, she could begin to pay off her mortgage. But Clara had other plans. Why worry about the mortgage so long as she paid the interest? Nobody could foreclose on a woman. As for the sums she had borrowed from Hedeman, he wouldn't take interest, and he didn't need his money. So Clara bought three more "forties" on mortgage.

A quarter section was more than Axel could work, but as the conventional homestead was a quarter section, four forties, one hundred sixty acres, Hedeman condoned Clara's land hunger.

Karl Hedeman came from Denmark in the early 1850s, a forerunner of the great Scandinavian immigration of the Sixties and Seventies. He had been born on a little farm that stood as a dry island in a great swampy heath. The farm was so inaccessible that it had never been drawn into the estate of a feudal lord. The Hedemans had never been serfs or tenants. The farm had passed from father to son through countless generations, under the quaint pre-Aryan custom that gave the farm to the youngest son, who assumed responsibility for caring for the aging parents. The older sons went out into the world to make places for themselves. Most of them went to sea. Karl Hedeman's heart was in the soil, and all Europe knew, America was a continent of free land. A fifty-seven-day passage in a sailing ship brought Hedeman to the city of New York, already growing so fast that the farms around Washington Square were being cut up into building lots. There were jobs to be had for immigrant workmen, but Karl Hedeman was not interested in city life. By steamboat on the Hudson and the Erie Canal and a steamship on the Great Lakes, he made his way to the Middle West, where he worked at one job after another, looking about for the farm home of his heart's desire.

There was an active Danish immigration in the early Sixties. The Germans had made war on Denmark and had taken away Holstein and Schleswig. Holstein was mostly German, but Schleswig was half Danish. The Germans were trying to make Germans out of those Danes, who, when they could, fled to America. In the southern part of Jutland there was a vivid fear that the Germans would soon grab them too. Many were emigrating to America.

Karl Hedeman heard, at the grocery store, that a group of Danes from Jutland had come over and were being entertained by the Boyesen family, three miles from his homestead. It was Sunday, and as a rule Karl kept out of the field on Sunday, though in emergencies he might cite one of the few Biblical texts he knew, "The Sabbath is made for man, not man for the Sabbath."

He hitched up his horses to the buggy and went over to call on the Boyesens. There he found several families of new immigrants, and among them a girl of about twenty, tall and robust, brown haired and as he saw her "quite good looking." He was introduced. She was Ingeborg Juhl.

"Juhl," he said. "My grandfather's grandfather was an Admiral Juhl, a great friend of the Dutch Admiral van Tromp."

"He was my grandfather's great grandfather, too," said the girl.

"Then we are a kind of cousins. Do you know the city of Ribe?"

"Yes, it was the big city of my childhood."

"Mine too," said Karl. "The last time I was there you could see fourteen storks' nests on the house roofs."

"There were only twelve when I last counted them," said the girl.

Karl Hedeman's heart felt livelier than it had felt for years. This girl was talking to him and he was talking to her in the antique dialect of South Jutland. No American can know what that means. Your old, old dialect, when far from home you hear it, is like your sweet mother's voice in a dream.

"Ingeborg—excuse me, Miss Ingeborg—would you like to see a Ribe house in America? I have built one.

It's two hours to dinner. We could ride over and take a look at it."

"That would be nice," said Ingeborg.

They explained to their host and drove away.

"Oh!" cried Ingeborg as Karl drove up to his house. *"Bindwerk!* Like the Burgomaster's house in Ribe."

"Yes, but small."

"Big for me. But how could you find carpenters who understand Bindwerk?"

"I couldn't. I did all this myself. It took me two years."

"But it's home." Ingeborg sighed. Two tears ran down her cheeks to her humiliation. Karl had felt that way too about home.

Bindwerk was the architectural specialty of the late 17th and early 18th century. You hewed square oak beams, eight inches thick, and mortised them together in triangles and parallelograms to make the complete outline of a house. Then you filled in the spaces between the beams with concrete. The beams showed on the outside and the inside. The effect was so charming that suburban architects still to our day tack boards in angles and parallelograms on plaster walls and call the buildings Queen Anne cottages. Karl Hedeman had built the only honest Bindwerk building in America.

"Take me back to the Boyesens'," said Ingeborg. "This Ribe house makes me want to cry."

They drove over the prairie.

"Ingeborg— Miss Ingeborg— Oh hell, Ingeborg. Would you like to live in that Ribe house?"

She remained silent long. But finally she said:

"Yes." And then she blushed, beautifully.

"I will come with the buggy for you tomorrow at nine. We can go to the courthouse and be married."

She turned pale. "Yes," she said, after a long interval, and blushed again.

Next morning she was ready when Karl appeared in his buggy. As they drove over the prairie he tried to find something to say. Even in Jutland dialect his effort went flat. They found a humorous old judge, and Karl explained what they were after. The judge expedited, and in half an hour kissed Ingeborg as Karl's wife.

They drove back to the Boyesens', trying to talk but with nothing to say. Karl explained matters to Mrs. Boyesen, who congratulated him, while Ingeborg was bringing out her little trunk. They drove across the prairie, with still nothing to say.

In the pioneer world courtships were very brief. Marriage, yes, but honeymoons, for two young people to learn the inadequacy of passion, no. Marry today and do chores tomorrow. And those casual and quick unions had the peculiar character that they lasted. Survey a hundred square miles of prairie; you wouldn't discover one "grass widow"—divorcee.

Karl Hedeman was a good farmer. He was not one who worked himself to death, but one who used his head. He never sowed small grain over frost in the ground, nor failed to have his seed in the ground for the spring rains. He planted only as much corn as he could tend well. He studied the native meadow grass and learned that when it is first in flower it is packed with nutriment which four weeks later is all lost in seed. The wild grasses flowered in August, a month of uncertain weather. On a bright morning Karl would be out at dawn with his mowing machine and cut some acres of grass. Under the August sun the new-mown grass would by noon be dry enough to rake up and build into cocks that could shed most of the rain that would come in the afternoon. On such hay his cattle kept fat through the winter, as if they were on rich pasture.

Karl and Ingeborg were one in their passion for self-sufficiency. Their bread was from their own wheat, their meat from their own cattle and hogs. Ingeborg produced enough butter and eggs to cover all purchases at the store.

Every year Karl would have a carload of fat hogs and another of cattle for sale. Prices were low; Karl didn't care. He got some money, real money in gold, which he banked in the kitchen clock. He had it ready to lend to a neighbor in distress, without interest; for it earned no interest in the clock; why should it earn more in a neighbor's hands?

Karl Hedeman loved the prairie. He would say to his son Bertil, "You can go hundreds of miles, east, west, north, south, all good plow land. There are a half million square miles of it, every square mile good for four quarter-section farms. Two million of them where any good farmer could make a comfortable living."

By the time Bertil was ten he was as ardent a prairie lover as his father. He, too, dreamed of the two million farm homes practically self-sufficient, like his own home, making very little money but not caring to make money.

In slack seasons of farm work Hedeman would make up a pretext for a long drive over the prairie. It was a principle of the family to eat bread and Johnny cake only of flour and meal from wheat and corn kept clean and dry in their rat-proof granary. When the flour and corn meal in the kitchen ran low, Hedeman and Bertil would fill a sack with wheat and a smaller sack with corn and drive off to a water mill, where they could be sure it was their own clean grain that was ground if they watched the miller and the miller boy, "with one hand in the hopper and the other in the sack." If they were not watched they would substitute for Hedeman's good grain mouldy and ratty grain from their big bins.

There was a perfectly good water mill three miles away, but Hedeman and Bertil would make themselves believe that there was a better mill thirty miles west over the prairie. After a mile in the valley the road ascended to the crest of one of the long grassy ridges that dominate the rolling structure of the prairie. On either side were spurs dropping lower till they reached a long valley. Between the spurs were little valleys, often choked with thickets of sumac and wild plum, and occasionally with the prairie type of walnut, more than a bush but not quite a tree.

As the little valleys widened they made space for homesteads.

"Bertil, look at that place. That little white house and big red barn. That is a Maine man. You can see, he is successful. He has put twice as much money into his barn as he's put into his house."

The next valley showed a ramshackle shanty, the barn roofed with a stack of straw. A steep slope had been broken and was already showing yellow-bottomed erosion ditches.

"That, Bertil, is probably the homestead of a Civil War veteran. They were my comrades in Sherman's Army and I ought to think well of them but I can't. They were probably industrious farm boys when they went into the Army. They came out after three years like this homesteader.

"You see how it is. In the army you're not expected to do any thinking for yourself. You get up when the reveille sounds. You eat when the bugle tells you to. You get ready for bed at tattoo and you put your light out at taps. Two or three years of that, and you won't get up when the cock crows, nor listen when the cows bawl to be milked or the pigs squeal. You don't say to yourself, 'The ground is dry enough; I'll sow the wheat.' No, you say, 'Hell, it's pretty raw; I'll wait a day.' And then you get ten days of rain, and it's too late to sow wheat.

"Now look at what this fellow has done. He broke up

a steep slope because it is near his shanty. A hundred yards above there is a big stretch of ground nearly level. It is good ground; you can see from the big compass plants. This fellow felt he'd have to walk a hundred yards to get to his field. Too much for him."

A mile farther on they stopped to look at another forlorn homestead, an unpainted shanty, sheds with straw roofs. Down the valley from the house, the well. Behind the house on the north, a steep little spur of hill.

"There's another no-good farmer. I don't think he is a Civil War veteran but just a small-town boy who never learned anything. See how he put his well below his house. Any dirt from the house will go into the well, and the women will have to carry the water up hill. He could have put his house below his well and could have piped water into the house.

"And see, he put his house under a steep hill spur on the north. He thought the hill would break the wind for him. One of these days there will be a blizzard. The crest of the hill will make the wind drop its snow on the leaside. He'll wake up some morning in a house under a thirty-foot snowdrift.

"He can't be a veteran. No such fool could have lived through the war."

They drove on past a half dozen homestead failures and stopped to survey a promising farm down a widely expanding valley. Two half-grown boys and a buxom girl were working in a garden.

"This farmer is a German," Hedeman said. "See those sheaves? They are barley. What do people grow barley for? To make beer."

"Beer!" Bertil said, with disgust.

"You don't like the taste. But you can be sure, those boys you see in the garden, and the girl, too, do like it.

"On a German farm, when everybody in the field, man, boy and girl, are feeling worn out they all go to the house and sit under the shade trees, and the mother brings up a pitcher of cool beer from the cellar, and black bread with butter and some awfully strong cheese. Everybody eats the bread and cheese and washes it down with beer. Then they go back to work, feeling fine.

"Those boys will grow up to be good farmers, and the girl to be a good farmer's wife.

"You see, Bertil, there is no such thing as a permanent farm population that doesn't have beer or wine. That's so all over Europe where you find farm families that have lived on the same land for a thousand years."

"Well, Father, why don't we have beer or wine, and black bread with strong cheese?"

"Because you are already lost to farm life. You dream of going to college, and Mama dreams you will, and so do I.

"There's something else to consider, Bertil. Here are all these farms of veterans and town lazybones. They are all going to be bought up by speculators. And the land will be put into big lots and farmed by big men with hired labor, who will try to make money. As I see it the only real value of a farm is as a home. As a business it is pretty poor business. I'm glad you will strike out for something else."

Bertil was six years old when Clara and Axel descended upon the Hedemans, to be guests until their own house could be patched up. Bertil was not, in his own opinion, a mere child, but the only son and a potential man. His parents had the same opinion of his status and treated him with the respect due to the clear promise of a man. If there was something they wanted him to do, they put their wishes in the form of a request, not a command.

To Bertil Axel was just a stranger, with a thin voice and thin gestures, a person one could hardly notice. But

Clara was something else. She was huge and noisy. She didn't get up from a chair; she bounced up. She romped around like a six-year-old girl. She had a shrill voice and was very voluble in a language Bertil couldn't at first understand and that made difficulties even for his parents.

She had hardly got into the house when she caught Bertil up to mother him against her deeply cushioned bosom. He must have protested, for she set him down and boxed his ears.

Bertil was outraged. Not even his own parents would take such liberties with him. For the rest of the stay of the visitors Bertil kept out of sight as well as he could. Meal times were hard to manage. Clara did succeed in catching Bertil and mothering him to her breast. "Sweet Poigie," she'd call him and inflict a heavily salivated kiss on his cheek. And Bertil's was a family in which nobody kissed.

Fundamentally Clara didn't approve of Bertil— "Poigie." Bertil's mother had taught him to read when he was three, and by the time he was six, he had covered much literary ground, particularly a huge *Child's History of the Bible.* He was now attacking the King James version, by no means beyond a six-year-old intelligence, though sometimes using peculiar words.

Bertil's father had opened a limestone quarry, and there he had shown Bertil the shells of primitive clams and oysters and other shellfish dating back to the time when all the prairie was an ocean, millions of years ago. And this was in sharp conflict with the chronology of Genesis. Bertil had to go through the conflict of science and revealed religion in his six-year-old head.

Clara thought Bertil's parents had done him a great wrong in teaching him to read so early. He had lost his childhood. She said he walked like an old man, his head bowed forward as if he were thinking. So he was, in fact.

It was Clara's idea that every male boy or man should run. She made Axel run to the barn to feed the horses and run back for breakfast. Bertil wouldn't run unless he saw reason to run.

Clara's disapproval of Bertil's literacy did not abate as he grew older. But she found a use for it. She could not read English, Bertil doubted that she could read Swedish, for when a letter came to her from Sweden she would have Ingeborg read it to her. Ingeborg didn't speak Swedish, but her Danish met the requirement.

By the time Bertil was ten he could understand Clara's Swedish perfectly. She had a small vocabulary and used the whole of it over and over. Bertil could have learned to speak Swedish, but Clara made so much fun of his accent that he forbore, using Swedish words only when he had to do it to make her understand a letter. It was her habit to buy everything she needed on credit and to delay with payment. And so she had a profusion of dunning letters. At first she had Hedeman read them and write replies. But that gave him an insight into her business. Bertil could explain the letters to her as well, and she had the naive notion, he wouldn't be able to understand her business.

Any day she might stand on her porch and shout, "Poigie. A letter."

One day she shouted: "Poigie! A letter. A terrible letter."

The letter was from the county treasurer. She hadn't paid her taxes.

Bertil read the letter to her.

"The scoundrel! I have paid those taxes."

Clara was lying. She always began any discussion with a lie. Bertil's father said it wasn't very wrong to lie if nobody believed you. He was always right in Bertil's opinion, but Clara's lies were hard for him to assimilate.

"The taxes are $20," Bertil said calmly. "He says they

are due the 29th. That is next Friday."

"I'll have to go up Saturday. I'll pay the scoundrel."

"There is a ten per cent penalty if you haven't paid by Friday. Two dollars."

"Oh, the robber! I won't pay him anything. And if he comes here they'll tar and feather him."

"No, they don't tar and feather tax collectors. You had better go Thursday and pay the taxes."

"You, a ten-year-old Poigie, ordering a woman?"

"Yes. If you don't pay your taxes the loan shark will pay them for you. He will get a tax lien on your place, as good as a mortgage. Nobody can buy your place without clearing off the tax lien. You'd have to get a lawyer—."

"No, a lawyer. They are robbers and thieves and scoundrels."

"So, you'd better go up Thursday and pay your taxes."

"Because Poigie is ordering me."

"No, because you don't want a tax lien plastered on your place."

She sighed, "I'll go."

Clara was developing a voluminous correspondence with a man who signed himself "Billy." She had Bertil read his communications to her and write some kind of reply. She wouldn't address the letter of reply, because she didn't want Bertil's father to know what she was doing. She had no notion that Bertil knew very well. "Billy" was William MacGregor, a Scotchman who had come into the country with a lot of money, set by rumor at half a million sterling. A bachelor in his fifties, with neither chick nor child he cared for, either here or in Scotland. But he was a man with a theory.

Billy's theory was that the prairie was destined to be a region of large farms, a square mile in size, four of the quarter sections Hedeman considered the ideal unit. A man with a sense of business, and with capital enough to get good farm equipment, could hire new German, Scandinavian or even Italian workers, and make money on a square-mile farm. So Billy believed.

Karl Hedeman and Billy liked each other, though they totally disagreed about how the prairie should develop. Bertil liked Billy. He didn't just call the boy Bub and push him out of the conversation, but told him about the privilege a boy had in being educated in Scotland with Latin and Greek two additional mother tongues. Bertil was struggling on his own to master Latin, but Greek was in the clouds. Billy presented Bertil with a history of Greece, by a Doctor Timayennis, perhaps not a very good history, but to an adolescent a Greek fire.

"Father," Bertil said one day, "do you know Clara is buying two farms? The one north of us and the one north of her own farm?"

"Yes, and if she could buy our farm she would have the square-mile set-up Billy wants. Our farm is the key; we have the road. You'll see, Clara will come after us. And she won't get our farm."

"She's also after a group of homesteads out toward Winchell's. She's buying four of them."

"Yes. Billy is financing her."

"If he wants the homesteads, why doesn't he buy them himself?"

"Well, you know everybody thinks, Billy has half a million sterling. If he goes to a homesteader that fellow thinks, 'Oh, he can pay $2500 for my farm.' That may be what the place is worth. But if Clara goes to him and tells him, a bunch of poor Swedes are coming over and she could pay a thousand dollars for a quarter section, she gets it—for Billy."

"But that's a fraud," said Bertil.

"Not exactly. You see, Bertil, those homesteaders are frauds. They put in their claims and got title to land that would make good farms. They never intended to make real farms out of them. In a certain time they could 'prove up' and the land was theirs. They could sell it for $500, a thousand, possibly more, and go on to California or try their luck in a city. Clara is just a part of the process and will get a little money out of it. And you know, Clara's dream of life depends on money."

Bertil knew all about Clara's dream of life, and thought nothing of it. But his parents did. In the sound judgment of an adolescent, Bertil's sweet parents were romantic.

Clara's dream was planted on a farm in Sweden, the Farm by the Lake. There was a beautiful large field running from the hilltop forest down to a lovely lake, with wooded hills on the other side. There was a noble house dating from the 17th century, with a wide veranda overlooking the lake, a manor house in English terms. The gentry of the house led a life of delightful leisure. They had a manager of the farm and a well-trained maid and butler. These employees ate socially in the kitchen. There was a permanent farm hand who counted for little and his wife, the cow girl. The cow girl was not the milk maid of romance but a hard-working woman who not only milked the cows and carried the big wooden buckets on her head, but also saw that the cows got their feed, cleaned out their stalls and put in fresh straw to bed them, and led the cows to grass and tethered them.

Cow girl and her spouse, man of all work, had a little cottage alongside of the barn. They cooked their own food. The cow girl brought the milk to the dairy in the basement of the manor house, where the dainty maid of the house accepted it, holding her nose, for the cow girl stank.

Clara had been that cow girl and Axel her suppressed spouse. They should have been contented; their lot was the lot of generations. But a whiff of the French Revolution had entered Clara's nostrils. She and Axel would save their few dollars of wages and when they had enough for steamship fare they would go to America, make money, and come back and buy the Farm by the Lake. God help the snooty maid of the house, when Clara came back!

Clara's speculative transactions grew wider and wider. Bertil was kept busy in his little leisure time looking after her correspondence, which she still dreamed he didn't understand. But she was coming through to her dream. One spring Axel did no plowing, Clara's cows disappeared. Next the team was gone. Wagons came and carried off the farm machinery.

Clara came to the Hedeman house and said, engagingly, she had to go back to Sweden. She belonged back there; she never could know English. A little place in Sweden would be right for her and Axel. They would work hard and make their bread.

The liar! Bertil knew she had straightened out all her speculative relations with Billy MacGregor. Billy had taken over all her property and was paying her $17,000. He was ready to pay Hedeman $1000 besides for what he had spent on Clara.

The Farm by the Lake was to be had for $12,000. The owners were old. Their son was high up in Stockholm civil service. Their daughter was married to another high-up civil service official. The old folk wanted a little apartment in Stockholm, near their children. The Farm by the Lake was for sale. And Clara bought it.

"The last of Clara, thank God," Bertil thought. But no. The next spring Clara descended upon the Hedemans.

"You wouldn't imagine," she said, "what happened to Axel. You know I bought him a nice suit of store clothes when we went off to Sweden. When we got to

Stockholm he went to an English tailor and had him make a gentleman suit, cutaway coat, striped pants, a flowered light vest, a string tie, spats. Think of it, spats. And all charged to me.

"All charged to me. I hollered, but he said, 'This is Sweden and a man is a *mandsperson*' (a man personality).

"I bought the Farm by the Lake. With my money. Would you believe it? In Sweden a woman is nothing. The farm is Axel's.

"You know we have a lovely lake, and in the summer the young people of the city come to bathe in it. They have hardly any clothes on. And you wouldn't think it, that old fool Axel dresses up and with his cane walks down by the lake. He says those girls jump around so, they may burst a shoulder strap."

Ingeborg interrupted. "Axel must have a lot to do managing the farm."

"No. We have a manager. I tell him, we do so and so in America. He says, 'America has a lot to learn.'

"Think of it, the cow girl and her husband thought they ought to be allowed to eat in the kitchen, with the maid and manager. But I put them in their place.

"But Sweden is terrible. A man is everything, a woman nothing. It was my money bought the place. It is Axel who is lord of it.

"You wouldn't know Axel. He is America in Sweden. He has parties, and he tells about the big trees in America, so big a whole corporal's guard can get inside a hollow tree. He tells about poker games where he and the other three had six-shooters for anyone who cheated. He tells about dances where he steps on a lady's skirt and tears it. She says, 'Gee whilikins,' and he says, 'I beg your pardner.' And her pardner says, 'O.K.'

" 'If it were in Dalecarlia,' says a guest, 'the partner would be out with his knife.'

" 'In America,' says Axel, 'we don't use knives. We use six-shooters.' "

"I wonder where Axel got his stories," Karl Hedeman said. "He was never away from the farm. And I never heard of his reading wild west stories."

"Oh, there was a Swede on the boat, going over. He had been rolling around the country for ten years. A big liar. He got thick with Axel, because Axel paid for the drinks. With my money. —I'll tell you why I came over. A woman is nothing in Sweden. I want to come back. You will be selling your farm when Poigie goes off to college. You could sell it to me. I'd bring over a Swedish farmer to help me work it."

"I don't know I'll ever want to sell the farm," said Karl. "Ingeborg and I have to live somewhere, and we like our house. Besides, Bertil may change his mind about college. He may want to stay with the farm."

"Oh no!" said Clara. "Poigie must be a schoolmaster. He will have a good living and never have any real work to do. He can read books all the time."

"Well, maybe. I have thought of getting a Danish family to come and live on the place, and farm it on shares."

"No," said Clara, "that would be terrible. There are no Danish farmers that are any good. They go to Folk Schools and Cooperatives and want to get into the Riksdag. Let me have your place and I will bring an honest Swedish farmer I can depend on."

"I'll think about it," said Hedeman. But it was clear to Clara that there was no chance of an immediate decision.

She rose to go. "I'll come in to see you again."

"Papa," Bertil asked, "do you think Clara is really coming back here to live?"

"No. All that talk of Axel getting her property away from her is just one of Clara's stories."

"Then what did she come for? Just to buy our farm for Billy MacGregor?"

"She would have liked to do that, too. But Billy has his eye on a lot of clusters of homesteads in the counties west of us. He can use Clara's technique of buying them for groups of new immigrants. Buying them cheap. Clara can make two or three thousand for herself, in a few months' work."

"She'll be here to pester us again," Bertil said.

"No, she knows it wouldn't be of any use. We've seen the last of Clara."

It wasn't quite the last. For a Swedish neighbor dropped in on Clara in Sweden.

Axel was still playing gentleman. But Clara had gone in for business. She was a marvellous expert on knitting, and she had assembled twelve girls, to knit for the tourist trade. They were the twelve homeliest girls that had ever been assembled in a land of prevailingly beautiful girls. Cross-eyed, birthmarked, scarred with small pox, or just congenitally homely. And Clara had turned the parlor into a workroom for these frights. Axel had to put up with a so-called study on the second floor.

Clara had developed a wonderful specialty. It was a sock with an individual lobe for each toe. Any member of an American Chamber of Commerce visiting Stockholm would buy a dozen pairs of those socks to present them to good Americans who had never really thought through the problem of toes. To fuss with each individual toe? That was a joke on the rising captain of industry.

But Clara also did sweaters of remarkable design. And her Swedish-American friend had brought with her a sweater for Poigie.

The body of it was sea green. But on its breast were two sea monsters, blood red, with long black claws, long white tusks, threatening each other across a row of reindeer horn buttons. Clara wanted Poigie to wear that sweater in college; other boys would order sweaters from her.

"Me wear that?" thought Bertil indignantly. He wrapped it securely and put it into the deepest corner of the deepest drawer in the house. And years later when he dug it out, he found that moths had destroyed about all of it except the blood red monsters, whose dye must have been poisonous. Bertil took the thing out to the burning pile, where the family disposed of all sorts of rubbish.

That was for Bertil the last of Clara. Later he was sorry about the sweater. He should have kept it for a museum of folk art.

EQUAL
TO
ANY
MAN

"HE WAS such a nice baby," sighed the melancholy Mrs. Forbes. "He never cried or made any trouble. I thought sure he would grow into a fine man." "He is a fine man," asserted Dr. Harrison, professor of pedagogy in the nearby university. "There isn't a man in this community more anxious to do what is right as he sees it. There isn't a man who is more cheerful under whatever weather than Link."

"But he can't hold a job," Mrs. Forbes wailed. "I can keep the wolf away by taking in washing. But suppose I died. What would become of him?"

"You are far from dying. One of these days Link will get a job he understands. He will prove so faithful to it, his employer will want to keep him forever."

"Maybe," said Mrs. Forbes, sighing deeply.

Lincoln Forbes grew from a good baby into a good little boy, anxious to please and to do what his mother or anyone else wanted him to do. But he was strangely late in acquiring speech. His mother would talk to him and he would try hard to make sounds that seemed to him like her speech. The sounds were just as unintelligible to her as her speech was to him. She would scold him and he would cry.

By the time he had reached school age he had mastered "yes" and "no," "good" and "bad," but rather by intonation than normal sound. The word "good" covered his little face with smiles and the word "bad" cast down his spirit.

"Feeble-minded" was the comment of the teacher at first meeting him in school. She would have liked to send him back to his home at once, since the community had no institution for the feeble-minded. But she couldn't do that, for she and all the other teachers were under the domination of the brilliant young university instructor in pedagogy, Dr. Harrison.

There was a new educational philosophy sweeping the country, issuing from the chair of Professor Terman in Stanford. Everybody had always known that the children of man differ in abilities from Simple Simon up to Shakespeare.

It was the great achievement of Professor Terman to develop the vague conceptions of superiority and inferiority into exact data of definite mathematical value. This he did through subtly conceived intelligence tests. The average mind would rate 100. Below were the ratings of the mediocre, the dull-witted. Below the dull-witted you came to the morons, but there was no use for refinements there, since all morons were educationally hopeless. Above 100 were the fairly talented, the highly talented and at the very top, with ratings around 140, the budding genius.

The consequence for education was segregation of pupils, if their number made it feasible. One class for the low-witted, another for the mediocre, one for modest talent and one for high talent, with very special treatment of the budding genius.

To Dr. Harrison, Terman and all his works were anathema. What happened to a child if he were formally set apart as dull-witted? He was humiliated and his dullness went deeper. What happened to the mediocre? They were discouraged from striving for high places. Had we not had Presidents, great generals, celebrated divines who would have fallen into Terman's mediocre class, where they would have stayed under the discouragement of formal classification? And what of the highly talented? Every boy or girl has the seeds of egotism ready to sprout. They would grow luxuriantly under the talent classification. And as for the budding genius, he might go through college with high honors; he might become a famous scientist, but a true scholar he never could be, for a true scholar must think of himself last and rate his achievements with honest humility.

Dr. Harrison was a devotee of the venerable democratic religion of the essential equality of all men. The democratic religion recognized the disparities of talents among men, but conceived that men were endowed with talent to be helpful to their fellow men. The student with talent should make it his business to help the student without talent. He would gladly, Professor Harrison believed, if he were encouraged to take responsibility. Then when the lesson was too easy for him, instead of being bored he would be thinking, "This is pretty hard for my protégé Johnny Jones. But I think I can make him see it."

Of course the bright boy would occasionally bully

his protégé if the protégé seemed incapable of understanding. It doesn't hurt a boy to be bullied by a boy. He expects it. But to be bullied by a teacher is another matter. That may crush a child.

Under the sway of Dr. Harrison the whole school was humming at recess and noon with children helping one another. When the primary teacher presented Link and his problems to Dr. Harrison he patted the boy's head and said,

"You are a good boy, aren't you?" Link immediately fell in love with him.

"Harry," Professor Harrison called, "and Peter." Harry and Peter, two twelve-year-olds, ran to him.

"Boys, I want you to help us. Here is a nice little boy who finds it very hard to learn. I want you two boys to take him in hand. It will take time, but you will be patient with him."

"Yes, sir."

"Now Link, you will try to do everything Harry and Peter ask you to do."

"Yes," said Link. He hadn't understood, but "yes" seemed the right thing to say.

What Link most wanted to do was to play with the little children. They had all sorts of games, and Link tried to get into them. But always he violated the rules of the game, and there are no rules so binding as those little children adopt. After a very few minutes Link would do something fatally wrong and be driven away with exasperated cries of "Goof!" ringing in his ears. And the little children substituted Goof for his name Link.

The primary teacher felt Link's pathetic desire to be just one of the little children and had him sit in her singing class. For a few minutes he was happy. He joined in the singing with a high monotone which he conceived to be identical with the ditty the children were

singing. That broke up the singing. The class was overcome with laughter and the teacher had to lead Link
away.

When Link was ten his two faithful monitors, Harry
and Peter, went on to high school. They had carried him
far. He could read, "If at first you don't succeed." He
could write his name correctly on occasion but usually
it came out Linkun Forbs. Harry would bully him into
writing his name correctly ten times, but the eleventh
try brought Linkun Forbs again. He knew the order of
the alphabet down to the Rs. The letters beyond R were
sowed broadcast in his mind and could follow any order. In arithmetic he could add the lower integers but
he could not subtract. He knew the muliplication table
through the twos and early stages of the threes. He could
divide integers by two. Manipulating the figure 8 he
came out triumphantly with 4. But if 9 were put up to
him he came out 4 with 1 over. He felt that he had
made a mistake and filled his slate with 9s divided by 2s.
Now, where did that 1 come from, and what could be
done about it?

He could spell simple phonetic words and a few with
silent letters. Peter had been so bold as to try him on
words pronounced alike but spelled differently. Link's
struggles gave the little children a means of pestering
him. They would surround him and chant, "Bill Wright
the millwright can't write 'rite' right." Link's face
knitted up with perplexity and the children went off
with gales of laughter.

Professor Harrison appointed two new monitors for
Link. The boys worked hard on him, but Link had
reached his farthest north. All the monitors could do
was to check retrogression. And the school was much
relieved when Link reached his sixteenth birthday and
left the school, to look for a job.

His first job was with a gardener who set him at weed-

ing long rows of cabbage plants almost ready for trans-
planting. The weeds were mostly a kind of grass with
very tenacious roots. Link got down on hands and knees
and attacked the grass with vengeance. In his zeal to
get all the weeds he occasionally pulled up a cabbage
plant. After two hours the gardener came to see how
the work was going. There were long lines of massacred
weeds, but the gardener's eye fixed itself on the dying
cabbage plants.

"You fool! You've pulled up two dozen cabbage
plants. They're worth twenty-five cents a dozen. Get
your hat and clear out. I was going to pay you fifty
cents. You've destroyed fifty cents' worth of plants.
We're even."

Link tried to explain to his mother why he returned
so early and without pay. She scolded him severely, and
he cried.

His next job was to deliver bottles of milk by push-
cart along a row of houses. He had a slip of paper with
the house numbers and the number of bottles to be delivered at each doorstep. He could get the house numbers all right, and the number of bottles of milk to be
delivered. But keeping house numbers and bottle numbers together was too much mathematics for him. He
settled the matter by delivering four bottles to every
house and found to his perplexity that his supply of
bottles ran out long before the house numbers. When he
got his cart back to the shop many complaints were
already roaring in by telephone. He was ignominiously
fired without pay and got scolded by his mother till he
cried.

But sometimes Link did a job well enough to take
home his pay. Always his mother moaned because it
was so little. That depressed Link, but it didn't make
him cry.

So matters ran on for three years. Link was now a

young man, rather handsome but still persecuted by Fate. She did her worst for him when he was taken on as a plasterer's helper.

The plasterer was stuccoing a huge new three-story house. All Link had to do was to carry buckets of mortar from the mixing trough to the plasterer. This he did faithfully and successfully so long as the plasterer was working on the first floor. But when that floor was finished the plasterer moved up to a scaffold. The buckets of plaster had to be carried up by a short ladder which trembled when you stepped on it. Link managed to carry the buckets up, but the plasterer kept telling him he was slow as seven-year itch. That did not trouble Link seriously, as he had never heard of seven-year itch.

The scaffold was raised to the third floor. It had to be approached by a long, shaky ladder with rungs of inch-thick iron pipe. The rungs looked very fragile and slippery to Link. But he bravely started up the ladder with a pail of mortar held in one hand while the other clutched the slippery iron rung. He was half way up when one of his feet slipped and his leg thrust itself far out between the rungs. Link tried to recover it, when the other foot slipped and followed its mate. Link held on with his one hand, but he couldn't hold the bucket of mortar longer. He let it go, and with the innate perversity of inanimate things, it turned upside down and fell into the plasterer's lunch basket.

"You damn fool!" the plasterer roared at Link, now at last able to climb down the ladder. "You're fired!" And then, as first he realized the tragedy of his lunch basket, he stormed down the ladder with the trowel in his hand. "Damn you, I'll—I'll . . ." He was too enraged even for curses. He started for Link brandishing the trowel.

At first Link couldn't realize that the plasterer meant to hurt him. But sudden fear came upon him and he ran for the gate, the plasterer pursuing him, shouting curses. Link outran the plasterer and got out of the gate. He kept running, pursued still by curses.

Link was crying. He could not see a man moving rapidly toward him. But a friendly hand slapped his shoulder. It was Professor Harrison.

"Well, young fellow, you pretended you didn't see me."

"He chased me. He chased me with an ax."

"Who did?"

"My boss. He chased me with an ax."

"Well now, he shouldn't have done that. But say, Link, could you help me out? My lawn needs badly to be mowed, and I haven't found anyone who could mow it."

Link's eyes dried immediately. To work for his beloved professor! "I will," he said eagerly.

Professor Harrison led Link to his house. It was a small house, but it had a big lawn. The professor got out his lawn mower and did the first swath. He turned the machine over to Link. What pleasure could Link ever have equal to that of pushing his friend's lawn mower?

The professor retired to his study, but came back when the sound of the lawn mower ceased. Link had been over the whole lawn, but the swathes had not coincided well. There were many long strips with narrow angular ends where the grass still flourished.

"Just the way it is when I mow the lawn. I always have those strips to bother me. But you'll go ahead and take them out."

Link grabbed the handle of the mower and eliminated a neglected strip, then another and another until the professor pronounced the job perfect.

The professor handed Link a dollar.

"Say Link, I have a pile of logs I have to cut up for

my fireplace. It's pretty hot weather for sawing wood, but do you think you could do it for me? Tomorrow?"

Could he? With joy, even if the thermometer proclaimed a hundred and forty degrees.

Professor Harrison had intended to let the pile of logs lie until October, when they would have given him a little pleasant morning exercise. Well, the wood would dry better if cut now.

In the morning Link appeared, blithe as a lark. The professor got out the bucksaw from the tool room and helped Link put the first log on the sawbuck.

"Now Link, my grate is narrow and can't take logs more than fifteen inches long. Here is a measure. It won't hurt if some of them come out less than fifteen inches. But don't let any of them be longer."

The professor went on to his morning class. Link siezed the bucksaw with joy. Soon he had a pile of fifteen-inch pieces encumbering the end of the sawbuck. In throwing them back he lost his measuring stick, but he thought he knew how long the logs should be.

Link had cut six logs by free hand when his eye fell on the measuring stick in the sawdust under the sawbuck. He measured the six pieces he had just cut. They were all an inch too long. He'd have to cut that inch off.

A sawbuck isn't adapted to the accommodation of sixteen-inch logs. But Link held the pieces fast with his knee and tilted the saw to an angle. When the professor came back he found Link's face dripping with perspiration and six disks of wood one inch thick. He saw immediately what had happened.

"What nice little pieces of wood! They will come in handy winter evenings, when the fire is low, but it's too near bedtime to build it up with big logs. These pieces of wood will be just right for a brief flame. But come in now for a short bachelor's lunch. I have to be back for a class in an hour."

The bachelor's lunch consisted of cold ham, toast, a banana and coffee with plenty of cream. It was a Delmonico feast to Link. Too soon over. The professor went off to his class and Link back to the sawbuck.

When the professor returned he found Link proudly pointing to a pile of inch disks, three feet high. For a moment the professor was astonished, but then he remembered his praise of the inch disks.

"That's fine, Link, but we have enough of them now. It's quitting time now; come back tomorrow and cut the rest of the logs into fifteen-inch pieces. Then we will make a pretty pile of them, so they'll dry. And here's the dollar you've earned. Take it to your mother."

As Link walked cheerfully away, the professor went up to a seat on his porch, where he liked best to sit and think.

"You can't say there wasn't any intelligence in his cutting all those disks. Some intelligence and more good will. It's a shame the way the poor boy gets kicked around. Somebody ought to take him on and build up his intelligence by one simple job after another.

"Somebody. That's me. But my salary won't carry a handy man, however unhandy. But wait. I'm to have a raise in February. Yes, I'll take him on then.

"What can I put him at? Well, for one thing I'll have him spade up a wide border all around the lawn and put it in flowers. And I'll find other things."

The next day, while Link was sawing wood, Professor Harrison called on Mrs. Forbes and told her what he meant to do for her son. He warned her not to send the boy on jobs he couldn't do. It was all right to get jobs at sawing wood, or shovelling snow in the coming winter. But she was not to mind if he sat around the house with nothing to do. That did not make him unhappy.

But an event loomed darkly over the early winter, an event that would cancel all plans, good or bad. War with

Germany was visibly inevitable. It came with President Wilson's declaration of war. The declaration was followed promptly by a draft act designed to draw millions of men to the colors.

Professor Harrison was too old for any draft except in a late desperate demand for men. But the commandant of cadets at the university had pointed out that there was a frightful shortage of officers for the enormous army forming. Officers trained at West Point would make hardly more than a skeleton file. All National Guard officers would be called in; not only those presently active but anyone who had once been commissioned. Professor Harrison had been a captain in the cadet battalion in his senior year in college. As was the custom, he had been commissioned an officer in the State National Guard—a first lieutenant. He had kept his commission in storage for twenty years. He would not have known where to find the document. That didn't matter. The Government would find his record in the university record office.

He was summoned before a committee of Army officers and informed that he was to be commissioned first lieutenant in Company B, of the Fourth Illinois. He had the right, as a professor, to refuse the commission. But he reflected, what kind of man would he be if he refused to serve, a bachelor with no dependents and in perfect health.

The draft reached into Mrs. Forbes' cottage and ordered Link to report at the recruiting office. Mrs. Forbes ran to Professor Harrison.

"They can't take Link," she asserted vehemently. "The poor boy wouldn't know how to take care of himself in battle."

"I'm going myself. I won't know how to take care of myself in battle. We'll all take our chances. But Link will have to go through examinations and they'll probably throw him out. But if they take him he'll probably be in the same regiment with me and I'll try to look after him."

Cold comfort for poor Mrs. Forbes who now realized how dear Link was.

The next day Professor Harrison—Lieutenant Harrison—led Link to the office for the medical examination. The doctors found him physically perfect and equipped with iron nerves if any. True, his intelligence seemed wanting, but what do doctors have to do with intelligence? They passed him.

Next Link was presented to a board of officers who were to determine his morale and patriotism—particularly to find out whether he had been corrupted by pro-Germanism or pacifism. As to those points Link was perfect. He had never heard of either. But he had never heard of Washington or Lincoln or Woodrow Wilson. He had never heard that there was a sea to cross before you could fight Germany.

The Board consisted of a West Pointer and two officers drawn in from the National Guard. The two were ready to throw Link out. But the West Pointer spoke first.

"We can't take this man. He's a born fool."

It was a common rule, in those days, for officers from the National Guard to oppose West Pointers on any matter whatsoever.

"I don't think we should throw him out," said one of the ex-Guardsmen. "I don't believe in sending our Phi Beta Kappas to the firing line and leaving the morons at home to breed."

"But our country is in peril," declaimed the West Pointer. "She has a right to the best blood we have."

"West Point hogwash," said the Guardsmen to themselves.

"Certainly she has a right to our best blood, yours and

mine. There isn't enough of it. We have to take ordinary blood, even sub-ordinary. At the front this fellow will dig a grave or stop a German bullet as well as any Phi Beta Kappa. I'm for passing him."

The other Guardsman agreed. The West Pointer screwed his face into a look of Old Roman virtue and left his seat.

Link was thus a full-fledged soldier. No, not fledged for he had yet to get his uniform. He was told where to report, but forgetting the address he ran to Lieutenant Harrison, who went with him to the store handling uniforms and picked out one that fitted Link perfectly. The lieutenant showed Link himself in the cheval glass. Link stared. Could that be himself? It was a fine figure of a soldier, tall, straight, chin in and head erect. Link's heart sang within him. For the first time in his life he felt himself the equal of anyone.

At drill he felt different. There were so many points where you could do the wrong thing. He knew right from left, in the abstract, but in action he was never certain which was which. "Right face" was likely to be "left face" for him. "Right about face" meant to him left face around the clock, ending to the rear of his comrades. "Present arms" meant to him to give his gun to the officer commanding the company, and he presented his gun stock first.

In the first week he had made a hundred mistakes according to his captain. One receives with reserve round number statistics. Maybe Link had made more mistakes or less. In any case he had demoralized his squad of fours and had pushed his company to the lowest place in the regiment.

The captain called a council of the officers.

"That man, what's his name?"

"Lincoln Forbes," said Lieutenant Harrison.

"That man is an idiot. We can't possibly make a soldier of him. I propose to ask the colonel to discharge him."

"May I present another view?" said Lieutenant Harrison. "We never can make a parade-ground soldier out of him. But we are soon to entrain for Boston, to take ship for France. There will be no drilling till we land in France and none there. The French don't care whether our privates keep step or not. They will draw us up in long lines and count us, to make sure America isn't gypping them on man power. Then they will devote themselves to us officers. We'd better keep our manuals of tactics and strategy handy.

"Before we know we'll be at the front. There will be no drilling there; only hard and dangerous work, simple as sudden death. Link will stand up to that kind of work with the best of men.

"Meantime I beg that Link be assigned to my tent, to do any work I can think of for him. I know a lieutenant has no right to an orderly, but the colonel won't object. And for the future I'll take full responsibility for Link's performance."

The lieutenant had not intended to sound authoritative. But how else can an ex-professor sound? The captain and second lieutenant were both college graduates, with genuine though semi-humorous respect for professors. They accepted Lieutenant Harrison's suggestions without further question.

And now life was again sunshine for Link. He could see his beloved chief, the lieutenant, every day. He could bring his chief's plate from the mess tent, rarely losing items on the way. He could give his chief's shoes a polish very brilliant in spots. Awake at night he could hear his chief breathing hard sometimes in sleep and sometimes sounds very like groans as the lieutenant dreamed of probabilities of the front which he refused to think about in the daytime.

The order to entrain was not long in coming. The lieutenant was able to keep Link near him on the train and on the transport.

The voyage was rough and most of the men and officers suffered severely from seasickness. Not Link, who remained blithe as a spring morning.

"Seasickness is a matter of the head," grumbled the captain. "That fellow hasn't any head. He can't be seasick."

As Lieutenant Harrison had foreseen, the French put the officers through a forced course of training. It was brief, for the French were in a hurry. There was a section of trenches where a French division had been held too long. The soldiers were grumbling and near the point of mutiny. The American division was hurried forward by train and then by truck, and debouched on a gentle slope under a low rise. Beyond the rise there was another gentle slope ending with the French trenches.

Two hundred yards behind the trenches the French had emplaced guns at short intervals, to throw contact shells into the German trenches, to explode and prevent any concentration of German soldiers for an assault over no man's land. The guns had done their work well, and the French reconnaissance reported no concentration in the German trenches paralleling the French trenches to be turned over to the Americans. To be sure, the Germans had dug many deep caves in both walls of their trenches, and there were German soldiers in these shelters. Not enough, however, for an offensive assault, the French maintained.

Under cover of a dark night the French joyfully evacuated the trenches and the Americans moved in. It was not an attractive residence. The floor of the trench was muddy from recent rains and there were horrible stenches, probably from men inadequately buried.

But by the morning light the trenches did not seem so depressing. They were of varying depth, sometimes so shallow that a tall man could look over the edge and fire his rifle. Where the trench was deep there were benches in the wall for the riflemen to stand on. And there were dark caves for the men if the German shelling became too severe.

Lieutenant Harrison was made gunner of one of the French guns. The French had left five shells at the base of the gun. The lieutenant tried his hand. The first shell overshot its mark. Lieutenant Harrison lowered the muzzle infinitesimally. The next shell fell into the trench. And the next. But it was time to get more shells.

Lieutenant Harrison had a squad of ten men who were to be on hand if the Germans poured out of their trenches and succeeded in crossing no man's land. A column would make for the gun, and the squad was to stop them with rifle fire. In the meantime they had nothing to do and were amusing themselves by digging little trenches with their bayonets to lie in, immune to sharpshooter fire.

A man had to be sent up over the crest to get more shells. It was a dangerous job. For most of three hundred yards, going and returning, the carrier would be exposed to sharpshooter fire.

The colonel had presented the order in which the men of the squad should be chosen for this job. But to Lieutenant Harrison it seemed more humane to call for a volunteer. He called. There was at first no response. Then Link jumped up, all eagerness, "I'll do it."

The lieutenant hesitated. Was it fair to send on so dangerous a job a man who did not realize the danger? But realizing the danger would not diminish it. The man who understood the danger would merely have fear joined to the risk. The lieutenant accepted Link and sent him on to bring as many shells as he could carry, perhaps fifty pounds.

Link ran gaily up the slope, got his load of shells—he made it a hundred pounds—and ran back, not in the least disturbed by the bullets whistling around him.

There was now another job to be done. Every shell was carefully wrapped in paper. The paper had to be stripped off. Sometimes shreds of paper stuck to the shell. They had to be stripped off, or the shell would jam in the gun. And the Army could better afford to lose a gunner than a gun.

For the delicate job of stripping the paper Lieutenant Harrison could have chosen any member of his squad. But he chose Link. What was needed was small skill but steady nerve. The skill was not beyond Link, and no other member of the squad had as steady nerves.

Lieutenant Harrison had been instructed by the French at St. Nazaire as to what he had to do if the shell jammed the gun. The gunner was supplied with two poles, one with a wrench at the end, the other with a blunt end. The percussion fuse was screwed to the shell by an octagonal nut. The gunner was to insert the wrench pole into the muzzle of the gun, move it about until the wrench engaged the fuse nut, unscrew it and draw out the nut and the dangerous fuse. Then he could take the other pole and hammer back the jammed shell.

Simple to specify; but if the gunner touched the fuse in his blind search for the nut the shell would blow up the gun and the gunner would be in eternity.

Lieutenant Harrison had fired a half dozen shells, to good effect. But the seventh shell jammed. It was plain what had happened. His poor protégé Link had got tired and had left a scrap of paper on the shell. Well, the best explanation was useless. The lieutenant ordered his squad, including Link, to retire three hundred yards and over the crest. If the shell should blow up there was no reason for letting other men be killed besides the gunner.

He inserted the wrench pole, pushed it slowly deeper into the muzzle of the gun. If his arm twitched and he touched the fatal fuse—But he was now feeling the tapering end of the shell. He drew his pole back by an eighth of an inch. Another eighth, another. What! Could it be the wrench was actually engaging the nut? He twisted the pole slightly. Something was yielding. He twisted more—and more. The nut with the fuse was free. He drew them out and laid them on the ground.

His arm was shaking violently now, but no matter. He took the other pole and hammered the inert shell back out of the gun. He ran back and examined the shell, rolling it over and over. Not a scrap of paper on it. He swabbed out the gun barrel. No sign of paper.

He again examined the shell. On one side appeared an almost invisible ridge, with bright metal at the end, where the shell had been forced against the barrel. It was not a matter of paper at all, but a shell inadequately tooled.

He began to reflect on the irremediable wrongs Fate may inflict on innocent men. If the gun had blown up, the squad and later the Army would have felt certain that it was the failure of Link to strip off the scraps of paper. A man crawled out from under the gun. It was Link. Link had made up his mind if his beloved chief had to die by his fault he would die too.

For a week the German trenches remained quiet, and the air reconnaissance kept repeating, No concentration. Then suddenly one morning the Germans poured out of their trenches, tens of thousands of them. The gunners lowered the barrels to strike the ground under the feet of the advancing Germans. Where the shells hit them were great holes in the German masses. But they came on until the American machine gun and rifle fire became too withering. By a megaphoned order from the slope beyond the Germans halted, about faced and double quicked—quadruple quicked—back to their trenches, leaving no man's land writhing with the dead and dying and the desperately wounded miserably trying to crawl back to the trenches.

But American casualties were heavy too. The distant German guns had got the range pretty well and had thrown shells into American concentrations in the trenches. The German gunners were trying hardest to hit the French guns and shells fell all around them.

Fragments of a shell shattered Lieutenant Harrison's right leg. It had to be amputated at the hip. But Lincoln Forbes was now at last the equal of any man. He was killed.

MOUNTAIN
FEVER

OLD JOEL HARRIS eased his rheumatism over the side of the bed. "William! You up and dressed?"

"Yes, Dad."

William had been up an hour—long enough to dress. It is an engineering feat to put on your clothes when your legs are nothing but heavy bones, with no working nerves or muscles, a dead weight to carry around when you manage to get up on your crutches.

"Ain't nothing in the house to eat, William. You go out to the store and get something. Got to get it on credit. We ain't got a cent in the house."

William got up on his crutches and hobbled to the door. He was slow, but he knew that his father wasn't really hungry. In an hour William was back, with two packages and a bottle of milk.

"Let's see, William, what you got. Meat? For the Lord's sake, sow belly. Can I eat that? Corn meal? Let me smell it. Musty, by gosh. I reckon that milk is sour."

"No. But he said we got to drink it quick, or it will be sour. And he said the meal will be all right if we cook it well, with plenty of salt."

"What the pigs won't eat Joel Harris can eat," said the old man in mock tragic tones.

"The pigs would eat it," William asserted humorlessly. "He said he couldn't sell us anything on credit if he could sell it to anybody else. People don't buy sow belly. It's been taking up space in his ice box for months. They don't buy musty meal. And he had more milk than he could sell."

Old Joel cackled a dry laugh. "Lucky I have a son to provide for me. Who was going to raise a stake for me in my old age." He sang:

> "Oh Daddy, Daddy darling,
> Oh, Daddy, for your sake,
> I'll go to Californy,
> And try to raise a stake."

William got back into his chair and looked straight ahead, seeing nothing. Life was opening for him, at fourteen. He'd never be anything but a cripple. People might be good to him and give him, out of charity, musty meal and unmerchantable sow belly. Why didn't the doctors let him die?

And the worst of it was, it was all his own fault.

From the time his mother died he had been his father's slave. Chores, errands, begging food on credit, for his father seldom had any money. There had been a time when his father was in great demand, as a dancer and fiddler for surprise parties and other dances in farm houses. The young people no longer danced in farm houses. They came to town and danced in the big hall in the court house, or in the parlor of a rich contractor. They had new dances, new music William's father couldn't do. Sometimes, but not often, an old farmer would invite Joel and his son to a family party, and perhaps reward them with a fresh ham or a string of sausages. But between such events there were months of short rations.

And William couldn't see any way out. He had never gone to school and could barely write his name, which he spelled Wilyum. He had never read anything; indeed, he couldn't read. Before his terrible illness he might have got a job as chore boy on a farm, but he hated the thought of farm work.

A fleet of prairie schooners bound for Oregon had camped at the edge of the village. William squeezed himself into the circle around the camp fire and heard entrancing talk about the wonders of Oregon. Trees as big around as a house and four times as tall as the steeple of the village church. Apple orchards with ten inches deep of luscious apples on the ground, for anyone to take a bushel or a wagon load, if he could use them. Orchards of those wonderful plums that are dried and sold in the East as prunes. Fifty-pound salmon working their way up shallow gravelly streams; you could wade out and take them by the waist. No gold there yet, but no long way down to California where they were always finding new gold fields.

The temptation to go along with the caravan was too strong. William managed to slip into a prairie schooner, and stowed himself away among the baskets and pots and pans making up the back load.

After a day and night of clattering with the pots and pans hunger drove William out. The driver of the

schooner was surprised. But he looked William over: a
nice bright boy, why not? He invited William to share
the camp breakfast and had him share the spring seat.
Soon he tried turning the lines over to William, who
found guiding the team no difficult task, for the horses
appeared to know the road as well as the drivers.

The caravan followed the northern branch of the
Mormon trail, heading southwest over the boundless
grassy plain of Nebraska, fording rivers occasionally,
something that made the trip more exciting. The broad
valley of the Platte; the winding rather uncertain road
up the North Platte to the Pathfinder Falls and above
the Falls the road along the lovely clear Sweetwater,
fenced on one side by jagged palisades, but on the other
side edging a sunny plain tilted to a long haystack mountain, with little antelope bobbing around like mechanical
toys. Ahead the two cones of the Tetons.

William had never been so happy in his life. He
played around the caravan, over short grass and
through sage brush and would have liked to have the
journey continue forever. But one day he found himself not quite well. He could not eat, and from time to
time he would be a bit dizzy on the spring seat. Next
day his face was burning with fever, and from time to
time he'd drop into delirium.

His host detached himself from the caravan, drove
back to the Pathfinder Falls and by a devious rocky
road to Casper, where there was a hospital. The jolting
was so hard on William's poor aching body, he thought
his end was coming. But whatever he had left of his
body was tough.

The doctors at the hospital were disagreed about his
case. One thought it was infantile paralysis. The others
thought it was mountain fever—tick fever. Whatever it
was, William's legs were gone. When the doctors were

sure that this was all they shipped him back to his father.

Joel Harris wasn't born cruel, but life had made him bitterly unkind. Every day he would twit his son. "You were going to make a pile and take care of me in my old age. Ha, ha, ha!"

William said nothing. The one thought always in his mind was:

"Why didn't they let me die?"

William was cooking the corn meal and frying the sow belly for what would be either a late breakfast or an early lunch.

"Gosh!" said old Joel, "that musty meal stinks. And that sow belly never came off a sow. It came off an old boar. I can smell that. It gags me."

William said nothing. The musty corn meal smelled like any other boiling corn meal; the sow belly smelled like any other frying pork. But the old man was unusually out of sorts.

There was a thundering knock on the door. William crutched his way to the door and opened it. A huge man who looked like a picture William had seen of a Viking King. More than six feet tall, a huge barrel of a chest, legs like columns. His tangled brown hair receded from a high brow over large, steady blue eyes and arcs of pink cheek holding their own against a cataract of red brown beard that tumbled to his waist. He carried a big brown parcel, which he set on the table.

"I'm Kurt Oberwaelder. Farmer now, but born educator." He sniffed. "Smells awfully good, your lunch."

"Yes, my son is a born chef. They say a good French chef can make a delicious meal out of an old shoe. William could about do that."

"What a lie!" said William to himself.

"I'm taking the boy home with me. I'm a born educator, and have nothing to educate but my poor little daughter Greta. It isn't fair to her for me to turn all the force of a born educator on her. So I am drafting your son. I'll have him ready for college in two years."

"You can't educate William. Why, he's never been in school. I used to beg him and pray him to go to school, but he wouldn't go."

Another lie. William had always wanted to go to school but his father wouldn't let him go near the school. Book learning, he maintained, took the spirit out of a boy. It made him unfit for dancing and fiddling.

"The harder a nut is to crack, the sweeter the meat," said Kurt Oberwaelder. "You'll see, in two years the boy will be well on the way to being an educated man."

"I can't let you have him. We two poor cripples have to stick together. We'd wither away, separated. My William is the apple of my eye. And he does all kinds of chores for me, runs errands for me, helps me into bed when the rheumatism ties me up hand and foot. No, I can't let you have my boy, my only son."

Why did his father have to be such a hypocrite, William asked himself.

"I know how you feel," said Kurt in a gentle voice. "My little daughter is the apple of my eye. It will go hard with me when she leaves me. But I'll be able to stand it, if it's for her own good.

"I can't make up for the loss of his company, though it's only three miles to my farm and he can come to see you or you may come to see him. But what he does for you in chores and running errands, I can make that up. I'll pay you two dollars a week, and for that you can always get a chore boy for a few hours a day, or a girl to keep your house cleaned up and your pantry full."

William eyed his father narrowly. Joel had been very envious of Civil War veterans who had managed to make out that they were suffering disabilities from their military service and had got pensions of six dollars a month. On that they could live without a stroke of work. Housing, such as it was, cost hardly anything; perhaps two dollars a month. Fuel cost nothing. You only had to ask the corn buyer to unload corn cobs at your front gate instead of hauling them out two miles to the burning pile. Food cost next to nothing, and clothing never wore out if all you did was to sit around.

Never in his life had old Joel had a steady income of eight dollars a month.

Joel cleared his throat. "That looks fair. But a stranger boy to help you is not the same as your own flesh and blood. Still, if it is for William's good I can't stand in his way."

William felt that his heart was jumping. He'd be free to go with this big German? Away from the constant jangling of old Joel.

Kurt Oberwaelder picked up his package and broke the string. "My Greta got up at four this morning to prepare dinner for her new fellow student. She dressed two chickens and roasted one in a hurry for me to bring to Mr. Harris, if you people hadn't started dinner. She put in some French fried potatoes and a glass of the wild grape jelly she makes so well. And some asparagus tips and a few pickles."

"She is very kind," said old Joel loftily. "But you can tell by the smell, we are having a mighty nice dinner. Can't you sit down with us?"

"Lord!" thought William. "Sit down to that musty corn meal and sow belly."

"Thank you," said Kurt. "Greta will have dinner all ready for us. We can get there just in time if we start right off. You can use the stuff I brought for supper. Get your things, William, and we'll be off."

His things! William hadn't any things but an extra

shirt and some handkerchiefs. He put them into a paper bag. How was he going to get into the carriage? Maybe he could climb up over the wheel.

Kurt Oberwaelder solved that problem. He picked William up like a little child and set him in the carriage seat, with the crutches beside him. After his illness William did not weigh much more than a little child. But William's depression came back on him with redoubled force.

"I'm nothing," he thought. "Helpless. Just a child."

The team was picking up speed.

"Mr. Oberwaelder," William began.

"Just call me Kurt. That's name enough."

"I was going to say, you are making a mistake. You can't teach me. I don't amount to nothing. My Dad doesn't amount to nothing. His Dad neither. Nor his Dad's father. Just fiddlers and dancers. That was what Dad was making of me. Just nothing."

"My boy, you've got things all wrong. Dancing and fiddling aren't just nothing. They are arts, about the oldest and most honored of the arts.

"When I first came to this county I went to a dance out on a farm. Your Dad was fiddling some old-time piece like 'Saint Patrick's Day in the Morning,' and it was nice, the way he played it. Everybody danced but old Mr. Mapes who was doubled up with rheumatism, and Grandma Mapes, who was lame and walked with a stick. But then your Dad began to improvise. He played the most intoxicating music I ever had heard. He danced himself while he was fiddling. The new music, which had never been heard before and would never be heard again, got wilder and wilder and so did the dancers. Old Grandpa and Grandma Mapes got into the dance. And there was a little three-year-old boy dancing a solo and singing. His panties came down and he kicked them off and kept on dancing like a wild little cherub. You could hear the horses stamping in their stalls; the old dog on the doorstep singing a long contralto howl and the coyotes on the hill doing a staccato chorus. And I thought, 'By the Devil, this is Orpheus.' "

"Who is Orpheus?" William asked.

"He was an old Greek musician who played so well everything danced, even the oak trees trying to get loose from their roots."

"Oh." William's tone was skeptical.

"If your Dad had put up such a performance in a Berlin beer garden, next thing he knew he'd have been on the stage of the Royal Opera, with tens of thousands of people crazy about him. But this country hasn't become civilized, yet.

"The old art of the dance is gone and the new art hasn't come on. The young people dance, in the court house or the Masonic temple. They have professional musicians with spectacles, reading the scores as they play, to have the music exactly right. Music that is exactly right isn't music. The dancers hop around without much attention to their steps and carry on sweet and daring conversation. Love talk. Pfui!"

"Maybe I didn't lose much by losing my legs. But what have I got left? Nothing."

"Listen, William. There are people who say there is nothing to a fiddler and dancer but legs. They say that for a dancer the head is nothing but a button to finish off the spinal cord. That's nonsense. Nobody could ever stand up as a new Orpheus, as your Dad did, without a good brain. And a good brain can be put to new uses. You have a good brain and I'm going to make something of it. Something worth while."

"Maybe you can. But Mr. Ober—Kurt, you want me to call you—why are you going to all this trouble about me? I'm not worth it."

"I'll tell you. I have education in my blood as you

and your father had the fiddle and the dance. My father was a professor; so was my grandfather. Farther back there were great professors on my mother's side.

"I went through the university and got my doctor's degree, *summa cum laude.* I wrote my *Habilitation* essay, which was unanimously approved by the Faculty. I could offer a course as a *privat dozent,* the lowest teaching rank, from which you rise through the rank of professor extraordinary to the professorship. It might take me six years, but then a lifetime tenure and the greatest honor anyone outside of the nobility could have.

"I was walking to the university, along a narrow sidewalk. I saw ahead of me a man coming my way. The sidewalk was wide enough for two, and as the man came up I flattened myself against the wall, to let him pass.

"He was an Army lieutenant, and I could see, he was of the higher aristocracy, which I hated. There was room enough for him to pass, with me flattened against the wall, but he might have brushed his aristocratic coat against me. He ordered me to get out into the gutter. I told him to go to hell. He hit me over the cheek with the flat of his sword. Next second I had him down and was scrubbing the dirty gutter with his pretty curly head.

"I went on up to the university, and thought I ought to go to the Rector's office, to report the incident. I had just got there when a police officer came in to arrest me. The Rector sent him away. I was under the jurisdiction of the university, not of the city. Any charge against me had to be lodged with him.

"When the police officer was out of hearing, the Rector said:

" 'This is a very grave matter. That lieutenant is of the very highest aristocracy and a favorite of the Kaiser. I don't know how long the university can protect you.

But there is a train that leaves for Hamburg in an hour. Be on it. There is a ship that sails for New York at midnight. Be on it.'

" 'How can I?' I said. 'I'd have to go to my bank for money and that wouldn't leave me time to make the train.'

" 'How much money have you in the bank?'

" 'About a thousand marks.'

" 'Make me a check for 600 marks and I will cash it from my safe. Go, my friend, and God be with you.'

"The voyage was not pleasant. I had thrown myself out of my career and out of my Fatherland, by a few minutes of hot temper. I thought, however, there were many universities in America that would welcome a well-trained young German doctor. They would let me offer courses as a *privat dozent*. Later I found they do not have *privat dozents* in America. And while American universities sometimes import established scholars they have no place for a beginning scholar like me.

"I came out here and bought a farm. It is a good farm and I've been happy on it. But I am dying for an opportunity to teach.

"I've been thinking, history is full of examples of scholars known only for a single student they taught. I ought to be able to find one student and make something of him. And at last I have found you, William. I will make something out of you, perhaps a great lawyer like George Norris."

It sounded fantastic to William. To become a great lawyer, or anything else that was great? But this mighty German looked equal to anything. For the first time since the fever struck him William felt in his breast the pleasant stirrings of hope.

They were driving up to Kurt's house. It looked more like a town house than a farm house. It was large, two stories, with two one-story wings. There was a welcoming porch, and from it you looked into a bay window with pots of geraniums in flower. Kurt opened the door and led the way into the living room, a large sunny room with polished bare floor. Kurt looked at the floor as if puzzled.

"Greta!" Kurt shouted. A girl of twelve came tripping in from the kitchen. A pretty girl, thought William. Blue eyes that seemed brighter than blue, lips redder than lips, rosy cheeks, two long neat braids of yellow hair, a dress of violets on a light pink ground, violets in bouquet bunches, in wreaths, and many scattered on their own. A little starched apron fringed with embroidery.

She offered her hand to William. It was scrubbed pink; William's own hand seemed to him intolerably grimy.

"My daughter, Greta," said Kurt. "She don't look like anything much, but she's bright."

"I can't look like anything much to Papa until I am six feet four and so big around." She indicated a circle with a diameter of four feet. "Then he won't look anything much to me."

"You're always getting ahead of me, Greta. That isn't filial. And this young man must be warned. Trust not the fair sex." He sang:

"O Maegdelein, O Maegdelein, wie falsch ist dein
        Gemüte.
Du schwörst mir Treu in meinem Glueck,
Nun arm Ich bin gehst du zurück—

"That says, 'O maiden, how false is your temper. You swore me faith when I was rich, now I'm poor, you back out.' "

"There's always another side to things," said Greta, and sang in her sweet, clear voice:

"Beware, young girl, he's fooling you,
Beware, oh, take care,
Trust him not, he's fooling you,
Beware, oh, take care.

"And here's one for Papa:

"He gave me a ring, my ma,
He gave me a ring, my ma,
He gave me a ring, but don't you tell Pa,
For it's none of his business, now is it, my ma?"

Kurt put on his most formidable frown. "You'll see, he'll make it some of his business."

"You'll see, we'll be too quick for you."

"We!" It meant nothing, but sounded sweet to William. Both laughed, and William laughed too. What a jolly family. If he and old Joel had teased each other like that he would never have run away.

"Greta, what became of the rugs?"

"They were too dusty and need beating. So I rolled them up and put them in the wood shed."

Kurt stepped over and patted her head. Dusty, no; she had taken away the rugs in anticipation of crutches. William realized that too, and felt grateful, but farther removed.

"I've got to go and unhitch, and water and feed the team. I won't take long. You children sit down and talk over our program. Then we'll eat."

Greta drew a big comfortable chair up to the smoldering fire and bowed to William. She placed a smaller chair near it.

"I am to teach you reading and writing, and German."

"Can you talk German?"

"Of course. Papa is German and my mother was German."

"It must be awful hard to learn German."

"No, it isn't. It's lots of fun to learn a foreign language. Every language has different ways of saying things. I'm learning Swedish now. From Grandma Jakobsen over the hill. They call a grandmother Bestemoder, or something like that. I think it means best mother. And that would be right about her."

"I don't even know what Swedish sounds like."

"I'll sing you a little song, Bestemoder said it fitted me." She sang in her sweet, clear voice:

"Lille Klara var den Flicka
Stedy, livly, rask ock snil,
Hun kun spin ock sye ock sticka.

"That means, little Clara was a good deal of a girl, steady, lively, quick and smart; she could spin and sew and knit. Well, I can spin and sew and knit. I made this dress for myself. How do you like it?"

"It's lovely."

"Papa says, I have to teach you reading first in poetry, because the sense of rhythm is strong in you, and you'll feel every word is just where it ought to be. That will help to understand it. Listen:

"Then up spake brave Horatius, the keeper of the gate:
'To every man upon this earth death cometh soon or late;
And how can man die better than facing fearful odds,
For the ashes of his fathers and the temples of his gods?'

"You wouldn't change any words around, would you?"

"No, I wouldn't know how to do it."

"Papa says that an old Latin poet says, to change around the words of a true poet is to make cannibal hash out of the poet himself. I'll give you another piece of poetry. From Shakespeare. Macbeth is saying it, when he knows terrible things will happen to him:

" 'Duncan is in his grave. After life's brief and fitful fever, he sleeps well.' "

William shuddered. "Is all poetry about dying?"

"No, but some of the best. Don't you sometimes feel, since you have to die why am I here at all? I do."

"You?" William was astonished. "You think about dying? Such a pretty girl, with such a wonderful father, such a nice home, everything your own way. You think of dying?"

She put her little hand in his. "So do you. We can't help it."

The door flew open and Kurt came in. "What! Holding hands already! But it's none of my business, now is it, my ma? Greta, did you show William his room? No? Come along, William. We'll look at it while Greta puts the chicken on the table."

It was two doors behind the living room. The room was bright, with a big western window. There was a bed with the covers turned back, showing the whitest sheets William had ever dreamed of. A desk, a book case, two comfortable chairs.

"Lord!" thought William. "I'm not clean enough to be put in such a room."

On the little table were two objects the use of which William couldn't divine. Kurt picked them up.

"These are dumb-bells. You use them like this—" and he did some exercises. "Every morning when you get up throw off your night shirt and exercise with these. Open the window; get cold, but exercise hard enough to overheat yourself. A half hour of the dumb-bells in the morning; another at night before you go to bed. It will give you thick, strong arms and a big strong chest. And that means a big strong heart, and that means everything.—We'll go and eat."

The table looked fantastic to William. A chicken waiting for Kurt to carve it, potatoes peeled and roasted brown with the chicken, radishes and young onions, hot biscuit, and waiting at the end of the table a big pie emitting steam from its eyeless eyes.

"William," the host said as he tried the edge of the carving knife, "our rule here is 'Don't let your modesty wrong you.' You may think you have eaten as much as looks right, but you could eat a little more. Do it.

"I've hefted you. You weigh about eighty pounds. You've got to lay on weight. You've got to weigh 120 pounds when I introduce you at the university."

William was nothing loath and put away more food than he had ever eaten in a week of dinners. Kurt pressed more on him and he ate it, but relaxation was coming upon him.

"We're not going to work this afternoon," Kurt declared. "We'll both take a little nap. Then I'll take you around the yard and introduce you to the horses and cows. Nobody can be an honest lawyer who hasn't known horses and cows. They are the only people that never bear false witness."

William found it very hard to go to sleep between the white sheets. Could anything like this really happen to anyone? Waking from a doze he would ask himself, wasn't this just delirium? He had known a vast variety of delirium experiences, mostly unpleasant but seeming as real as this. Not absolutely. There never was in a delirium anything like Greta's little warm hand in his.

In the morning William was put under Greta's instruction in writing and reading. First she made him copy long columns of letters. His pencil wavered too much and he had to copy letters over and over. Greta's pedagogy did not permit keeping the learner at a task until he hated it. Soon she passed over to reading. Her text was a collection of Tennyson's poems. There might be deeper poets, she agreed with her father. But none that could match Tennyson for rhythms.

> "A prince I was, blue eyed and fair of face,
> Of temper amorous as the first of May,
> With wealth of yellow ringlets like a girl"—

"Sounds all right," William said. "But I don't know what it means. There are too many words I don't understand."

"Well, let's see. You understand the first line."

"Yes."

" 'Of temper amorous.' "

"Hold on," said William. "What was he mad about?"

"Mad?"

"When a man has a temper he is awfully mad."

"Oh, that isn't what temper really means. You can have hot temper or mild temper and almost anything else. The prince had an amorous temper."

"And what does that mean?"

"It means, whenever he saw a pretty girl his heart went pitty-pat."

William felt himself blushing, but Greta's eyes were fixed on the page.

"How can I ever find out what all those words mean?"

"You keep reading. You come to a word you don't know. You guess what it means. Next time you see it you guess again. Maybe the meaning seems a little different. After a few more guesses you get it straight. That's how everybody learns the language."

Kurt opened the door. "May I have William now?"

It was nearly as delightful to work with Kurt as with

Greta. To Kurt teaching was exciting, inspiring. William was virgin soil. What farmer does not get a special delight from turning over virgin soil? William could hardly multiply two by three and get a result he trusted. Kurt turned the multiplication table into a fascinating game. Kurt couldn't wait the proper length of time before introducing his pupil to geometry—Euclid, he insisted on calling it. For Euclid first of mankind had shown how you can calculate distance without the tedium of foot by foot measurement. Euclid had won the mastery of space for mankind. That gave William almost a religious feeling.

But Kurt's pedagogy required frequent change of scene. From mathematics he skipped over to Latin, the Latin still a living language of scholarship in his Europe. "Amo, amas, amat," yes, for a little while, but then reading, and not of Caesar's *Commentaries* nor trivial little biographies of Cornelius Nepos, but Nicolas Klimmaeus, *Iter Subterraneum,* a *Utopia* far more instructive than Sir Thomas More's. In a few brief weeks William, who had thought he couldn't read English, was reading Latin with intense enjoyment. After Baron Holberg he was reading Seneca whose style, Kurt said, became the model of all European scholarship, to stand for 1600 years.

Time goes very fast, if you work every day, including Sundays and holidays. William had a feeling he was only beginning to learn, when Kurt declared, "You are prepared for college now. Next week students are registering at the university. We will be there."

William had been growing fast, not only in his head. The dumb-bells and good food had given him powerful arms and a torso big enough for any kind of heart. He could get around now on his crutches about as quickly as any boy could get around on his sound legs. The psychology of the cripple had mostly evaporated from his mind. Everybody, he thought, has a lot of things to overcome. He can overcome them if he makes up his mind.

The University of Nebraska was still new. Kurt and William made their way from the station to a square enclosed by an iron fence. Before them, University Hall, a big building with wings under mansard roofs and a square tower over the whole. To the right a building William later knew as the Chem laboratory, and beside it the Gym and Armory, and farther back Nebraska Hall, for the biological sciences, with a museum where you could spell out the whole development of the Nebraska mastodon's teeth, from smooth surfaces good for grass in the humid periods of history to the highly corrugated surfaces that came in when drought hardened and toughened the grass. The show piece in the museum was a giant clay screw, discovered by Professor Barbour and named by him, *Demon helix,* a devil of a screw. Tragically for him the biological world was more classical than he and made over his *Demon helix* into a *Daemonhelix,* a name by which the poor thing is known to this day.

Kurt introduced William to the registrar and departed. The registrar was a sweet old lady, enemy of irregularities, but eager to help a cripple. She sent William to one professor after another. The professor of Latin asked him to quote a piece of Latin, and William made a Latin speech the professor couldn't understand. But fortunately he could correct the German pronunciation of Caesar and Cicero. The professor of ancient history made him make a little speech on Greece and encountered a terrible puzzle. Who was Tookydiddes? What! Thucydides? He could pull that off in class.

The professor of German was full of astonishment and pleasure to find an American-born youth who could speak German correctly. The mathematics professor set

William down as a born mathematician.

Ma Smith, the registrar, sent for William, who was waiting in the lobby. "From what the professors tell me, you can register as a Freshman. They say you are really too far along for that."

College life, William saw, was bound to be very pleasant. He liked the professors under whom he was to work. Perhaps their scholarship was not of the highest order. A new institution can't expect to set up a highly distinguished Faculty. But these professors loved their work. The Great Academic Grouch had not infected them. The professor of philosophy was not distressed by the fact that the head of the city garbage collecting organization had twice his salary. The professor of literature was not driven sour by the fact that the butcher he patronized had twice his income. What the deuce! The professor of literature could live all the days of his life with Milton and Shakespeare, Wordsworth and Browning and Tennyson, discovering new ideas, new beauties every day. How big a salary would make pig-sticking outweigh Hamlet or even Elaine?

All the professors treated William like an honored guest. The professor always set aside a seat for him, the best in the class room. He never fired surgically edged questions at William, but rather seemed to consult him as a colleague. The students would have resented such a privileged position if it had not been for William's crutches.

William was not sociable by nature and made few friends among the students. But he had a pleasant room near the campus, where he would coach poor devils who feared that they would fail in the examinations. And on Sunday evenings, if the thermometer registered figures below zero, William was likely to have his room crowded with students from unheated rooms.

The college years passed in a flash and the two years

in the law school were equally fleeting. William had his degrees of Bachelor of Arts and Bachelor of Laws.

The Dean of the law school informed him that there was a clerkship open in Judge Pound's firm, a golden opportunity for a young lawyer. William was not interested. He was committed to his own county.

William and Kurt were in town, looking over the office Kurt had rented for William.

"Looks all right, doesn't it?" Kurt assumed a judiciously critical tone to cover over his enthusiasm for a really fine office such as one doesn't expect to find in a country village.

"It's a fine office. Big. I'll rattle around in it."

"When I told your father about it he had a great scare. If you were coming back to town, he feared, I could see, that the two dollars a week might drop off. But I assured him, they will keep on till you can make it four dollars.

"You wouldn't think it, but your father has saved money out of that two dollars a week. He has saved $400, and he's been putting it out in short-term loans to farmers at eight per cent. But now he's getting the thrill of a big capitalist. He asked me what I thought of U. P. as an investment. I said the road was running down, Atcheson or Northern Pacific were better bets. He got a pad and put down some kind of symbols he could probably read."

"My father has hardly recognized me when I've come to see him, in these last years. He seems to be dozing all the time."

"Yes, until he hears the word money. The one thing that prolongs the life of intelligence. Gold, gold. Spurned by the young, hugged by the old. I'm glad the poor old fellow has something to hug to his breast and warm his old heart."

"I'm not clear where my clients are coming from,"

said William. "The legal business in this county is all sewed up. There are six lawyers who divide it up. If a client can afford Shreve, he wins his case whatever it is. Shreve doesn't really know any law, but he is in with the machine. So is Harlow, but not so tight with the powers. He wins most of his cases. And so on. So far as I can see, every case is treated as political, and the law mumbles in the dark."

"That's true. You've got to begin on a hopeless case, and win it. Then you'll be on the map. And I have a hopeless case for you.

"There's a dirty scoundrel being tried for buying votes. He is guilty as hell. Everybody has seen him buying votes as openly as you buy strawberries in spring. The prosecution has all the witnesses it can use. And the scoundrel hasn't money enough for a fancy organization lawyer. You take his case."

"A case I can't win."

"There's no such case, if you go all out."

William took the case.

The case was, if anything, worse than William had anticipated. His client was the slimiest crook he had ever seen, and it gravelled him that in talking about his case the client kept saying "we," unctuously, as if his lawyer were compromised with him. The jury was made up of farmers who looked like honest men. The county attorney had been so sure of his case that he had not taken the precaution of packing the jury.

The witnesses were called. William had the right to cross-examine them, but that was of no use; the testimony was unimpeachable. Then the county attorney made a high moral speech on the crime of corrupting the electorate. It was for William to answer him, if he could.

"Honored Judge Wilson, my honored colleague the county attorney, gentleman of the jury:

"I have been taught since childhood that the ballot box is the most sacred instrument of American democracy. It is the only means by which the will of the people can manifest itself. Who corrupts the ballot box is enemy of the people and deserves to be treated as such.

"My client is accused of bribing voters in the last election. You have heard the testimony. I recognize it as unimpeachable. You have heard the noble exposition of the meaning of the crime from our honored county attorney. There is one angle of the problem, however, the county attorney did not touch on. I wonder why.

"It has been proved against my client that he bought not only the votes of our own home-born loafers and drunks and scalawags, but also the votes of even lower elements, imported by the Republican Party to vote in our elections. Those imported scalawags were the private property of the Grand Old Party. Bribing them for the Democrats was a plain violation of sacred property rights.

"If my client had been buying votes for the Republican Party he would not be here before us. You know and all the world knows, there were four men buying votes for the Republican Party, as openly as you buy potatoes at the grocer's. These men are not before us.

"Gentlemen of the jury, your faces and demeanor show clearly you are honest men. Bring in an honest verdict. If you convict my client, find him guilty not merely of bribing voters, for that is hardly a punishable offense with us. But guilty of bribing voters for the Democratic Party."

"Your Honor," shouted the county attorney, "the attorney for the defense has suggested to the jury that they alter the terms of the indictment. Will you instruct the jury, they must convict on the indictment as it stands?"

"It is so ordered," said the judge. "The attorney for the defense has overstepped the bounds of legal decency."

"I offer my humble apologies to the court. I had meant only to help the jurors define the gravity of the offense. It is the law that they must convict on the indictment before them, or acquit."

As William pronounced the word "acquit" his eye caught that of the foreman of the jury. It was round with understanding.

The jury retired to the jury room. The sound of laughter came in over the transom. The judge fidgeted in his chair.

Soon the jury filed in.

"Not guilty," the foreman declared.

"Not guilty!" roared the judge. "That man is guilty as hell. The county made a perfect case against him. Go back and find a decent verdict."

"Your Honor," said the foreman, "once a jury has found a verdict it cannot lawfully change it."

"And you call yourself a jury," said the judge bitterly. "You are a disgrace to the county, the state and the nation. You ought to be punished. Mr. County Attorney, can't I declare this jury in contempt of court and put them in jail?"

"I'm afraid you can't. The law is very sensitive about the position of the jury."

"Well, I'll order a new trial. And you, Mr. Attorney for the defense, I don't like the way you handle a case. If that is the way they are training lawyers at the university we don't want any of them here."

William bowed. He had expected to be cited for contempt, and fined, if not jailed. He was getting off easy. As for a new trial, it would never be ordered, now that the political issue had been opened so forcefully.

The client sidled up to William. "You did a good job,

Judge, and here's your fee." He held out a soiled $50 bill.

"No, thank you," said William, "I don't take dirty money."

The client's face fell. In a moment he recovered. "All right. I can use it myself."

Kurt was bubbling with good humor as he drove William home. "You're made, my boy. The whole county has seen you stand up to the Republican machine and beat it."

"Not much law in that."

"No. But in this county politics comes first, law next, if at all."

The next Sunday morning William and Kurt were sitting in arm chairs on the porch, enjoying the early September sunshine. Greta was clearing off the breakfast table.

"William," said Kurt, "aren't you going too fast?"

"Too fast?"

"They tell me you are setting up a citizens' party, to throw the Demo-Reps out. You haven't quite two months before election day. Hadn't you better give yourself more time? Say a year or two."

"No. If I allow myself a longer time to put my party together I'll be allowing the gang a longer time to pull it to pieces."

"Greta says you have your slate practically finished."

"Yes. With Greta's help. She analyzed the voting forces for me. There are three hundred German votes, as many Scandinavian, four hundred Irish. That makes a thousand, and the whole vote of the county is two thousand, plus two hundred hoodlums from the cities the Republicans import to vote. There are two hundred and fifty farmers from New York State and one hundred and fifty from Maine and Vermont. That brings us up to fourteen hundred, enough to win the election even if all the rest voted for the gang. And they won't.

"There are five offices to be filled, treasurer, county clerk, sheriff, judge and county attorney. Greta and I picked out a German for sheriff, a Scandinavian for county clerk, an Irishman for judge, a Yankee for treasurer. We haven't been able to find a lawyer not tied up with the gang to run for county attorney. I may have to take that job myself, though I don't want it."

"And have you got your men committed?"

"Yes. Greta and I drove over to call on Blume. You know he was a drill sergeant for half a dozen years in the German army. Of course he said no, with full German force. But Greta put up so good an argument on his duty as a German to help his country get rid of the crooks and scalawags that were disgracing us. He wanted to see the slate, approved it, and agreed that if the others accepted he would. Then we drove over to the Swede, Hindahl, who said—or sang—never. I reminded him that he had been auditor for a big company in Stockholm and would be a wonderful county clerk. And Greta suggested that since we'd have the German Blume for sheriff, we'd need a Swede to hold him down. Hindahl laughed and said he'd do it if he didn't have to make speeches. I said I was monopolizing the speech-making business.

"Then we drove to Father MacCrae's residence and asked him to name us an Irishman for county judge. He shouldn't be a lawyer, but every educated Irishman has spent a lot of time arguing points of law. We wanted a just man, firm but kindly. And we knew that Father MacCrae could name us such a man.

" 'A Roman Catholic?' the Father inquired.

" 'Of course.'

" 'Might not the Pope influence his decisions?'

" 'We'd be proud to have the Holy Father look in on

our dog cases.'

"Father MacCrae laughed. "Your man is Aloysius Sullivan, proprietor of the hardware store, an honest man all his days and intelligent. He can't afford to take the job, but he will. He has two boys who can run the store.'

"We got Aloysius committed that afternoon and drove over to the Maine community, and had our treasurer, Horace Clapp, signed up before we left. That's where we stand now. We are planning a dozen local meetings and a big mass meeting on the court house lawn about the first of October."

The mass meeting project was a frightful headache for William. He could present his candidates, but each one specified he would not make a speech. All the known speakers in the county were tied up with the two old parties. He had invited the Republicans to provide speakers and present their candidates for the offices. They had not decided on their candidates, but they would have the Congressman of the district, Cyril Blake, speak for them. William persuaded a Unitarian minister to preside. But if there was to be any speaking for the Citizens' Party he would have to do it, and his opinion of himself as an orator was low.

To add force to William's worries, the meeting turned out to be huge. He had counted on three hundred and had provided benches on the lawn for five hundred. They were soon filled and there were more than six hundred milling around. Fortunately the meeting would be brief. He asked the chairman to proceed at once to introduce the Congressman.

Congressman Blake was a large, comfortably well-fleshed person with a face made up pleasantly and a persuasive manner. He began with well-finished compliments for an electorate that turned out in such numbers to consider serious questions of politics.

He had known of dozens of instances in which well-meaning but misguided citizens threw in their lot with fragmentary parties, peoples' parties, citizens' parties, farmer parties, labor parties, even vegetarian parties. Nothing had ever come from such attempts at political reform. America was a land of two parties. If you really wished to reform political life you would throw in your lot with the one great party, the Republican Party, which had saved the Union and had created conditions under which America had grown great.

No doubt among his hearers were many sound Republicans who had come out of curiosity. What did they think of a fancy party that had to offer them foreigners for their three most important offices? And did they not realize that every Copperhead in the county was quietly hissing around among them?

The Republicans had met ignorant and traitorous opposition before. They were marching now. He intoned, "Tramp, tramp, tramp the boys are marching."

"You have not forgotten Andersonville. You have not forgotten the Fort Pillow massacre. You have not forgotten that it was a Copperhead who assassinated Lincoln." Again he intoned, "We shall rout the Copperheads and Rebels once again."

William had admonished himself again and again not to lose his temper, no matter what an opponent might say. He rose on his crutches.

"Gentlemen, we have come together not for the pleasure of listening to well-polished rhetoric but to consider the state of this county of ours. It could be, and should be, one of the richest counties in the state. It has some of the best soils and a whole population of good farmers. But our county is poor. It can't pay its bills promptly and regularly. You who have served on juries know that the county pays by warrants you can negotiate with a usurer for fifty cents on the dollar. If a contractor builds a bridge for the county he is paid in warrants, and of course he puts his bid up correspondingly. We are known to pay twice as much for every public improvement as our neighbor counties pay.

"And why? Because our big property owners do not pay their taxes. There are taxes ten years in arrears. I have made a hurried examination of our books and have found $150,000 in unpaid taxes. If we collect these taxes we can pay all our bills and have enough over to improve our roads, now the worst in the state, rebuild our court house which is falling to pieces, give our schools a chance of life. That is what we propose to do and will do after the next election. (Mild applause).

"I had thought the bloody shirt had been consigned to the old clothes man. Our honorable Congressman has seen fit to wave it over our heads. He may be excused, for that bloody shirt is his private property. He got it off the body of the man he hired as a substitute when the Civil War draft touched his own tender skin."

"A lie!" roared the Congressman.

"If it is a lie let him sue me for slander. I could be of some help to him, for I have the transcript of his record from the Archives of the War Department."

The roar of applause could be heard a mile away. The Congressman marched off the stage muttering about pettifoggers and rabble.

As the applause died down the chairman pounded his gavel for silence.

"Now since the late honorable Congressman Blake has left us—" What more he meant to say is unknown, for a shrill woman's voice from the audience recited, "All the king's horses and all the king's men can't put the Honorable together again." The applause awoke with redoubled fury and ended only with the dispersal of the crowd.

*   *   *

It was the day after election. William and Kurt sat before the fire reading the newspapers.

"I'm somewhat disappointed," said Kurt. "You won, but only by 1,730 votes against 310. Do we have 310 crooks in our population?"

William laughed. "There are 150 delinquent tax payers that we wouldn't want to vote for us."

"Now you've got started in politics you'll be running for Congress."

"Not if I can help it."

"It's coming. But I want to take up another matter. When are you going to settle that Greta matter?"

"What Greta matter?"

"Why, marriage."

"My dear friend Kurt, even supposing Greta would take me, would you throw away such a beautiful and brilliant daughter on a poor cripple?"

"You're not a cripple in your head nor in your heart. That's all that counts with me, and all that counts with Greta. Crutches are an acquired characteristic and don't go with heredity. There is more danger that my grandson will inherit the dancing legs of your family line. But if he does we'll send him where people appreciate art."

"But, Kurt—"

"Greta." Kurt's voice sounded through the house.

Greta appeared in the doorway. "Yes, Papa."

"William and I can't decide on the day for the wedding."

"Not before Wednesday. I won't have my dress ready."

It was hard for William to find his tongue. There were so many things needing to be said and they interfered with one another.

"Lovely Greta," he said at last, "I never dreamed that I could win you. I don't believe it now. I never would have dared to ask you to be my wife and I don't dare now."

"Dear William, you were proposing to me the very first time I saw you, and I was accepting. You have proposed every time we met since and I have accepted. It wasn't a matter of words. Words can be false. Silence can't be."

She opened her purse and drew out a ring of copper wire. She slipped it over her finger, drew it off and gave it to William. "That's the size," she said, and sang, "But don't you tell Pa."

Kurt picked up the tune: "For it's all of his business, now ain't it, my ma?"

"My dear father," William said, "what can I say? How can I thank you and Greta? I am your creature. All I am or can ever be, you and Greta created."

"And the mountain fever," Greta laughed. "Some day we'll set up a monument to mountain fever."

MY
HERO

WHAT CAN BE SO exciting to a school boy of eight as a new boy, perhaps a year older but of exactly the same height? Especially if the school is small, far out in the country and has had not a single boy of eight-year size, but only bigger boys who wanted to bully you and smaller boys you needed to bully to keep them in decent form? Johnny Blake was exactly my height. A big boy had proved this by laying a geography book on our heads.

Equal in height, but there equality ended. Johnny was brilliantly handsome; I considered myself just short of being homely. Johnny had dark brown hair forming in large lustrous curls; my hair hovered between ash and tan, and rose in bristles when the schoolroom got very cold. His eyes were shining brown, mine a flat blue. He had a delicate little nose, I a nose merely utilitarian. He had a small mouth with rosy lips slightly pursed; I had a big mouth and lips too thick. Johnny walked on his little feet with an engaging strut; I merely covered space efficiently with feet too big.

I was just a clodhopper who had never traveled more than twenty miles from home. Johnny was a boy of the world, who had traveled with his parents by prairie schooner to Puget Sound and back. He had seen rivers so full of salmon you could walk dry shod across on their backs. He had seen trees so big that if they were hollow you could put a whole house inside them. Above all, Johnny was a hero.

In passing through the Blackfoot country Johnny's father had put up for a few days at a ranch. Johnny had borrowed a pony and a cavalry carbine and rode out to get an antelope. The ranchman said, nobody had ever shot an antelope with a carbine. Johnny meant to show it could done.

He hadn't ridden far when he saw about twenty Indians following him. He could see they had blood in their eyes. They wanted his scalp to hang on their lodge pole. Johnny spurred his pony and galloped on, the Indians galloping after him. But one Indian pony after another got winded and dropped out, until there was only the chief following. Johnny turned in his saddle, aimed his carbine. Bing! The Indian chief tumbled off his horse, good and dead.

Then Johnny remembered, he was out for antelope. He rode on for a few miles and saw an antelope on the hillside, a quarter of a mile away. He aimed his carbine. Bing! The antelope dropped dead. He rode up and picked it up.

"It was very good eating."

I had thought myself in love with little Helga, new to the school, whose parents had just come over from Copenhagen. Her curls were true gold, and her eyes violet blue. She wore the prettiest dresses ever seen in Nebraska, and broken English issuing through her pretty lips sounded like music. But now Johnny, boy of the world and hero, had appeared on the scene. I fell into the Jonathan and David pattern. I loved Johnny with a love surpassing my love for little Helga—indeed, extinguishing it. Johnny, like David of old, had too much ego in his cosmos to be very ardent about anybody. But he approved my admiration of him and my spacious receptive ears.

I had an old friend in the school, Charlie Woodward, by seven years my senior. Charlie's father and mine were cronies. And so from my first day in school Charlie held me under his protection. If any boy felt like teasing me into a fight he first looked at Charlie, caught Charlie's fierce eye and saw his instant fist. He gave up any idea of fighting me. For Charlie had a reputation of ferocity as a fighter. When he was twelve a big drunken tramp stumbled into the schoolroom and tried to kiss the teacher. One blow from Charlie's fist was enough for him. Charlie seized him by a foot, dragged him out of the room and threw him into a snowdrift.

I had read a dozen novels before I was eight and so was in command of a fairly wide vocabulary. Charlie, who had never read anything, had to struggle hard over the essays and poems in Hilliard's Fifth Reader. Often he would ask me to read a passage and tell him what it meant. Usually I could do it. If I could not I'd commit it to memory and ask my mother to tell me what it meant.

Charlie was laboring over a long didactic poem on the "Evil Influence of Skepticism." Most of the poem he could understand, but the final lines were Greek to him, and to me. I committed them to memory to lay them before my mother. Here they are:

"Ah me, the laurel wreath that murder rears,
Blood nursed and watered with the widow's tears,
Seems not so foul, so tainted nor so dread
As waves the nightshade o'er the skeptic's head."

The next day I supplied Charlie with my mother's interpretation. The "laurel wreath" stood for the crowning of Napoleon as Emperor. The blood was that of the million men killed in the wars Napoleon waged to win the glory of the Emperor's throne. The skeptic was anybody who didn't believe everything that was printed in the Bible.

"Gosh, then my dad is a skeptic, as that poet fellow sees it, worse than that man Napoleon. My dad says the Flood can't have reached Nebraska. It would have drowned out the skunks. And even if Noah had taken a breeding pair aboard and skunks had swarmed over the Old Country, they never could have got here. They'd have had to swim the Atlantic.

"I think that poet is a damn fool. But say, Dick, you've got a mighty smart ma. She's Scotch, and Scotch women are smart. And you take after her."

I felt like purring. But Charlie continued:

"Don't get too close to that Johnny boy. He's no good. He's just a blowhard."

My hero just a blowhard? Almost my friendship for Charlie died on the spot. At recess, when Charlie went out to play ball, I took my books out of his desk and moved down the aisle to take the seat beside Johnny.

My life at school entered upon a new phase. I had always been quiet as a mouse, reading other children's books when I had worked sufficiently on my next lesson, or puzzling over arithmetic problems far in advance of the assignment to my class. But Johnny had a world of amusing things to whisper to me, and I could not keep from giggling, and whispering replies. The teacher began to look disapprovingly at us. That pleased Johnny, for to him the teacher was the pupils' enemy, and to annoy her was the pupils' right and duty. It was a new idea to me, but I espoused it eagerly. Johnny knew the world.

My father was building a new house. The walls were up, the roof on, the windows in. The three floors had been laid, even being planed down. The second floor was as smooth as glass. No partitions had been set up, and the floor was for the time a single hall, thirty feet by twenty-eight, except for the stairwell in one corner. As might be expected the young people in the neighborhood wanted to have a dance there. My father consented.

For the first time Joseph Blake, Johnny's father, visited us. He had lived in the county since the fifties, but at some distance from us, until now he had moved to a worn-out farm and a ramshackle house a half mile below us. It was the rumor of a dance that brought him. He was sure my father would not know how to fix up the house for a dance, and sure that he could do it just right, being a man of the world. My father was quite willing to hear Joseph's advice, though not caring much for it.

Joseph Blake was a large man, rather overweight, who limped painfully when anybody was looking, otherwise hardly at all. Inhabitants of territorial Nebraska had not been subject to the Civil War draft. Some men crossed over to Iowa and volunteered. Joseph Blake was one who remained on the prairie.

But it was rumored that Confederate agents were stirring up the Sioux Indians in Dakota to go on the warpath. And the inhabitants of Nebraska Territory got together a battalion to march into Dakota to watch the

Sioux. Joseph Blake joined this battalion.

They were transported by boats up the river, landed and set up camp. The Sioux in fact had no intention of going on the warpath. The battalion sat in camp through a terribly cold winter, and came home in the spring. All they could show of casualties were a few frostbites. Of these the most eminent was Joseph Blake's loss of four toes on his left foot.

With the brutal humor of amateur soldiers, his comrades alleged that on a night when the thermometer registered 28 below zero he had beeen dead drunk and had let his foot wander out from under the blankets. However that might be, the toes were gone. Now, after nearly twenty years, he declared, his foot hurt him terribly at every step. The neighbors doubted it. What use were the little toes except to grow corns, in those days of ill-fitting cowhide shoes?

The government was pensioning veterans for the loss of toes in the Civil War: five dollars an ordinary toe to seven and a half for a big toe. Joseph felt that he ought to have a twenty-dollar pension. But unfortunately the pension laws did not stretch over the Territorial Battalion, irregularly formed and never inducted into the Army.

But the climate for pensions had greatly improved. The Democrats had come near carrying the country with Tilden. Nebraska was traditionally Republican, but the farmers were growling about the low prices after the deflationary return to the gold standard. They might not vote Democrat, but they might not vote at all.

Every pensioner could be counted on as a staunch Republican. The political arithmeticians calculated that every pensioner was good for four votes, his own and those of relatives and intimate friends.

And so pensions were flying around freely. If the claimant did not fit under the general law an obliging

Congressman might work out a special bill for him. Such bills always passed and were always signed by the President.

Joseph Blake had at last come within sight of a pension for his perished toes. A bill had been passed and was only awaiting the President's signature.

Money in his pocket. He could almost feel it.

But now he was bent on having everything right for the dance. The platform for the fiddlers must be in such and such a place and be of such and such a height. The benches around the wall should be of two-inch plank, because the country girls who would sit on them were inclined to be buxom. There had to be a canvas-walled dressing room on the first floor near the stairway where the ladies might retire to replenish the powder on their hot faces. There had to be a looking glass and a lamp with a stand of defined height. And there should be another canvas-walled booth where the boys might retire for a nip when their spirits began to tire.

"No," said my father. "If the boys need a nip they can take their bottles outdoors."

Joseph Blake was visibly disappointed, for he had intended to preside over the nipping booth.

There had been dances in our old house, surprise parties with two fiddlers, sometimes only one. But this dance in our new house promised to be something quite different. There would be about forty couples, the organizer said. My father set posts for hitching all around on the bare ground that was destined to be our lawn, and managed to borrow four lanterns to hang around among the posts. There was to be a party of twelve or fifteen couples in single-seated buggies from the town and its vicinity. They wanted to be hitched together, and my father set apart fifteen posts to the left of the house and asked a boy who came with the organizer to keep other carriages away.

It was hardly dark when the first guests arrived. Soon they came in droves. My father and Joseph Blake had taken their stand near the stairway to welcome the guests as they came. Soon the fiddlers arrived, three of them, one with an oversized fiddle. They walked around the room drawing sweet sounds from their fiddles as the guests ranged themselves on the benches along the walls.

I was burning with excitement. I had never seen so many people together. I had never seen such pretty dresses. The fiddlers now began to sing snatches of nonsense foisted upon the tunes they were to play:

> "Oh swing that girl, that pretty little girl,
> The girl I left behind me."

And

> "Ha ha ha! 'tis you and me,
> Little brown jug, don't I love thee?"

And

> "Round and around the vinegar jug
> The monkey chased the weasel,
> That's the way the money goes,
> Pop goes the weasel."

This was life, I felt.

And now a tall man on the fiddlers' platform, the Caller, I was told, shouted, "Choose your partners." Young men and women sprang up from the benches and soon there were two sets pirouetting around to a tune we knew as "Happy is the Miller Boy," later re-christened "Turkey in the Straw." Most of the dancers did their steps right but there were greenhorns who got tangled up amid general laughter in which I joined though not clear on the points in the case.

Johnny, who had been circumnavigating the benches, smiling into the face of every pretty girl, now came up to me.

"Dick, this is a rotten performance. Those fiddlers can't play. They are out of tune. Doesn't it hurt your ears?"

I had liked the fiddling; indeed, it had seemed to me perfect music. How green I was! Of course Johnny, boy of the world, was right.

"Let's go outdoors," said Johnny. "We can have some fun. . . . It isn't just fun we're after," said Johnny as we stepped out into the dim lantern light. "Those town boys have a plot against their girls, and we've got to stop it."

"A plot?" I asked, aghast.

"Yes. About every boy has a bottle of whiskey in his buggy. You'll see. They mean to have the girls drink it on the way home. The girls will be drunk and the boys can do anything to them they want to."

"But what do they want to do?"

"Don't you know? Then I can't tell you. But it's horrible. If the plot succeeds those girls will be crying for a week. Bawling."

I tried to think what it could be. The boys would kiss them, no doubt, but girls don't bawl for a week for that. But whatever it was, Johnny had said it was horrible, and Johnny was authority.

We went up to the first buggy hitched at the left of the house. Johnny put his hand under the lap robe and drew out a bottle—a hip flask, he called it. The owner had probably taken a little nip already, for the cork had been drawn so far one could pull it out with his fingers.

"Want to taste it?" Johnny took a mouthful and handed the bottle to me.

Gosh! What a nasty taste! I spat it out, and yet choked. Johnny had swallowed his mouthful manfully, but in the dim light I seemed to see tears in his eyes.

"Tastes bad till you're used to it," said Johnny. "My dad and I took nips regularly when we drove home from Puget Sound. Keeps up your strength."

Boy of the world! What couldn't he do?

The next carriage produced a quart bottle.

"Gee, she must be a resistant gal," said Johnny. We proceeded to the next buggy. Another hip flask. Now we worked fast and soon had a pile of twelve bottles on the ground, five of them quarts, seven hip flasks.

"Now what are we going to do with the stuff?" Johnny asked rhetorically.

"Let's pour it into the swill barrel."

"And get the hogs drunk?" Johnny laughed. "Ever seen a drunk hog?" He dropped on his hands and knees and gave a realistic representation of a drunken hog.

"But that won't do. The boys would smell the swill barrel and raise Cain. I tell you what. We'll put the bottles into Dad's buggy. He'll drive home early on account of his foot. He'll know how to get rid of it. Maybe throw it in the creek when the water's high."

That seemed a good way out. We carried the bottles to Joseph Blake's buggy and packed them carefully in the straw on the buggy floor. Then we returned to the dance floor.

The dancing was going on with spirit. The fiddlers were working themselves into a perspiration and the caller was shouting "Allemand right," whatever that meant. My father caught sight of me.

"Dick, it's long past your bed time. Run back to the old house."

"But Johnny can't go to bed yet."

"Joseph Blake is looking after Johnny. I'm looking after you. Trot."

I trotted, reluctantly, through the dim lantern light and the pitch-dark lane. But I felt exhilarated. I had been privileged to share a heroic exploit with my hero Johnny.

A week later my father returned from a trip to the town. His face was grave, but he said nothing until the family were assembled at dinner.

"Something happened that night of the dance that looks bad to me," he began. "Nobody holds me responsible for it, but it was on my place.

"Those town boys had some whisky in their buggies to warm their way home. Somebody went through their buggies and stole it. And they thought it was Joseph Blake, because he's been drunk ever since, and nobody knows how he could have got money to pay for all the whisky he is drinking. Blake had left the dance early. But I told them I took him to his buggy, on account of his foot, and saw him drive away. He couldn't have looted the boys' buggies.

"But I wouldn't wonder if he had a confederate. Some town loafer he had asked to come and get the stuff, on shares."

I addressed myself vigorously to my beefsteak. I could feel my cheeks growing warm but I had too deep a sunburn left over from the hot weather for my blushes to be very evident.

That old fool, to make a hog of himself on all that whisky! But Johnny and I had saved the girls.

In the next school days Johnny and I let our war with the teacher smolder. There were so many amusing experiences of the dance party to be discussed in whispers and giggles. Katy—we no longer called her "teacher," but either "Katy" or "the O'Sullivan woman" —kept an eye on us but seemed to accept our minor disorder passively.

"The trouble with the O'Sullivan woman," Johnny

whispered, "is that she is getting awfully fat."

I hadn't noticed that. But now I saw, her arms filled her sleeves so tightly they reminded you of big sausages.

"See how tight her waist is," Johnny whispered.

I looked again. Yes, the cloth formed little wrinkles as it approached the buttons.

"One of these mornings," Johnny whispered, "those buttons will fly off and she'll tumble out and show how fat she is."

The picture of the buttons shooting to right and left, and Miss O'Sullivan's confusion was so funny that my throat was choking with laughter. I tried to keep it down but it burst forth, loud and long.

The teacher marched down upon us. "You boys are having too much fun here. Richard, I'm changing your seat. Get your books." Richard. She had always called me Dick. Next she would be using my full name, Richard MacIntyre. How elegant Johnny Blake sounded in contrast.

I piled my books on my seat. Miss O'Sullivan seized my arm and half jerked me out of the seat, as if I were resisting her command. She led me across the aisle and planted me in a seat beside Annie Brinton—Mean Annie, we called her—the most terrible girl in the school. If you gave her the least little pinch she yelled like a Comanche and clawed both your cheeks with her finger nails, which she kept long and sharp. You would have four little rivulets of blood on each cheek.

Nor did you have to pinch her to set her finger nails in action. She was always looking for a *casus belli*. You laughed—you were laughing at her. You put on a grave face—you were turning up your nose at her.

I seated myself as far away as I could from Mean Annie and looked across the aisle to see what Johnny was doing. He was going through a pantomine of waist buttons flying off. He was very funny, but I could not laugh with Mean Annie's cat-like eyes narrowed to a slit, watching me, her thin fingers closing and unclosing eagerly. I'd best sit quiet as a mouse.

I opened my arithmetic and began to study the next lesson. No, that was what my enemy the teacher wanted me to do. I closed the book.

The next day I sat listless in my seat—no, Mean Annie's seat—and listened to the Third Reader class making hash of some fair poetry. Johnny was called on to read.

"The boy stood on the burning desk—"

"Desk!" shrieked the teacher. "Read that again."

"The boy stood on the burning desk—"

"Johnny! Do you know what a desk is?"

Johnny nodded.

"Did you ever see a desk?"

Johnny nodded, and pointed at the teacher's desk.

"That boy stood on a desk like that, and it was on fire?"

Johnny nodded. "That's what the book says."

"Take your book, Johnny, and go back to your seat. Tomorrow you'll read in the primer class. Maybe you'll be able to understand 'The cat has got a rat.' "

I was a bit shocked. My hero, mistaking a deck for a desk. I looked across the aisle. Johnny was smiling triumphantly. And then I realized he had read desk just to harass the teacher. How slow I had been! I hadn't been able to conceive that feigned illiteracy is a lawful weapon in the war upon the teacher.

The Third Reader class was droning away on the boy on the deck. A subdued air was floating in the room. Of course it was Johnny, who held his hands before his mouth. The air was just distinguishable but the first words were not. But then they came with faint clearness.

"My mother and father are Irish
And I am Irish too."

Miss O'Sullivan stood with her back to us, but I could see her neck reddening.

The air went on. And

"They keep the pig in the parlor,
And that is Irish too."

Miss O'Sullivan strode down the aisle with long steps, and boxed one of Johnny's ears and then the other. It was not the half caressing stroke with which a girl quiets a lover's too hot enterprise. It was a box from the Old Sod, and the stove pipe overhead rang with the sound.

Johnny tried bravely to smile, but in spite of himself his eyes flooded his cheeks. As the teacher turned back to her desk, Johnny flew to the door and from the window I could see him threading his way through cornfield and meadow to his house.

I felt I ought to demonstrate my solidarity with him. At least I ought to stand up and yell. But there was Mean Annie, watching me like a cat. I remained quiet. Afterwards I was deeply ashamed of my weakness.

Johnny did not come to the school the next day. I sat uneasily at the end of Mean Annie's seat, her cat eyes watching me for a cause of action. It was a dreadfully long day, but all days come to an end, sooner or later. The next day was Saturday, no school and no relief to my anxiety for Johnny and his poor ears.

But on Sunday my parents and I walked over the hill to visit our friends the Woodwards. There was a span of skinny horses and a battered old buggy at the gate.

"Well," my father said regretfully. "They have other company. The Blakes."

Oh joy. My friend Johnny was there, as blithe and

handsome as ever. Mr. Blake was telling a story. The old fraud! It was the story of Johnny's heroic encounter with the Blackfoot Indians. But Mr. Blake had revised it to make himself the hero. He had been riding out on a roan stallion, with a Winchester rifle, to get a shot at a bighorn. The bighorn, he explained, was a kind of wild sheep or goat with curving horns a yard long and thick as a man's thigh. It lived on steep mountain sides and if it came to a precipice, even two hundred feet high, it jumped over, fell on its horns and got right up to graze the mountain grass.

Mr. Blake returned to his story. A troop of Indians had pursued him, but his roan stallion was too swift for them. One by one they dropped out until only the chief kept up the pursuit. A well-aimed shot from Mr. Blake's rifle finished the chief. Mr. Blake rode on and soon saw a bighorn about a mile away on the mountain side. He fired, and the bighorn came tumbling and rolling down the mountain. Mr. Blake took it back to camp. He meant to take the horns back to Nebraska as a souvenir, but there wasn't a bone saw in the camp.

I listened with boiling indignation. The old reprobate, stealing his own son's heroic exploit! I wanted to shout the truth at him.

But Charlie said: "Come boys, we'll go down to the barn and have some fun." Charlie led the way, Johnny and I following arm in arm.

Without a word Charlie saddled and bridled two enormously tall horses.

"We're going to have a horse race. There will be a prize for the winner. Dick says the old Greeks gave a prize to the loser too. That's right and I have a prize for the loser. Johnny and Dick will race. Come on, Johnny."

"No" cried Johnny. *"No!* NO!"

Charlie caught him by the collar and the seat of his pants and threw him up on the horse like a sack of potatoes. Johnny shrieked, louder and louder and tried to get off the horse. His leg was too short to reach the stirrup, and he didn't dare to drop to the ground.

"Come on, Dick." Charlie formed his two hands into a stirrup. I put in my foot and Charlie lifted me up. I got astride the saddle and grabbed the pommel with both hands. I was scared. I had never ridden a horse, and such a terrifyingly tall horse!

Johnny was gripping the pommel squirming and shrieking.

"The goal will be that elm tree down the lane," Charlie said. "When you get there yank the bridle strap on the right and the horse will come back." He picked up a blacksnake and gave each horse a mighty blow. The horses made wild leaps and started off in a horrible gallop which simmered down to a jerky trot as we approached the elm tree. I pulled at the bridle strap and my horse turned around and galloped back to the barn. Johnny's horse ran on for a quarter mile, then turned and trotted back. Johnny's shrieking had given way to the deepest sobs I had ever heard.

Charlie pulled us off our saddles. "Dick won the race. Here's the prize." He handed me a big red apple. "But the loser gets a prize too. Hold out your hands, Johnny." Johnny, still sobbing, held out his hands. Charlie dropped a live toad into Johnny's cupped hands.

Johnny shrieked and ran for the house.

"Dick," Charlie said, "we'll wait here a few minutes. They will have to take their crybaby home. Poor little devil, he'd never been on a horse.

"You heard his old man tell a story about how the Blackfoot Indians chased him and how he shot the chief. Johnny tells about the same story. I've heard it before. It was about a Canuck half-breed fur trader seventy-five years ago. The Blackfoot Indians are mild as a Sunday school today, but they were mighty mean in those days.

A bunch of them chased the Canuck, but he outrode them, all but one, and the Canuck shot him."

The house door opened and the Blakes came out, and went down the path to their buggy. Mrs. Blake was carrying her sobbing son; her step was uncertain as if her knees were giving way under the weight. Charlie and I stepped back into the barn to be out of sight.

Charlie had been brutal to my beloved Johnny. I should have felt outraged. I did not. Just a fake hero. To think that I had believed his tales. To think I had let him make a nuisance of me in school, warring on the teacher who had always been kind to me.

His handsome face—as I thought of it now—was a sissy face. His beautiful curls—sissy curls.

Still, was there not one heroic exploit of Johnny's and mine that could not be brushed away as mere fiction, the saving of the girls? When doubt finds entrance into a boy's mind, it does not know where to stop. Did we really save those girls? Suppose the boys tried to make them drink all that whisky. A girl's mouth and throat were as tender as mine. The first mouthful would have made a girl choke and spit, as it had done to me. The boys couldn't have made them take another mouthful.

What would have happened was that the boys would have drunk the whisky themselves. Then the girls could have done whatever they wanted to do with the boys. And what would the girls have wanted to do? As every boy of eight thinks he knows, what a big girl most wants is to get engaged, just what a big boy least wants. If we had left the whisky to its owners about a dozen engagements would have been announced the next day.

We had saved the boys, not the girls. And that was nothing to brag about. Every boy and man regards the hooking of a reluctant bachelor as a great joke, and a good thing. It takes him out of circulation and puts him to work.

My love for Johnny had flown away, like a wild goose in autumn before the arctic wind.

Monday morning I came early to the school house. I gathered my books in Mean Annie's desk and carried them to Charlie's desk. Charlie came early, too, and we resumed our old discussions of the Fifth Reader text. Charlie was reading Marco Bozzaris and was discontented with the poetry.

"Look at that:

> 'But Bozzaris fell
> Bleeding from every vein.'

"There are a hell of a lot of veins. He couldn't have been wounded in a way to cut them all."

"Well, this is poetry," I said. "The poet couldn't say, 'bleeding from thirteen veins.' "

"If he couldn't say the truth he shouldn't have said anything."

Miss O'Sullivan came in. She paused and looked at me gravely. I had left Mean Annie's desk without permission. But then Miss O'Sullivan looked at Charlie. Plainly he wanted me there, and nobody, not even the teacher, cared to cross Charlie's will. She smiled at me and went on to her desk.

She wasn't too fat. She was plump as a woman ought to be. She wasn't a tyrant as Johnny had made me think. She was kind and helpful. What a fool I had been to join in Johnny's war on her.

Across the aisle Mean Annie was staring at me through her cat eye slits. She looked disappointed. I had been in her power and she hadn't clawed me once.

Johnny did not come to the school, but that

afternoon, when I was feeding the chickens, Johnny appeared, blithe as ever, with the strut I no longer considered distinguished.

"That was a horrid time we had yesterday. Those weren't riding horses. They were plow horses fit only for convicts to ride. I didn't want to ride, because I had an awful earache from the blows that O'Sullivan woman gave me. When you have earache you can't keep your balance, and it's dangerous for you to be on horseback. I tried to tell that to that brute of a Charlie but he wouldn't hear me. Well, when I get my growth I'll give him the licking of his life."

Empty sounds, but Johnny was my guest, and I had to assume a credulous air.

Johnny changed the subject. "Did I ever tell you about the time I climbed Whitestone Mountain in Idaho? It was awfully steep, and I about wore out my breath climbing it. But what a view! You looked south and you could see the Gulf of Mexico; you looked north and you could see the Arctic. I was looking east and saw lots of big cities; I was trying to pick out Washington when there was a terrible clap of thunder overhead, and the lightning smashed a big boulder into gravel, not ten feet from me. And the fumes of sulphur nearly choked me."

Again I tried for an air of credulity. There was no mountain so high you could see so far as that, I commented to myself. If the lightning had smashed a boulder ten feet from Johnny, he would have been dead. As for the sulphur fumes, I knew where they came from. There were in the neighborhood two hill-billy families from Arkansas, entirely illiterate, their minds encrusted with superstitions. When the lightning struck near them they said they smelled sulphur. My father explained that those hill-billies thought lightning comes from Hell and that Hell is a big lake of burning sulphur.

Satisfied with the apparent success of his story, Johnny wanted to begin another. "Did I ever tell you how I ran over the Falls of the Missouri in my canoe?"

"No, but we can talk while I go on with my chores. I've got to go to the cornfield and get a basket of purslane for the hogs."

"Oh, the hogs don't need purslane. They can eat grass."

"But they're crazy about purslane."

That was true, and it was true the hogs didn't need it. But Johnny hated chores; the purslane might shake him off. I got a bushel basket and led the way to the cornfield, Johnny following reluctantly.

It was no problem to fill the basket. Purslane carpeted the whole field. When the basket was full I gave Johnny his choice of right or left handle.

"I'm sorry, I can't use my hands. That brute of a Charlie put a toad in my hands. He knows toad poison covers your hands with warts. My mother washed my hands with turpentine to kill the toad poison. They're sore."

I looked at his hands. Turpentine would have made them red. They were white. Anyway, Johnnie's mother wouldn't have turpentine in the house. As for toad poison and warts, that was some more hill-billy lore. I carried the basket myself.

I threw the purslane into the pig pen. The hogs devoured it instantly as it fell among them.

"I'll have to get another basketful," I said.

Johnny looked at the sun. "I've got to run home. There are some chores my mother wants me to do."

He was gone. But he'd come again the next day. Was I saddled with him for life?

But as a Methodist would say, deliverance would come. When I returned to the house I found Mrs. Blake with my parents. She was crying bitterly. At first

I couldn't conceive why she was crying. The first pension check, twenty dollars, had come in. Was that something to cry about?

It was. The Blakes had moved into the unoccupied farm next to ours, without paying anything on the rent, having nothing to pay with. They had lived on nothing. Every evening Mrs. Blake had come to our house to get a gallon of milk my parents gave her out of neighborliness. For a month the Blakes had lived on that milk and a little corn meal my father had given them.

Now that the Blakes had pension money, the owner of the farm demanded a rent of ten dollars a month. Half of the pension, as if he too had laid four toes on the altar of his country. Joseph Blake was outraged. He would move out.

And he could move out. The banker who cashed his pension check had an unoccupied house on the fringe of the village of Harlow, twenty miles away. He would rent it to Blake for twenty dollars a year. All the land that went with the house was a town lot, fifty feet by one hundred fifty, but why should a cripple want more land? Joseph Blake had accepted the banker's offer, and was now down in the saloon celebrating. The pension money would flow like water, Mrs. Blake said, and what would the family live on in Harlow with no kind neighbors to supply them with milk and corn meal?

"I'll tell you what you can do," my father said. "Joseph Blake will be treating the boys, fifteen or twenty of them. Of course he'll treat himself with each batch of boys that come in, and when he gets home he'll sleep like a rock. Get his wallet and take a little money for yourself. When he counts his money in the morning, he'll think he had been awfully liberal in treating. Even if five dollars are missing."

"But wouldn't that be stealing?" Mrs. Blake asked, somewhat doubtfully.

"No. The Government gives pensions to support veterans and their families. Half that pension money should go to you. You could appeal to the county court, and the judge would order a fair division of the pension money. But that would start a scandal. The way I suggest is better."

Mrs. Blake picked up her pail of milk, said good night, and set out for home. She had straightened up and her chin was thrust forward. She would do it, I knew. "There'll be reactions tomorrow morning," my father said.

Tuesday was a school holiday—Admission Day, to celebrate Nebraska's birth as a State. Late in the morning Joseph Blake appeared, his face flushed with suppressed rage.

"MacIntyre," he said, "your team ain't working today. Lend them to me with your big wagon. I'm moving to Harlow and I got to get my furniture out of the house before that skinflint landlord grabs it for back rent."

My father was used to lending tools, his plow, even his mowing machine, but he would never lend his team. Nobody but himself could handle his horses properly. Least of all a stupefied man as Blake then stood.

"I'll tell you what we'll do," he said. "I'll come with my wagon and take your furniture. You and the family can ride ahead to Harlow. Take a broom and a mop and the water pail; Mrs. Blake will want to clean up the house a bit. I'll come along then with the furniture."

"That'll do." Blake growled ungraciously. "Say, MacIntyre, do you know what those scalawags did to me in the saloon? I had been treating one bunch after another, and it was getting late. I had been working hard, yesterday, and I got sleepy. I sat down in an armchair and dozed off. Soon the saloonkeeper woke me up, it was closing time. He gave us a drink all around, on the house, and I drove home.

"Well, this morning I got to thinking, I had been treating a lot of boys; I must have spent a couple of dollars, maybe a little more. I reached for my coat and got out my wallet. The wallet was empty, by George! Some son of a meat ax had stolen the whole twenty dollars, while I was asleep."

My father put on his longest face, but I could see he was bursting with suppressed laughter.

"I drove down there this morning," Blake continued, "and I gave the saloonkeeper Hell for running a pickpocket joint. That scoundrel swore I must have lost it on the way home. Lost the paper money out of the wallet which stayed in my pocket! Well, he said, nobody could have taken my wallet out when I was asleep without a dozen fellows seeing it. That's right. They were all in cahoots. The whole kit and caboodle ought to be in jail, the saloonkeeper with them. I told him so."

"Too bad, too bad," was all my father could say. "But now you better go over and get your stuff ready. I'll be around with the wagon in half an hour."

"Dick," my father said. "Don't you want to ride out with your friend Johnny and me?"

"No," I said.

"You were awfully thick with him. Have you thinned out?"

"Yes."

"But anyway you have to go over with me and help me load. You have to bid Johnny good-bye. You won't see much of him after today."

My father was right. I'd have to put on a proper air of sorrow at parting. My father's standing rule was "If things don't go right with you, still you have to march off in style."

There was not much of a loading job. Three folding cots and some bedding. Half a dozen folding chairs. A folding table. A bushel basket of pots and pans and another of table ware. A five-gallon jar half full of corn meal, a covered pail with half a gallon of milk. That was all.

The loading done I bade Johnny an affectionate farewell. I promised to come to see him often, and he made a similar promise to me. Words written in wind and running water.

The order of the procession my father had prescribed was changed. Mrs. Blake insisted on riding with him in the wagon. The three Blakes on the buggy seat would be too uncomfortable. My father agreed and helped her to the wagon's spring seat.

Blake came over to him. "MacIntyre, you don't happen to have a little money on you? I could pay it back when I get next month's pension."

"No, I have only a couple of quarters, one for my lunch and one for feed for my team."

"You can feed your team in my barn. The banker said I'd find some hay there and a few bushels of oats. Lend me a quarter. We'll soon be going through Smith's Crossroads, and I can get a cup of coffee. I'm all in."

My father handed him the quarter. Blake climbed quickly into his buggy, touched his horses with a whip and was off for Smith's Crossroads. My father followed slowly with the wagon.

"Mrs. Blake," my father said, "you did a thorough job on his wallet. How much did you get?"

She began to cry. "I got what was left. He'd been pouring it out like water."

"Yes, but how much?"

"I got fifteen dollars. That was all he had except a nickel in his pants pocket. I left that. You see, I had to have some money. I've got to get flour and coffee and sugar. I've got to get a warm suit for Johnny, now cold weather is coming on. I ought to get a coat for myself. I've got only this thin dress and my underwear is all worn out. I might get pneumonia and die, and what would happen to poor Johnny?" She was crying bitterly.

"You did right," my father said soothingly. "But what will Joseph think when he sees you spending money? He'll want to know where it came from."

"That's all right. He'll think I got it from my folks in Illinois. I do beg them for money when we are starving, and they send me some. But they give me Hail Columbia for not making Blake work, as if I could."

"Everything seems to be all right," my father said. "But you'd better spend that money in a hurry, and hide whatever you don't pay out right off. Put it in a paper bag and bury it deep in the corn meal, for Joseph will be dying for a drink, and he'll hunt all through the house for money. A month on cold water is something he can hardly stand, now he has a pension."

"Oh, he doesn't have to go over to cold water. He has a lot of the whisky you gave him."

"The whisky *I* gave him!"

"Yes, at the party. A dozen bottles. He's got nine left. I carried the bottles up from the cellar. He couldn't go down on account of his foot. He has them in the buggy now."

"Oh, I see. But if he had all that whisky in the house why didn't he have his party there and save his money?"

"He says he can't have a party in our house. I spoil it like a death's head. I know I look pretty awful." She was crying again.

"You don't look awful. You're a fine-looking woman, if you have decent clothes. Mrs. MacIntyre says that too."

Her crying stopped. Gallantry through a big black beard is very convincing.

"I have another word of advice," my father said. "You can't have a saloon pocket-picking every month. You have a right to one half his pension, but I suggest that you get it by installments. He never knows how much he may have spent in an evening at the saloon. He wouldn't miss five dollars when he has just received his pension."

"I'll do that," she said. "My! I'll feel rich with ten dollars a month."

It was late in the evening when my father drove up to our house. He was in good spirits.

"They'll be all right. But I think it's the last we'll see of them."

What finally became of the Blake family? What became of the Arkansas hill-billies and the equally shiftless and illiterate families from the poverty-stricken hill country of West Virginia, Kentucky and Tennessee sprinkled over the pioneer communities in the early homestead period? They are gone. You can drive hundreds of miles through the Nebraska farm country and never see their mark, fields with sunflowers taller than the corn, horses with half a bushel of cockleburs tangled in their tails.

Drop anything in the river: the flowing water purifies it or silts it over. So it is too with the river of time. It purifies the family groups, or silts them over.

BEES

OF ALL THE FARMS in the community, the one I liked best to visit was that of Claus Jespersen, on the Missouri River bottom. Claus had two sons—two boys, Hans aged seven and Jorgen nine, and I was eight. We three made a natural group of tall, slender Danish-American boys. But Claus, the father, pronounced us deplorably skinny.

Claus was a huge man, of that Jutland Danish stock that produces men over six feet tall and thick in proportion. He wore his curly red beard three inches long and shaved his upper lip, to make sure, my father said, that the orders he roared at his sons would not be softened by filtering through a mustache. He didn't really like my father and my father didn't like him. But the two had been born in the same parish in Jutland, had used the same local dialect, unpopular with the Danes from the islands. A sense of tribal obligation led my father to visit the Jespersens, though at long intervals. The two farms were four miles apart by bee line, but six miles apart by the country road, which wound along a small stream from the upland and ran south along the edge of the Missouri Bottom.

Most of Jespersen's land lay in the Bottom and produced corn stalks so tall, it took a tall man to reach the ears. But behind the farm buildings there was an extremely steep, wooded bluff rising some seven hundred feet above the Bottom. A hundred feet above the level there was a limestone stratum twenty feet thick. It had been undermined by the river in some great flood and had broken off square, presenting a perpendicular face which we boys made into a mountain precipice. The top of the bluff was a narrow grassy plain with clear views up and down the Missouri, and far over the rolling plains to the east and the west.

Like all farm boys approaching the teens, we were homesick for the horizon and what lay beyond. But we disagreed on direction. The Jespersen boys dreamed of the Rocky Mountains, the gold fields of Nevada, the huge trees of Columbia. I dreamed of the great cities of the East, where people didn't live in houses but on huge shelves, one above the other, up to dizzy heights.

We would strike up a little song:

> "This long, long year
> A prisoner here, ah me
> I'd give a thousand guineas gay
> To be over the hills and far away."

Or we would sing, scornfully, the chorus of a song popular with parents:

> "Stay on the farm! Stay on the farm!
> Though profits come in rather slow,
> Stay on the farm. Stay on the farm
> Don't be in a hurry to go."

We'd laugh, "Profits come in rather slow, you bet!"

I was an avid reader of Scott and Dickens, and sometimes I offered to lend the boys my books.

"No, the Old Man would skin us alive if he caught us reading. And we don't care for stories of the dead Old World. Now, Gene Burton, who lives down the road, has lots of stories of the West. For one dollar he gets twelve complete stories, mighty good ones. Wish we had a dollar. But the Old Man wouldn't give us a red cent."

A month later, my father and I visited the Jespersens again. The Old Man took my father on the rounds of the farm; the boys and I scrambled to the top of the bluff. As we were recovering breath, Jorgen drew out from under his shirt what looked like a collection of newspaper Sunday supplements.

"Twelve complete stories. Real stories of the West. Look at them."

The first I looked at was *Black Tom, the Scout*. I ran my eyes down a column. What stilted English! Rubbish. I looked at another. *Six Buckets of Blood; or The Half-Breed's Revenge*. More rubbish.

"But here's one that is all true and tells just how it was done." *The Alton Train Robbery; or All's Well that Ends Well*.

"You see just how the boys could do it. There were a lot of farmers on the train, going down to Chicago with the money they got for their wheat, to have a grand spree. Well, there's a place where the Alton bends east, just where the Illinois Central bends west. Not ten miles from an Alton station to an Illinois Central station. Well, those two boys went down the train collecting wallets, jumped off at that station, borrowed a couple of horses hitched before a saloon and galloped across to the Illinois Central and got tickets for New Orleans. They turned the horses loose, to go back to their barns. Everybody thought they'd be in Chicago and the police hunted the town over. From New Orleans they got to California, bought a gold mine that was supposed to be exhausted, but it wasn't. They made millions and had somebody look up the record of the robbery. Said they were acting for two fellows that had been killed and who wanted to return the money they had taken.

"You know what? Those scalawags that were robbed claimed that they had lost twice as much money as they had. But they were paid what they claimed.

"You know, that could be worked here. The North-western bends west near Omaha, and the U.P. bends north. There are two stations not ten miles apart."

"It couldn't be worked here," I asserted dogmatically. "Too many railway police. If your heroes had tried that here they would soon have lodged in the Pen."

"Maybe." Jorgen folded up the literature and thrust it under his shirt. "Twelve complete stories for a dollar," he said with renewed appreciation.

"Where did you get the dollar?"

"Robbed the pocket of the Old Man, when he was asleep."

"But he must have missed it."

"I cut a hole in his pants pocket, big enough for a dollar to go through. When he picked up his pants, all his money spilled out on the floor. He hunted every corner of the room but didn't find the dollar. And of course he didn't tell us. He hated to have us know he had worn a hole in his pocket."

The Jespersens were a bachelor establishment. Of course there had been a Mrs. Jespersen. But as my father surmised, she had been a smart woman and had realized it was better to be dead than to live with Jespersen. She had died early, and the boys had no memory of her.

Jespersen, for years, did the cooking; now he was imposing it on his boys. It was simple. Corn meal mush or oat meal for breakfast, with plenty of milk. Boiled pork or beef for midday dinner, with boiled potatoes, onions and cabbage. Milk and bread from the grocery store for supper. But the slope of the bluff produced bushels and bushels of walnuts, wild grapes that turned into diminutive raisins on the vines, wild plums curing on the bush into sour prunes, black haws, a wild viburnum with the most delicious flat black fruit in red-stemmed umbels. And in spring there was an infinity of wild strawberries and raspberries.

Whatever the virtues or vices of their diet, the boys throve physically and shot up like young saplings.

My father timed our visits to the Jespersens to avoid their dinner table. But in the afternoon I ate walnuts with the boys, and wild fruits, fresh or dried on vine or bush. There was no such reservation on the part of Jespersen. He would drive up to the house just when my mother was preparing to serve dinner.

"Oh, horrors!" she would exclaim. "Here are the Jespersens!"

My mother took pride in her dinners. There would be a savory roast of pork, with potatoes baked with the pork. There would be leeks boiled like asparagus, and Brussels sprouts grown in our garden in spite of Nebraska weather. There would be in the offing a Danish red pudding, grape juice thickened with tapioca or sago formed in a cup into a beautiful dome which could stand, an island in a dish of cream.

"My boys can't eat anything sweet," Claus Jespersen proclaimed. "If you put honey on their bread it would gag them. And you couldn't hire them to touch that pudding."

My mother's face burned, but she said nothing. My father suppressed a smile under his beard. He knew the boys would make straight for the honey cask in the cellar as soon as their father went out with him to look at the crops.

This they did. I gave each one a honeycomb the size of a slice of bread. They devoured it, and we went down to the swimming hole, where they could purify themselves.

When we came back to the house we found the fathers in the living room. Claus Jespersen had picked up a book I had been reading—Stevenson's *Treasure Island*. He turned the leaves and read a few sentences.

"Juhl, I want to know, what good is your boy going to get out of a book like that? A farm boy doesn't need to read books. I never read a book, nor my father or grandfather. Or their forebears, as far back as is known. If I were you, I'd burn all those books your boy is wasting his time on. My boys wouldn't look at a book."

"Oho!" I thought. *"Six Buckets of Blood."*

"This is America," my father said. "You can't know what is good for a boy here. You can't say whether your boys will be farmers when they grow up."

"I can," Claus Jespersen asserted. "They are of peasant blood. They have peasant minds. They don't dream of anything but farming. Your son may be different. Your family had a peasant farm, but all the boys went to sea. Bones of your family are rocking around the Straits of Magellan."

"Maybe," said my father. "I don't think books are bad for boys. If they are good books."

"Good books! There are no good books but the Bible. And your son isn't reading that.

"In the old country," Jespersen continued, "we had to go to schools run by the Church. We had to recite, 'Ask, and you will be given. Knock and the door will be opened to you,' and other things that are not so. I was not going to have my boys waste their time going to school. But the chairman of the school board came to my house and said I had to send the boys to school. It is the law. And you call this a free country. Bah!"

The only reason my father had for visiting the Jespersens was my desire to climb the bluff with the two boys. Claus had a more cogent reason for visiting my father. He was always running short of money, and my father always had a store of gold pieces he kept in a box on the fireplace mantel. Claus could borrow small sums from him without interest.

Claus made money enough out of his farm, but he was bent on enlarging his fields. He had bought an additional forty acres, on mortgage, the terms of which permitted him to make part payment on the principal at the end of any quarter year. Any money he got hold of went into such payments. Then he would run short. Perhaps a dry season cut his corn crop too short for fattening his herd of steers. He'd have to buy corn. Or if his corn crop promised to be heavy he would not have steers enough to consume the grain. He would buy two or three more off grass, to fatten.

Or perhaps one of his farm machines broke down. He could get a new one by a very small down payment, with the rest of the price covered by installments running over two or three years. But he calculated that he would be paying interest at the rate of fifteen per cent on the installments. Better visit Juhl and borrow the money without interest.

My father had little concern about money. He would not sell wheat or corn, and produced only enough for our bread grain and for the stock. We had our own milk and butter and cheese, eggs and fowl, and indeed produced enough for the market to cover our ordinary groceries. When my father sold five or six fat cattle, or a dozen hogs, most of the price took the form of gold in the mantel box. Still larger sums went there when my father sold a horse. We always raised more horses than we needed. Grazing cost nothing, and it was easy to supply enough prairie hay and oats and corn to winter a dozen horses at different stages of maturity.

When Claus Jespersen came to borrow money, he always went through an almost ritual formula.

"Well," he would say, "I've got to go to town tomorrow to borrow some money from Nick Hanson."

"That usurer!" my father would exclaim. "How much money do you need?"

"I've got to get eighty dollars."

"Nick will make you sign a note for $100. He will make you date it back ten months. You will have to pay him, in two months, a hundred dollars as principal and eight dollars, a year's interest. Twenty-eight dollars on an eighty-dollar loan."

"Yes, Nick is a robber. But what can I do? I've got to get the eighty dollars."

My father would step to the mantel.

"Here you are," he'd say, handing Claus Jespersen four double eagles.

"I'll pay you eight per cent."

"No, you'll pay me the interest it would earn in the box."

"Juhl," Jespersen said, "how do you dare to keep all that gold in the box? Last week there were a couple of robbers broke into the Bergers', and tortured Berger and his wife with burning matches under their bare feet till they told where their money was."

"They didn't come here," my father said.

"The neighbors say, you sleep with one eye open and

have your old Civil War rifle handy."

"Yes, there's something in that," my father said. "Eight years of battle front, in Denmark against the Germans and here against the rebels, does something to your sleep."

A veteran from Sherman's army who had been a corporal in my father's company had visited our community and circulated a story of my father as a sharpshooter and one of the few men in the army who could aim a rifle in the dark. My father dismissed the story as mere gossip, but he did in fact have the capacity of awakening at any unusual sound. Sometimes I would awaken from sleep to hear my father's footsteps on the stairs. I'd hear him go through the living room to the rifle that stood behind his chair and pass out of the front door. Then I'd be unable to hear anything, for the beating of my heart. The door would open, I'd hear his military tread across the living room floor; I'd hear him plant his rifle in a military ground arms. Then peace and security and sleep.

Of course the Jespersens had to be invited to dinner, little as my mother liked it. The boys seated themselves and looked grimly at the food their father would let them have, meat and potatoes.

"Mrs. Juhl," said Claus Jespersen, "will you take those dishes of stewed fruit away from the boys? It disgusts them to see anything sweet. And will you put that plate of honey back on the end of the table? Honey! Not fit for food."

"Jespersen," my father said, "you amaze me. Danes have eaten honey since the old days. Why, they made a sweet honey wine the gods drank in Valhalla."

"The gods didn't worry about their teeth."

"I've eaten honey since I was a child," my father said. "I'm fifteen years older than you, and I have all my teeth. You have lost some of yours."

"But look what the honey did to your skeleton. How tall are you?"

"Five feet ten."

"You could have been six feet two."

My father laughed. "I've been shot four times in my shoulders. If I had been six feet two I'd have been shot in the chest and finished."

The conversation was becoming boring to the boys and me, but fortunately it was coming to an end. The fathers rose and went out to look at the stock; the boys and I raced into the cellar where I had a most wonderful honeycomb for them. It was dark brown, wild buckwheat honey. The wild buckwheat is a slender vine, growing at the edge of thickets. The bees must have gone over miles of thicket to fill a wild buckwheat comb.

In his eagerness, Hans broke his piece of comb and the honey spilled over his clothing. Terribly fragrant honey. There was plainly a whipping in the offing.

"I'll tell you what we can do," said Jorgen. "We'll go to the swimming pool. Hans can get in with his clothes on. We'll say he was scuffling with Erik and fell in."

An adequate solution. Of course Claus Jespersen roared. "Fool boys, to scuffle at such a place!" And Hans' summer suit was ruined. Sitting around with the suit wet, Hans would pull out seams. He ought to be undressed and ride home naked.

But that wouldn't do, morally. They drove away and the last I heard was a paternal admonition to Hans to be on his guard against Erik, that tricky boy who read books.

Two weeks later my father and I returned the Jespersens' visit. There was a faint veil of mystery over the boys' faces, but they had nothing to say until our two fathers walked away to look at the corn crop. There was a tract of land a quarter of a mile from the house where the cornstalks were incredibly tall. My father had to see them.

We boys went off into the wood, squeezed our way through bushes to what looked like a little clearing. There was a grocery box covered with a dusty window sash looted from the barn.

"What do you think we've got there?" said Jorgen. I tried to look through the dusty glass. All I could see was the floor of the box carpeted with wilted wild flowers. Oh, yes, in a corner under the glass were two angry-looking insects.

"Well, what are they?" I asked.

"Bees! We caught them with a net we made out of mosquito netting. We're feeding them flowers, and soon will have our own honey. They will lay eggs and soon we'll have a whole swarm working for us."

"These aren't bees," I said. "They're hornets."

"They *are* bees. They stung us."

"All sorts of things sting. But if they were bees they couldn't lay eggs. Only the queen bee can do that, and you haven't got a queen. And she can't sting."

"Listen, two of a kind can start anything! How many bees did Noah take into the ark? Two of a kind, of everything. Why can't two bees start a swarm now?"

"These can't. They are not bees, but hornets. You say they stung you. If a real bee stings you, the sting sticks in your flesh and tears off in the bee's body. That kills it."

"These *are* bees, Mr. Know-it-all. You'll see, we'll have plenty of honey for you, one of these days. But there's no use in talking to you. Mr. Know-it-all. Good-bye!" They pushed their way through the bushes and disappeared in the wood.

At first I was astonished at their behavior. My astonishment turned to rage. When I got back to the house my father and Jespersen had returned from the field.

"Papa," I said, "I'm ready to go home."

"Already! Where are the boys?"

"I don't know. They went off into the woods."

My father scanned my face, which was unpleasantly hot, and drew his own conclusions.

"All right. Jump in. —Jespersen! We're going. Good day."

"Gu dow," Jespersen shouted. He was always glad to see us go.

Two weeks later the Jespersens came to visit us. The two boys came up to me with such friendly faces that my anger began at once to thaw.

"Erik," Jorgen said as soon as our fathers were out of hearing, "you were right about those bees. They weren't bees. They died."

Sufficient apology. I took the boys down into the cellar, having first purloined two bath towels, out of the clothes chest, to serve as napkins. I found for the boys a particularly delicious pale honeycomb, late basswood honey. It was rare, and before the boys were through, nonexistent.

Visits between the two farms became increasingly rare. Jespersen had added his new forty acres to his field and had to stretch his manpower. Both boys were strong enough to handle a harrow or cultivator. Jespersen had now three teams at work in his field. His working day was from dawn to dusk, and the boys got tired long before sundown, but had to keep at work. When Sundays came they had no spirit for visiting. When they finished the chores—and the range of chores had grown wide—they liked best to retire to the barn and sleep on the hay.

Life was easier after mid-July, when the corn was "laid by." There were still oats and wheat to be harvested and hay to be cut, but such work was less wearing than the long grind of corn plowing. The boys would not be entirely exhausted on Sundays.

Jespersen still liked to raise small loans from my father as summer advanced and he began to buy cattle for fattening. So the visiting picked up, to flatten out when corn husking began. The boys' hunger for honey had not abated, and they still loved our swimming pool. I tried to get as much pleasure out of their company as I had of old, but changes were coming over my mind. I was devoting every hour I could spare to preparation for college. Hours of listening to a rehash of that same old batch of dime novels were wearying to me.

The stories were not in fact absolutely the same. They had undergone much revision in the teller's memory. In the story of the beneficent train robbery, for example, the railways were becoming less and less the Alton and Illinois Central and more and more the Northwestern and the U.P. The West to which the heroes of the story resorted was becoming less and less California, and more and more Nevada. And the heroes were growing younger. They had been just over 21. Now they were under 21.

Well, I thought, something like that probably happens to all stories if you tell them over and over. I had recently read *David Copperfield* and *Vanity Fair*. I did not feel that the David Copperfield at the end of the book was quite the same as David Copperfield at the beginning. I could not see, in *Vanity Fair*, any close kinship between Becky Sharp at the end and Becky Sharp at the beginning.

The next year another change came over the relation between the two families. A bank had been opened in our village. The Farmers and Merchants Bank. A smooth bank officer went from house to house, flattering the farmers and expounding the benefits of banking. My father would not bite. He said he never had enough money for a bank to count. Jespersen bit. He would get four per cent on his average deposit, and he could borrow any money he needed for short-term transactions at eight per cent. And he would find it very convenient to pay by check and to accept checks without worrying about them.

And so Jespersen came no more with a story of how he had to go to a usurer for a little money. And that meant that he and his boys would visit us seldom, if at all.

I wish I could say I missed them keenly. The truth is, I was glad they stayed at home. I was all bent on getting into the university. I had no high school training. My father visited the nearest high school and got from the principal a list of the text books used in the high school. He bought the books and I boned away at them every hour I could be spared from farm work. I knew that the university would not accept my home-made high school education, but I thought that they would let me in as an unregistered student. Once in, I felt confident that I would find my level.

It was many months since I had seen my friends, and in youth the dust covers memory too quickly. But one day I was astonished: the two boys turned up. They were tall as young trees.

"What! my friends, you here? I've been thinking of you. It's so long since we were together."

"Yes, our Old Man doesn't want us to see you. But he's gone out West, to see if he can't buy better cattle off the range. He left us to haul out a pile of manure and spread it on the field he will plow next Monday. A pile of manure the size of Pike's Peak. Well, we thought we'd come and see you and eat your honey."

"Fine! But did you come afoot the four miles over the hills and valleys? Why didn't you drive around?"

"Our neighbor hasn't anything to do but watch us. If we had taken the buggy, he would have reported on us to the Old Man."

I led the boys down into the cellar, where I had what I considered a special treat. It was a strange wild honey from late summer flowers I had never been able to identify.

The boys gobbled up the choice comb as if it had been just clover honey. Soon they were back on their dime novel stories. They told again the story of the beneficent train robbery, now quite Nebraskan in its terrain. But they were no longer dreaming of the gold fields. Their long legs itched for horseback, and they dwelt at length on the career of McMahon, the cowboy hero.

To say truth, Red McMahon bored me as much as the old tale of the train robbery. I loved the boys, after a fashion, but the teenage fashion may not be very ardent. I bade them good-bye with warmer regret than I felt and returned to my own books and problems.

In an hour I was drawn from my room by a great noise. The Old Man had driven up and was roaring for his sons. My father went out to mollify him.

"Those damn boys! They're hiding here."

"No," said my father. "They are on their way home. They left an hour ago."

"I ordered them to haul out the manure. And here they come over to your boy, on foot. Why did they come? Your boy feeds them honey. I've smelt it on them before, but I wouldn't believe it. They know what I think of sweets."

"I don't know why they came," my father said. "I thought they liked Erik. I know Erik likes them."

"Erik? Pooh! What they liked was honey."

"Well, if they did eat honey it never hurt them. You'll look far for two such fine young men as your sons."

"Fine young men, with honey in their minds instead

of manure. —As I drove up I saw two fine kinnikinick bunches along your lane. Makes the best rods for putting sense into a boy. You'll let me cut them?"

"For God's sake," my father said, "you aren't going to whip those boys? They're young men as tall as you."

"I can't, can't I?" He flexed his huge arm.

"If you touch them you will disgrace the Danes in America. No American father would touch those boys."

"I'll teach the American fathers something. And if you won't let me have your kinnikinick, there are fine clumps down the road."

Two days later, we heard from a neighbor of the Jespersens that there had been a great commotion at the Jespersen house, the Old Man beating to a pulp the two young men lying half naked on the ground.

"I'm through with him," my father said. "I'm through with his boys. They took it. Erik, I don't want you to see them again."

Of course I wouldn't go to see them. But what if they came to see me? In fact, they did on a day when my father was in town.

You would hardly have recognized them. They had new suits of striped tweed, well-fitting suits except that the pants and sleeves were too short. They had made-up ties and derby hats and carried themselves like young salesmen.

"Erik, we're going West."

"The Old Man is on his way to Chicago with a bunch of steers. We broke open his strong box and got some money. Not enough, but some money."

"Broke open his strong box! But he was keeping his money in the bank."

"He had been hearing the bank might bust, and he said, maybe your old man was smart keeping his money in the box. So he got a strong box and put some of his money in it. There was a lock, but the box was only sheet iron, and we chiseled a hole in it."

"That doesn't look good to me," I said moralistically. "It looks like robbery."

"Robbing! What has that old man been doing to us? For the last five years, we've been doing the work of farm hands. Damned hard-working farm hands. And what has he given us? Sometimes fifty cents for a new pair of overalls, or a dollar and a quarter for a pair of plowshoes.

"In five years we saved him a thousand dollars, each of us, a thousand dollars the hands would have cost. If there had been two thousand dollars in his strong box and we had taken it, it would have been fair. There wasn't that much money, by a long shot. We took what there was, just a small part of our rights."

There was no use in arguing the case. But the boys hadn't said all their say.

"You wouldn't have had to break open a strong box. You could go to your father's box and help yourself to his money. But you wouldn't. Not with your kind of Old Man. We wouldn't either.

"Remember the licking our Old Man gave us the last time we came to see you? We could still show you scars. He'll sweat when he finds us and some of his money gone. He ought to sweat."

Still, it was robbery, I thought. But one had to allow for the circumstances. The boys didn't look like wrong-doers. So tall and straight, with such blithe faces. I ran my eyes over their new suits. How well they fitted.

"What's that you've got in your hip pocket, Hans?"

Hans drew from his pocket a shining new revolver. Jorgen drew another.

"We're going out into a country where men have to defend themselves," Hans said, with a shadow of pride over his face. "But say, can you spare a few mouthfuls of honey? We've got three miles more to go, and we've got to get on the train at two."

We went into the cellar and the boys ate great combs of honey, the kind of lunch they would eat, they said, when they struck it rich.

And away they went, singing to the tune of *Oh, Suzanna:*

> "Oh Las Coras. That's the place for me
> You will never find go where you will
> So lovely a place as thee."

The second day after the boys left me, my father returned from town, looking uncommonly grave.

"Erik, I have bad news. Terrible news. Your friends the Jespersen boys robbed the Northwestern train. They jumped off at Cournot, stole a rig and drove over to Hamlin expecting to catch the U.P. for the West. Cournot had telephoned to Hamlin, and the Sheriff with a posse was there to pick them up. They are in jail now at Cournot. The trial is set for a week from today."

"If they are convicted—" I began.

"Of course they will be convicted. And they are likely to get long sentences. The railways try to get sentences of twenty years to life."

Those poor boys! They had taken the dime-novel story as a blueprint for action. Twenty years to life! Better be dead.

"I'm going down there to see if I can do anything for those poor boys. I found out that the judge was in Sherman's army. There was a man of the same name, a Sergeant Wykoff in Company I—Eye they wrote it, the 78th Regiment. I was in Company K and twice went out scouting with his squad. If it's the same man, maybe I can help the boys."

To his great satisfaction my father found that Judge Wykoff was actually the Sergeant Wykoff of Eye Company he had known. And the judge recognized him immediately and offered him a strong, warm hand.

"Private Juhl! Awfully glad to see you. I've been telling for years about the Danish soldier who could see in the dark and aim a rifle perfectly in the dark."

"I couldn't," my father said. "But I had been trained in the Danish army to catch sounds however slight and judge their direction. That gave me my reputation for seeing in the dark."

"Another thing I remember about you. We had marched all the way from Vicksburg and were coming up to Chattanooga, in the valley between Lookout Mountain and Missionary Ridge, and the rebels on Missionary Ridge were popping away at us, but Grant was ignoring them. He was in such a hurry to get us started on Sherman's march to the sea, before the desk generals in Washington could hear of the project and veto it. He was willing to stand a few casualties to gain a few hours' time. The soldiers didn't like it and stormed Missionary Ridge without orders, and cleaned the rebels out. Well, as I recall, you were first to start the charge."

"I wasn't. We were all first. Grant was willing to stand by and take casualties. But we were the casualties."

The judge laughed. "But, Juhl, what brings you here?"

"I've come down to beg you to let me say a word for two boys you are trying for robbing a train."

"Oh, the Jespersen boys. Do you know them?"

"I've known them since they were little shavers in knee pants. They are really good boys and I hope this lunatic folly of theirs is not to ruin their whole lives."

"They don't look to me like real criminals," said the judge. "I've talked with their father. When I summoned him, he said he wouldn't come. He had disowned the boys. I sent him word that a man can't disown minor children charged with crime: he would come or I'd send an officer after him. He came.

"You see, the boys have a right to trial by jury or they can plead guilty and throw themselves on the mercy of the Court. That is what they want to do, but as they are minors we have to have their father's consent. And he said, 'Do as you damn please; I wash my hands of those degenerates.' I had the court stenographer put down his statement as he made it and got his signature. Then he left. Maybe you would have liked to see him?"

"No," my father said. "I never want to see that wild boar again."

"Who is this boy Erik, Jespersen said corrupted his sons?"

My father laughed. "That is my son. The corruption he was guilty of was trying to make the boys read Dickens and Scott. The father considered all reading as of the Devil. But the boys got hold of a batch of dime novels, one of which told them just how to rob a train. And the other terrible thing Erik did, he gave them honey to eat, though the father had absolutely forbidden the boys to eat any sweets."

"You say they had a dime novel that told them just how to rob a train. You know, they might have got away with it? They left the train at Cournot, and everybody thought they would go on to Omaha and hide in the dives by the river. They commandeered a buggy to drive over to the U.P. They might have made it if they had taken a farmer's buggy. But they took Dr. Bond's carriage. The doctor was in the hospital having tea after a difficult operation. People saw his carriage galloping down the street and thought there must be some terrible accident somewhere. They ran to the hospital, and found the doctor sipping tea. Imagine how he stormed around when he heard his rig was galloping away. There was telegraphing, and a sheriff and posse to lay hands on the boys at the U.P. station. They were lodged in jail not for train robbery but for stealing horses and carriage. The idea that they were the train robbers came up only when they were searched and were found to have over two thousand dollars."

"So everything is clear," my father said. "What are you going to do with them?"

"They ought to be condemned to college. But the railways are insistent on long sentences for train robbers. If I give them less than ten years, the railways will try to impeach me. But I can make it four to ten years. After four years, they can be paroled if their behavior has been right."

"Good!" my father said. "And don't they teach men trades in the penitentiary?"

"Yes, carpentry, blacksmithing, shoe making, harness making."

"Judge, can't you recommend harness making for them? There are very few competent harness makers in the prairie states and we need them badly."

"That's what I'll do," said the judge.

And so we three boys set out for Lincoln in the same week. We were the only boys from our county that year to go off to Lincoln and our farm neighbors liked to tease my father by pretending to confuse the two institutions.

"When your boy gets out, will you have him look at my harness? I don't get the pull out of my team I think I ought to."

Poor wit, and my father didn't like it. To all such sallies, his tongue responded automatically, "Go to hell."

I visited the penitentiary and found my friends in a long room with tables cluttered with pieces of leather, shears, awls, peculiar flattened needles, balls of linen thread, wax and what not. Along the wall were mighty sewing machines, stamps, chests of material. The room was heavy with the smell of new tanned leather.

My two friends sat at a table punching holes in strips

of leather. They caught sight of me but looked away.

"Hello, boys," I said.

No reply. They fixed their eyes upon their work. And it was the same on later visits. They were dead to their old world.

We three were liberated the same year, I with my A.B. degree, the Jespersen boys with their parole. My liberation came three months earlier than theirs, and I went East, to work out my plan for further education. With his parole Jorgen set out for Seattle, where he found a job in a harness-making shop and promptly won praise for his energy and skill. Hans returned to our old village and took over an old harness shop which had been abandoned, with doors and windows boarded over.

My father had sold his farm and the family had established a new home in California. But I had a friend who still wrote me from time to time about the events of the community. Why had Hans decided to settle where everybody knew about his past? My correspondent thought that it was a kind of revenge on the Old Man who could not come down the village street without passing the shop of the son he always spoke of as his "penitentiary bird." The Old Man was selling out and meant to go back to Denmark to buy a farm, get a new wife and produce new sons who would "honor their father."

But I got a more human explanation of Hans' strange conduct in settling down in his old community. It was in a letter from Hans himself, a brief letter but friendly. A man's disgrace, he wrote, follows him wherever he goes, and gets taller if it has to go far.

I meant to visit Hans in my vacation. But when you are supporting yourself through a university, a summer job that can pay your next year's tuition has you by the neck. It was the same the following year.

But when I had just got started on my third, and I hoped final year of graduate study I received a letter in a slanting feminine hand, signed "Joan Yorkness."

"You don't know me, Mr. Juhl, but I am a friend of your friend Mr. Hans Jespersen. Something has come up he can't decide on. He says the only person who could give him advice is his friend Erik.

"He needs you. Will you come?"

She was wrong at one point. I did know her. When I was still on the farm I met her from time to time at the store, and I knew something about her. She was the daughter of a widowed farmer who was always sick and peevish against all the world. Nobody could stand him, except his faithful daughter. Nature had meant her to be pretty and charming, but she had given herself wholly to nursing that crabbed old man. He was dead now, but her devotion for him was still her life.

She had beautiful hair, but the only thought she had of it was to keep it out of her eyes. She had a beautiful smile, but she had kept it mostly for her father. She had a beautiful figure but she carried it as if it could serve only to carry drops to his bedside.

I had admired her from a distance. For she was three years older than I, and at eighteen a girl of twenty-one looks like a prospect for the Old Ladies' Home.

I arrived on a midday train. She was at the station to meet me. The same girl who didn't respect her gorgeous head of hair but kept it out of her eyes. The same strong little hands, so unlike the soft girl's hand made for squeezing, but yet thrilling to hold. She led me to her carriage. It would be a short ride, she said. She had something to say. Could she say it at once?

"Of course," I said.

"I want to marry Hans. He would like to marry me. But I'm too old, four years older than Hans. And he thinks a man on parole from the penitentiary can't marry. But he thinks you could advise us. You are a scholar, he says, and know a lot of things we don't know."

I was embarrassed. To be set up as an oracle while I was just on the threshold of scholarship. But I fixed my mind on Joan. She turned and smiled at me. What a very lovely smile, breaking from her unconsciously.

"Joan," I said, "I don't pretend to scholarship. But I love Hans. And I could easily be devoted to you."

We drove up to the harness shop. Hans came out to greet us. My same Hans, tall, slender, shy, extremely handsome.

"How fine of you to come," Hans said. "We need you. But let's drive up to my house."

Hans' house was a little frame cottage on a hillside above the town. Its entrance was flanked by two lines of hydrangea clumps, now turning purple. Hans took us by the house.

"Look," he said.

I looked. Four beehives.

"I bought them at your father's auction," said Hans. "He showed me what to do with bees, and next year I'll catch four more swarms. —Do you still eat honey? I have basswood honey that has been waiting for you since June. But listen to the bees. Doesn't their music carry you back to the old times when we were boys, homesick for the horizon?"

I had to wipe my eyes.

"Shall we go and eat?" Hans asked.

"No, let us talk first," I said.

"All right. This is the problem. I want to marry Joan."

"No," said Joan. "The problem is, I want to marry Hans."

"Well," I said, "where the deuce is the problem?"

"I am too old," said Joan. "I'm four years older than Hans."

"I am studying sociology under Professor Giddings," I said. "He likes to prove how wrong we usually are. He has a lot of statistics that show the most successful marriages are of young men with brides older than themselves.

"If a boy of nineteen marries a girl of eighteen, of course they fall into a row every Monday morning. If a boy of nineteen marries of girl of twenty-five, she just pats his foolishness down and they live happy ever after. Professor Giddings thinks it ought to be against the law for a very young man to marry a girl still younger.

"What I think, Joan and Hans, Joan may not be quite old enough, but Joan is Joan, perfect at any age."

"Thank you," said Joan. "I see you are a corrupt judge. But I've heard most good decisions are by corrupt judges."

"That's fine," said Hans. "But corrupt *my* problem. How can a man under parole from the penitentiary marry a woman so grand as Joan? At any time the State can pull him back into the penitentiary."

Professor Giddings had often criticized me because I thought too slowly. But he thought I was likely to think right. I was trying to think right just then.

"Listen," I said, "Hans on parole has carried himself as the inventors of parole hoped men might carry themselves. The whole community respects him, as a true and skillful workman. Nobody ever thinks about that parole. But we'll get up a petition to the Governor for a pardon. Everybody in the county will sign it and I'll go down and get the judge who sentenced him to head the list of signers. It will be easier to get his signature if I can say Hans is marrying so lovely a lady as Joan."

"We're putting you to a lot of trouble," said Hans.

"You're worth it," I said.

The next day I presented myself at the office of Judge Wykoff, a gray-headed, gray-bearded man with friendly eyes; I could have recognized him from my father's description of him, years ago.

"Judge," I said, "I've come to you in behalf of two boys, friends of mine, you sentenced to the penitentiary about six years ago, Jorgen and Hans Jespersen."

"Oh, yes. The dime novel train robbers. You know, they were just children. We shouldn't have put them in the Pen. We should have spanked them and sent them off to school."

"That's about what you did, Judge. After four years of excellent training, they got out on parole, perfect harness makers. The older one, Jorgen, went to Seattle where he is manager of a big leather goods establishment. I have a letter from him in my pocket." I handed it to the judge. "You see his name on the letter head?

"The younger boy, Hans, came back to his home community to face it out. Everybody says he is the best harness maker the county ever had, absolutely reliable, extremely skillful and intelligent. He is highly respected throughout the county."

"I'm mighty glad to hear that. Say, are you the son of my old comrade, Juhl? You look like him."

"Yes, I was the boy old Jespersen said led his sons astray, by trying to get them to read Dickens and Scott."

The judge laughed.

"I am going to ask you for a great favor. There is a young woman, the most admirable young woman in the county, who wants to marry Hans. He wants to marry her, but he thinks it isn't right for a man under parole to marry. The lady doesn't see anything wrong in his marrying under parole, but is prepared to wait the four years until his sentence has expired. I think it is a shame to put so fine a woman through such an ordeal. And I want to get up a petition to the Governor for a pardon. Everybody in the county will sign the petition, but what would really count is your signature. Will you let us have it?"

"Of course, those boys ought to be pardoned. But

maybe there's a quicker way to get at it. The Governor is an old friend of mine. I'll call him up. Suppose you step out into the anteroom and amuse yourself with the old magazines."

A half hour—what an enormous extent of time! But it was over at last and the judge called me into his office.

"The Governor says a petition isn't necessary. Those boys ought to be pardoned. I am to send him an abstract of the trial and the report I have on file of the boys' good behavior in the Pen. And you will dictate to my stenographer what you have told me about the boys' careers under parole. And stress the young lady who wants to marry Hans. The Govenor is very tender about the fair sex.

"He says if I get my report in tomorrow, he will sign the pardons and send them off. Hans will get his pardon on Wednesday, Jorgen not before Friday, because mails to the Coast are slow."

On the return trip, I rehearsed my announcement of the problem solved. Would I say, straight off, thanks to that wonderful judge and an equally wonderful Governor, the pardon will be here by Wednesday's mail? Or would I go into details, first, my calling on the judge, what he said, what I said? It's hard to fix your mind on anything in a railway car bumping over an uncertain track. The more I rehearsed my report on my success, the more I was discontented with my capacity for expression. I had something of vital importance to report to my sweet friends, and every way of saying it I could think of sounded flat in the ears of my imagination.

They were waiting for me at the station. Joan was very pale, and clinging to Hans' arm. Hans was trying hard to command a look of manly indifference.

"Congratulations, my friends," I said, forgetting my rehearsals. "Hans is a free man. The Governor will sign his pardon tomorrow morning at ten, Jorgen's pardon too. The pardon will be here in the mail on Wednesday."

Joan looked incredulous for a moment and then turned very white and clung with all her weight on Hans' arm.

"Treat 'em rough," my good old Professor Giddings admonished his students. "Women faint only when there are softies to hold them up."

"Joan!" I said severely. "This is no time to faint. We have matters to decide on. That marriage. I have to be there, but I can't wait days, cutting classes at Columbia. The best date is tomorrow."

Joan stiffened up and some color came back, first on her neck, then on her cheeks.

"But the pardon won't have come, tomorrow," Hans objected.

"That makes no difference. He has promised to sign it at ten tomorrow. You are a free man then. When the document comes is a matter of no importance. —Do you mean to be married at the courthouse or in a church?"

"In the courthouse," said Joan faintly.

"Yes, in the courthouse," said Hans. "The judge may understand better. The preacher might be worried."

"Exactly my opinion," I said. "Let's not stand around here talking. I'll have to run over to the courthouse and get the judge to promise to be on hand for ten-thirty."

I bade them good-bye for the time, hired a livery rig and drove to the courthouse. I was there in time to catch the county judge in his office, a good-humored man who knew as much about law as I did. He wasn't clear what he could do about a paroled convict, but I unloaded on him some lore I had picked up as a hearer in Columbia law classes and convinced him that the marriage law didn't care about parole. But my assertion that the Governor was signing a pardon next day was conclusive with him. Anyway he admired Hans, and Joan still more. He agreed to be on hand at ten-thirty, to tie the knot, which he said is easy to tie but hell to untie.

The next morning at ten-thirty we were all in the judge's office. He shook hands all around, produced some documents for Hans and Joan to sign, pronounced some formulas we all thought were preliminaries and declared Hans and Joan man and wife. He shook hands with Hans and kissed Joan and stood waiting for us to clear out.

"Erik," said Joan, "I'm going to kiss you, if Hans likes it or not. You have been our good angel."

I had never realized that a woman could be so beautiful as Joan was at that moment.

In two days I was back in my classes. In one I was hearing how wonderful good government could be and how persistent the forces making for bad government. In another I was learning how wonderful the natural economic forces were and how unfortunate the disposition of ignorant governments to interfere with them. In another class I was hearing that civilization came into existence when the long-headed men came down from the North and put the short-headed men of the South to work. Learning. I swallowed it in great gulps. But my mind would wander back to Hans and Joan, and their bliss, a sweet fruit of the sour plant of crime. And I wondered why there should be so wide a gulf between life and learning.

I meant to visit them the next vacation. But a young university instructor has little command of his vacation. There are summer classes to teach, research problems to advance, jobs with commissions, sometimes with publishers. Years had flown by and I had not visited Hans and Joan. But at last I had an appointment from the Bureau of Reclamation in Washington to make a survey of some Reclamation settlements in western Nebraska and Wyoming that weren't doing so well as they should. There was no reason why I should not stop off for a day or two with my friends in eastern Nebraska.

Hans and Joan met me at the station. They were my same old friends, Hans a little heavier but not quite heavy enough for his height, Joan with more complete calm on her gentle face. She had dressed her hair more carefully, and her dress became her better. Otherwise the same Joan.

The house was the same, but painted cream instead of white. There were a dozen flower beds flanking the path to the house, and Hans drew me past the house to see a whole battery of beehives. We had just settled down in the living room when two boys came storming back from school. Joan introduced them. They were Robert, aged eight, and William, aged six. Blond boys, very tall for their age, for all the world like Hans and Jorgen when I first knew them.

"They will eat dinner with us," said Joan. "I understand that in the East the children eat in a separate room."

"In some families," I said. "In English aristocratic families the children eat by themselves. And in the East people who want to live like English aristocrats have their children eat in the nursery, where they throw food at each other or out the window on the passersby. But I was brought up in an old-fashioned house. My father always said, eating together makes friends, and he wanted to have his children friends with him. I'm sure your children are your friends."

At table I looked across to four bright blue eyes fixed on me. The boys meant not to speak unless spoken to, but clearly expected to be spoken to.

"Do you like school?" I asked.

"You bet," said Robert. "We have the nicest teacher."

"Do you have to work hard?"

"You bet. The multiplication table is awful hard. But I can do it and Robert can do it up to six."

"And what do you read?"

"About the rooster and the fox. And the spider who kept climbing up."

"Do you read anything at home?"

"You bet. We read the *Boys' Handy Book of the Handicrafts and Industries of the World.*"

"Do you like it?"

"You bet. But there are awful hard words. But it told us how to make a kite. We made a good one, but it blew away."

I felt it was time to turn to the parents, but William had something more to say.

"Mister, Papa says you want to go out tomorrow to see your old home. But you can't go. It's going to rain tomorrow."

I looked at the pale blue sky through the open window. "Rain? But the sky looks as if it could never rain."

"The bees say it will rain."

"The bees?"

"You know, they buzz different ways. One way says rain."

"And how do the bees know?"

"They've got to know. They can't fly in the rain. Their wings would get wet and they'd have to crawl around, and the lizards would eat them. So they have to look out for the rain."

It was time for the boys to scamper back to school.

"What bright little boys," I said.

Hans cleared his throat. "You see, those poor boys favor my side of the house. They are almost the same as Jorgen and me. And my Old Man said we had peasant minds. Our family had had peasant minds for hundreds of years. We could be good farmers and artisans. But that was all."

"Your Old Man wasn't an oracle. There is no such thing as a peasant mind. There is a peasant mentality, a crust of custom, tradition, prejudice, superstition overlaying the mind and keeping it from working in a natural way. Your boys have good minds. But why do they have to read the *Boys' Handy Book?*"

"I don't like to have them read stories. Stories give you false ideas."

"Bad stories. Not good ones. Good ones give you a command of language, and that you have to have if you are to be educated."

Hans was silent for some minutes. "Erik," he said, "will you give me a list of the good stories the boys should read?"

"Certainly. And may I suggest they read them aloud to Joan. Make the reading a threesome. If there are words one boy doesn't understand, the other may. Or Joan may understand it. And if you don't, Joan, there is the dictionary.

"Remember: words are the tools of thinking. The small tools that carve out big thoughts."

It did rain the next day. I spent my time expounding to Joan everything I knew about education, and in addition, a lot of things I surmised.

For years a regular part of my correspondence consisted in answering inquiries of Joan on the matter of the boys' education. Her letters came thick and fast when the boys went off to the university. Joan had hoped that the boys would train themselves for teaching, or if not, for the law. But the boys wanted to be civil engineers. And there was no way, Joan said, of turning them away from engineering.

"Joan," I wrote, "it's their lives, and the decision is theirs. You are fortunate in having sons who have a clear idea of what they want to do. And probably they are right. Those boys are six feet two, and such tall men find life in a chair very trying. They are homesick for the horizon, and civil engineering may carry them to the far corners of the earth."

Sometimes I am right. I was right in this case. I had a letter from my friend Elwood Mead, who was putting through an irrigation and settlement project on the Murrumbidgee River in Australia, in which he mentioned with admiration two young engineers, the Jespersens, who had told him they knew me.

Hans had sold out his harness-making shop, and his house, and had moved to California. I still received occasional letters I had to answer through a complicated RFD address. And the next time I was in California I set out to find them. By train to Sacramento, by bus on a road, winding toward the Sierras, a bus stop at the foot of a grassy hill, and there were Hans and Joan waiting for me in a Model T Ford car, a car that could climb any slope, and climb it had to. But in the end we were at Hans' and Joan's new home.

A sweet cottage, all of redwood, at the center of a little plateau, nearly level, with very steep slopes on all sides. Behind the house was the longest file of beehives I had ever seen.

"Just our bees and the horizon," said Hans. "That is all the world, for us. I have escaped, at last."

"Escaped? From what? You were at home in Nebraska, weren't you? Everybody loved and respected you. Was it the Nebraska winds you escaped from?"

"No, it was the smell of leather. Ever since I was a little boy, I hated the smell of leather. I suffered terribly in the —— harness-making laboratory, as they called it. I hated it in my shop. I felt I had to stick to harness making, to pay for the education the state gave me, and in compensation for my —— foolishness.

"But now, no leather. You see, I wear canvas shoes, a canvas belt. Joan doesn't mind the smell of leather, but she doesn't wear any.

"We'll sit down on the verandah and listen to the bees. People think bees just buzz, always the same. That isn't true. They change their tune every minute. Listen. You never heard just that tune, did you? You won't hear it again, but another.

"And so Joan and I live here, listening to the bees and watching the light on the white Sierra peaks. The bees make us our living besides making the music of our lives. What more could we ask for?"

"Just one thing," said Joan. "That the boys would come a little more often and stay a little longer. But they are at home in the horizon."

A
MODERN
HORATIUS

NEWSPAPER READERS of long memory may recall an episode in World War I that proved Italy still produces men of the stamp of Horatius who held the bridge against the Etruscan army, in the brave days of old. Commendatore Rosetti with one companion, in a craft resembling an enlarged orange crate, penetrated a well-guarded harbor to attack the mightiest Dreadnought that was ever built, and succeeded. But the period was one of world-shaking events. The Central Powers were collapsing, and a mere feat of personal heroism could not hold public attention long. Like everyone else, I forgot about Rosetti, and never asked what became of him. Who ever asked what brave Horatius did with himself after his wounds healed?

Some years later my friend Professor Salvemini, the great Italian historian, refreshed my memory with additional details. Rosetti had indeed won world recognition. He had been offered the rank of admiral in the Italian navy, and corresponding rank in the French, British and American navies. He would not accept any naval post. Trained as a naval engineer, he refused to have anything to do with navies. An engineer, though specialized on naval problems, could surely have found employment in industry. Even for that Rosetti had no stomach.

The spirit and the exploit of Rosetti resembled that of Horatius more closely than one would think, considering the changes that have come over the world in twenty-five hundred years. The Etruscan army was marching down from the Janiculum hill to the bridge across the Tiber. If the Etruscans took the bridge there was no hope to save Rome. Horatius and two companions held the bridgehead until the bridge was cut down at the Roman end. What was involved in the Rosetti case was not a single city but all Italy.

The First World War was dragging to a close. The Germans had knocked out Russia, and Austrians and Hungarians had reduced the Serbian forces to guerrilla bands in the Balkan hills. Austria had invaded Italy, and after a long delay on the Isonzo had broken through, to be thrown back at the Pavia. Austria was exhausted and could go no further with her land campaign. Germany could spare no divisions from the Western front, now tremendously stiffened by the fresh American armies. But the Central Powers still dreamed of knocking Italy out, and although this would not mean winning the war it would immensely strengthen the Germans at the peace table.

Italy was vulnerable from the sea, but the Central Powers had no effective naval power in the Adriatic and

Mediterranean. The weak Austrian fleet had been bottled up in harbors by the stronger Italian navy. No German warship could get through Gibraltar, locked up by the British navy. But the Germans had a plan to build a mighty Dreadnought in the Austrian port of Pola, almost directly across the Adriatic from Venice. The Germans were working day and night to build this naval monster, which was to have greater firing power than any other ship afloat. Launched and cruising the Adriatic and the Mediterranean this ship, the *Viribus Unitis* (United Powers), could lay down such terms as it chose for sparing Venice, Naples, Genoa and any other Italian ports. The British might detach Dreadnoughts from the North Sea and Channel to destroy the *Viribus Unitis,* but could ill afford to weaken the naval forces that were holding the German fleet in check.

The Italian air reconnaissance reported the *Viribus Unitis* ready for launching. The guns had been emplaced, the magazines packed and workers on deck had given place to a naval crew selected from the best in the German navy. In a few days, perhaps a few hours, the *Viribus Unitis* would sail down the harbor and cross the Adriatic to Venice. To save Italy the ship had to be destroyed and Rosetti undertook to destroy it.

So much I knew about the case from the press reports and from Salvemini. One day Salvemini called me on the phone and told me Rosetti was in New York. Would I like to meet him? Would I? As any man in old Rome would have liked to meet Horatius.

Where could I call on Rosetti, I asked. It would be better, Salvemini said, if I could ask him to my house in Nyack, to meet nobody outside of my family, as Rosetti was not publicizing his presence in New York.

Salvemini passed the word to Rosetti that I would be delighted if he would come to my house at three in the afternoon of the next day and stay for dinner. He accepted my invitation and at three rang my doorbell. Before me was my ancient Roman. Not the type you may see at Tivoli, which you conceive to be what the Latins and Sabines were like. Not the Greek type of Southern Italy nor the occasional Etruscan of Tuscany, with wide shoulders, narrow hips, long narrow feet. Nor yet the Celtic type of Milan. Rosetti was of moderate stature, very slender, with narrow intense face, lofty brow, quick intense eyes. He was out of one of the hill towns of Northern Italy, from the region held by the Ligurians in Caesar's day. Was his type Ligurian? You see something like it in Genoa, also in Caesar's day a Ligurian city.

Rosetti loved his hill town. His family had lived there for many generations, how many he could not say. The same was true of all the other families. The houses had all been there for generations, and every inhabitant knew every stone in the pavement. Rosetti's first entry into politics was to fight some dreadful innovators who wanted to set up street lights. Only a few of them were threatened, but enough to destroy the glory of the moonlight. And why light the streets when every inhabitant could feel his way with security in the darkness?

I took his hand and brought him into my living room, where my children, still little or half grown, greeted him with the repressed excitement a hero arouses in the young.

"Doctor," Rosetti said as he seated himself before the fire, "we have much to talk about. Where do we begin?"

"I am most deeply interested in your attack on the *Viribus Unitis*. It is an historic event I know too little about."

"Very well. But I may be what you call long-winded."

"The longer the better," I said.

I wish I could reproduce Rosetti's account as he gave it. His English was good, with occasional Italian overtones that enhanced the beauty of his speech. His diction was better suited to an heroic exploit than mine, conditioned to recording the ordinary events of democratic life. But I have to content myself with plain reporting of the substance of his account.

Rosetti had worked out a plan for blowing up the *Viribus Unitis* as it left the ways. He would build a boat that would accommodate two men, which would show only a hand's breadth above the surface. It would carry at its sides cylinders with powerful time bombs calculated to float just under the surface. Compressed air would serve for motive power, but when the throbbing was likely to be perceived the power would be shut off and the two men would push forward with oars. Arrived at the vicinity of the *Viribus Unitis,* Rosetti would detach one of the cylinders, after setting the clock to time for the explosion. He would swim to the ship, attach the cylinder and swim back to his boat, if still alive.

The project looked hare-brained to the Admiralty, and they pigeon-holed it for months. But now the air service reported the ship had left the ways and was riding in deep water in the middle of the harbor. Rosetti's project was drawn from the pigeon hole, a boat—if you call it that—was built to his specifications and on a dark night a sailing vessel with dark sails towed the boat with Rosetti and his companion to a point as near the mouth of Pola Harbor as the vessel dared to go. Rosetti went on by compressed air until near the mole, a long masonry structure with sentries marching back and forth. Rosetti shut off the compressed air and rowed into the shadow of the mole.

Then he found a way to move forward even more quietly than by rowing. He and his companion with their fingers could catch the joinings of the stones composing the perpendicular mole wall. Once beyond the mole they could safely row for a space and turn on the compressed air.

Pola Harbor is narrow and extends several miles into the land. Air surveys had shown three buoyed chains across the harbor, each with its fruitage of contact bombs. As Rosetti approached the first chain he swam to the chain, pushed it deep under water while his companion rowed the boat across. They proceeded the same way with the second and third chain, and felt now they were free to push on in the harbor. But something warned them there might be another chain ahead. Rosetti swam forward. There was indeed a chain. The boat was rowed across.

Panic came upon Rosetti and his companion. Had they turned around in the darkness, and was this the third chain they were recrossing? They rowed forward cautiously as far, they judged, as to the second chain, if they were going back. Rosetti swam forward. No chain there. Clearly a fourth chain had been laid down after the air survey.

Now they had plain sailing. They turned on the compressed air and moved steadily up the harbor toward the *Viribus Unitis,* now brilliantly lighted. Searchlights were playing around it. They came as near as they dared. Then Rosetti released one of the bomb cylinders, set the clock for explosion in two hours, swam toward the ship with the cylinder. As searchlights approached him he dived. He reached the ship, dived with his cylinder and attached it, ten feet below the surface. He swam back to his boat.

But as he got aboard the searchlights fell upon the boat. Shouted orders set half a dozen boats in pursuit. The two men had barely time to put on their uniforms before they were called on to surrender. They were taken up to the deck of the *Viribus Unitis.*

Here, to their astonishment, they found a gala celebration. Scores of beautiful women were dancing with officers plastered with orders and dashing civilians in evening clothes. An orchestra was playing a succession of waltz tunes. At tables were refreshments and champagne in pyramids of bottles.

Rosetti demanded that he be taken to the captain. "For God's sake, Captain, get this party off the ship. It will be blown up, and soon."

"That is impossible," the captain said. "Every nook in the ship has been explored and watched. There is no possibility that explosives could have been secreted anywhere."

"Nevertheless, the ship is going to be blown up. You have barely time to get the company off."

The captain's confidence in the security of the ship was shaken. No wonder, if Rosetti spoke as earnestly as he did when repeating the conversation for me. The party was ordered to the boats.

But when almost all the party were in the boats, the word flew around that this was nothing but a hoax. The occupants of one boat climbed up the ladder, then those of another. Soon the whole party, including Rosetti and his companion, were on deck again. The orchestra played "Invitation to the Dance," dancing couples soon packed the space of the deck.

A terriffic explosion made the great ship tremble. There was a rush for the ladders to the boats. For the first time in his life Rosetti realized the potency of German discipline. The German crew took charge, dispelled crowding and eased the party to the ladders. After a few moments the ship began to list and the ladders on one side became unavailable. The crew guided the frightened women and men down the now sloping deck. Everybody was in a boat when the *Viribus Unitis* turned on its side and sank.

There was only one casualty. The boatswain of one boat lingered too long, to see if anyone else would come down the ladder. A hand spike came hurtling down from the sloping deck and dashed out his brains.

The two prisoners were taken to a guard house. How could this be? The officers were in Serbian uniform and spoke only Serbian, which Rosetti could not understand. But an officer who spoke Italian was sent for, who overwhelmed Rosetti with a report on the incredible change in circumstances. Austria had signed a treaty of peace with Italy and Serbia. At the very moment when Rosetti and his companion were fingering their way along the mole, the war had come to its end.

Austria had acceded to all Serbia's and Italy's territorial claims, surrendering to Serbia—soon to be Yugoslavia—all military and naval equipment in the harbor of Pola, including the *Viribus Unitis*. Our heroes had sent to the bottom a ship belonging to one of Italy's allies, the greatest ship any of the Allies had ever owned.

Whatever the grim humor of Fate, heroism is heroism and was recognized by the world. But Rosetti would never again be attached to any military organization. He meant to return to his hill town and live and die as his ancestors had done through a score of generations.

THE
FLYING
BUTTRESS

AT THE TURN OF THE CENTURY, a thin stream of graduate students was converging on Columbia University. Their elders had gone on to Harvard and Yale, institutions of much longer repute. But Columbia had circulated pictures of the Low Library, which looked to the Western student like the glory of Roman architecture restored to life. A Roman student could never rest until he had seen the Parthenon. The Low Library was the Parthenon to many Western students who could afford to go to the East for completing their studies and also to a host of others who could not afford it.

"Built for looks, not for books," the French professor said. But what looks! The domed building standing high above a colossal flight of steps, not yet tempered by Alma Mater. Noble columns, and within, a circular hall leading to a reading room where pigmy mortals wrestled with ideas under a space so high it strained your neck to look up. On the third floor, one entered the quarters of the School of Political Science, with pleasant classrooms and offices, and seminar rooms with access to the stacks, where you could help yourself to books you had heard of but never expected to hold in your hands.

A visiting scholar from Berlin commented, as he toured the building: "A place for dukes and young princes."

From the atmosphere of the dukes and young princes it was a short walk but a long way to the boarding houses. The boarding houses most graduate students lived in were scattered along the north end of Morningside Park, or over the flat land from Morningside Park East as far as Mount Morris Park. Sons of bankers and paving contractors lived in the better houses where they might pay as much as fifteen dollars a week for a well-furnished room and a fat table. The proletarian student couldn't do above eight dollars a week and usually had a poor room in a poor house, with the table poorest of all. In many houses there was no heat in the third-floor rooms. In very cold weather the student remained in the atmosphere of dukes and young princes until closing time, and on Sundays strapped his quilt around him and went on with his studies with a cool head. As for the food, the dinner was everything, breakfast and lunch mere sketches. The *pièce de resistance* at the dinner was likely to be Canada mutton, generally believed to be goat, three pounds for a quarter at Weisbecker's. It was nutritious if one's dentition was adequate. And if not, the student could comfort himself with the thought that those great educators, the Buddhist priests of Kashmir, required a student to fast two weeks before they plunged him into the depths of philosophy.

My third year of graduate work was beginning. I had to look for a place to board. The Columbia Secretary's office had a list of houses. As I went through it, I came upon the name Elizabeth van Bronk. She offered room and board for eight dollars a week, my usual limit of expense. The address was of a house on 115th Street, the second block from Morningside Park.

I went immediately to look at the room. The house was red brick, laid in neat patterns, the stoop was hospitable with easy steps, the brass fittings of the door were well polished. A neatly dressed maid admitted me and showed me the room. I was sure she was making a mistake. For the room was charmingly equipped with handsome mahogany furniture, an Empire bed with head and foot of beautiful picture mahogany, the chairs Chippendale so solid they must have been antique. There was an oval Hepplewhite table, a desk of rosewood fantastically carved, and in a corner of the room a "high boy" (probably spelled *haut bois*). I felt the blankets of the bed. There were enough for a night in an Eskimo igloo.

"Are you sure this is the room?" I asked the maid. "People don't furnish rooms for boarders with antique mahogany."

The maid laughed. "Some of the swells on Fifth Avenue have gone over to new furniture made to order. They have been selling their antiques at auction. Mrs. van Bronk loves antiques and has been buying them up for the big house the van Bronks are building out in Westchester. She is using the rooms here for storage, until the new house is ready to live in."

"Then any day all this furniture will move out."

"Not before next October."

I signed up. The room alone was worth eight dollars

a week. No doubt Mrs. van Bronk would make all the savings she could on the table. Well, I was willing to feed on hay, for such a room as that.

The dinner bell rang. I found the dining room resplendent with antique mahogany similarly on storage. My host stood by the chair at an end of the table, my hostess, looking very queenly, at the other end.

"I'm van Bronk," said the host, a big genial man one could easily be friends with. "You are?"

"Edgar Bates."

"Columbia student? Of what?"

"Political science."

"Good. I was afraid you might be studying philosophy. We have two of them there," he pointed at two young men on the right and left of the hostess. "When they talk they make your head spin. You'll sit here on my left and educate me in pure political science. This young lady, on my right, is Louisa Winthrop who teaches school and helps me to understand Mr. Woodward, on her right, a great engineer who is building a viaduct over the Manhattan Valley, to extend Riverside Drive. He's awfully deep, but Louisa sometimes makes me see what he means."

The soup was served—a soup that would have delighted Lucullus. The two philosophers picked up a controversy of several days' standing which promptly grew hot. It was about nothing. Literally nothing. They were discussing the nature of zero. One of the philosophers was a Neo-Hegelian, the other was a pragmatist. The Neo-Hegelian was insisting that zero has no existence. The pragmatist dwelt on the extreme importance of zero in mathematics. Before the Arabs discovered zero mathematics limped. If a man had to deal with even the simplest sum, he had to reach for his abacus, and if he didn't know how to work an abacus he had to appeal to an expert. No one would deny that zero is a tremendously important tool of mathematics, and so of all science. It works. And what better claim to existence has anything?

"Gentlemen," said our host, "I offer a compromise. Split zero in two and each of you take his half."

The two philosophers looked grim. Low humor is cold water on a philosophic head.

In the temporary silence, the engineer, Mr. Woodward, raised his voice, to discuss the way the great steel arches we saw on the slope from Grant's Tomb were bolted together. How vital it was to make sure that there was no flaw in a bolt, what stress each bolt might have to meet and what stress it was capable of meeting. All in engineering language the host and I could not understand. Louisa Winthrop translated the engineering account into words of four syllables anyone could understand. The intense ardor of her speech made one realize she considered the engineer an Archimedes at least.

I won't go into details on the dinner. I get hungry even now when I recall that dinner in memory. And the next dinner was equally sumptuous, and the next and the next.

We had finished our Sunday dinner. The other guests had retired to the living room. Mr. van Bronk and I were still sipping our coffee.

"What do you think of our table?" Mr. van Bronk asked.

"It beats Delmonico. But what I want to know is, how can such a table be supported by the boarders' meagre eight dollars a week?"

He laughed. "Some day you will have a wife. And you will find, wives nowadays want an income of their own. You can be just as liberal as you please, give them money whenever they ask for it, press it upon them when they don't ask, it won't help.

"My wife saw a way to earning money of her own by

taking in boarders. I was willing, provided she'd set as good a table as I was used to having. I pay the maid and cook, and the grocery and meat market bills. That leaves to my wife the boarders' eight dollars free and clear."

"That looks to me like just an expensive way of giving a wife money."

"You will come to know families where the wives go out and get jobs, any old jobs that pay them salaries that amount to half the pay of the woman who is hired to manage the home. The husband pays the woman. Yes, it's an expensive way of giving a wife money, but she doesn't see it. She doesn't want to see it."

I dropped into the habit of lingering over my coffee. It was fun talking to that good-humored cynic van Bronk. What was his business? Most certainly something yielding easy money abundantly.

There was a van Bronk, Patrick if I had his name right, who was the Tammany leader of our district. He was regarded by the Faculty of political science as a particularly corrupt boss. Probably my Mr. van Bronk was a relation and so was put in the way of lucrative jobs.

We were sipping coffee. "Does the university know you are boarding here?" he asked.

"Of course I've left my new address at the Secretary's Office."

"That's all right. But don't tell the profs you are boarding at the house of Patrick van Bronk, the Tammany Boss, they usually say corrupt Boss."

I was a bit shocked. This genial man the corrupt Boss Patrick van Bronk whom I had conceived of as a sinister cross of fox and wolf?

"Your professors wouldn't like it. They have been dusting your mind over with big words that don't mean anything, to keep you from seeing the real facts of politics. The dust cover isn't complete yet and you are in danger of seeing real facts. That's terrible."

I laughed. "My teachers insist on our getting the facts."

"Yes, facts dolled up to sit on a lady's mantel. My district runs from 110th Street to 135th and from river to river. It's hard to keep track in so big a district of all the people trying to break into politics. The Columbia professors are helpful to me. When they come out for a man, I know that's somebody I have to put down, if I can."

One afternoon a week later I saw from my window a woman mounting the steps. She was crying aloud—rather musically. She was admitted to van Bronk's office, whence issued more violent sounds of crying. But van Bronk was soothing her with his kindly voice and the lamentations ceased. After an hour I saw her trip down the stairs of the stoop, apparently light of heart.

I was impatient for coffee-sipping time, because I was sure van Bronk would tell me all about the woman's visit, for my education. And he was evidently eager to put the case before me and impatient with the dilatory eating of the other boarders.

Finally we were alone.

"You saw that woman come wailing up the steps," he said. "It was Mrs. Melograno, who runs a boarding house in our Little Italy, over there near the East River.

"You know, for thousands of years Italians have lived mainly on bread and wine. They eat their bread dry, with wine to wash it down.

"They can't afford to buy wine at the liquor stores. So they make it themselves. In the grape season you will see truck after truck loaded with grapes in the streets of Little Italy, and the whole region will smell for weeks of fermenting grape juice. It isn't entirely lawful for them to make wine without a license, but they think it can't be more unlawful than making bread. And usually we let them alone.

"Those Italians are the hardest workers in New York. They do all the work on digging trenches, repairing cobblestone streets or replacing cobblestone with Belgian blocks or asphalt. You see them throwing cobbles around as if they were rubber balls.

"Where do they get their energy? Their breakfast is a piece of dry bread and coffee. On that they work like Trojans all morning. At noon they sit down and chew up half a loaf of dry bread, with a pint of wine if they can get it. At night they have a dinner of spaghetti with grated cheese, some meat, a bowl of mixed vegetables and a pint of wine. An American couldn't work on such a diet. The Italians couldn't work on it if you cut out the wine.

"Mrs. Melograno supplied her boarders with a small loaf of bread for lunch and a pint of wine. She had no notion there was anything wrong in that. But a new cop came along, inquired about it, declared she was selling wine without a license and took her husband off to jail.

"What did I do about it? I called up City Hall and asked, 'Why in hell are you losing me a thousand Italian votes?' I explained. They apologized and had Melograno out of jail and returned home. And I had them assign that too conscientious policeman to Staten Island, to watch for smugglers.

"Corruption, you'll say?"

"No," I said. "It sounds to me like good sense, since the law is what it is. But can't the law be made to fit the facts better?"

"How could you make a law that would be right for a city of many colonies like New York? There is an Armenian colony that makes their own beer. It you taste it, you'll say, 'Nothing but a horse can drink this!' But it's what they want to drink, and they have to make it. Against the law, but the police look away.

"I could give you stories of law violation in the Spanish colony, the Russian colony, the Serbian colony. They do not mean to violate a law. They think what they are doing is what everybody has a right to do. Our policemen are human and keep their eyes closed, as a rule. When one of them gets too legal, as the policeman who arrested Melograno did, van Bronk, the corrupt Boss, is likely to be called in. And what does he get out of it? Votes. You are studying economics. Someday we may try to figure out what votes are worth in money."

It had been a gorgeous November day, and everybody at the dinner table was in the best of humor, even the philosophers. Woodward, the engineer, for the first time since I came into the house, really showed signs of animation. And his faithful interpreter Louisa Winthrop sat lightly in her chair and looked as if she would have to hold herself down.

The Riverside Drive viaduct construction was ready for a great surge forward. Two of the great steel arches that were to support the roadway were lying complete on the grassy slope north of Grant's Tomb. Louisa Winthrop's Archimedes had to tell us in detail how they were put together, what pieces of steel were welded together, what pieces put together with bolts. And the engineer supposed we wanted to know all about the careful examination of the bolts, to see that there were no hidden flaws in the steel, and how often nuts had to be rejected for screw interiors that were not perfect up to one tenth of a millimeter.

You could see that the philosophers' minds were wandering, but that is the normal habit of the philosophic mind. Van Bronk and I had no technological imagination, and with the corner of my eye I could see that van Bronk was winking hard to keep off sleep. So was I. But Louisa Winthrop was plainly in intellectual heaven as she interpreted the technical terms. From time to time she would involuntarily put her pretty hand on the engineer's hairy wrist.

But all this was just a preliminary. The overwhelming fact was that rails had been laid to the edge of the viaduct approach and a ponderous movable structure with a mighty steel arm was now in its proper place. An arch would be rolled down from the slope. Then—as van Bronk and I understood Louisa Winthrop's interpretation—the steel arm would take the arch by the scruff of the neck and swing it out over the abyss of petty traffic of the Manhattan Valley. Then it would gently let the arch down until it rested squarely on the concrete footings that had been set up. A pair of arches would be hooked together and hooked to the approach structure. All the metal that would support the roadway would be welded or bolted in, a temporary roadway would be laid, the machine with the great steel arm would move forward and more arches would be rolled down to swing their way to the prepared concrete footings.

The engineer seemed to imply that this was an unprecedented way of building a viaduct. I wasn't sure of that, but Louisa Winthrop was sure beyond the remotest doubt. And while you could not pick out from his technological discussion any claim that he had been the inventor of the method, Louisa Winthrop took that for granted, and her soul lay prostrate in admiration at his feet. But I remembered, he was one of a dozen engineers on the job.

I was young, then, and more interested in the unacknowledged romance before my eyes than in the technological facts dinning in my ears. Louisa had been a very pretty girl and was pretty still, with a ripe beauty. The philosophy students likened her to a pear that had remained too long ripe on the tree and desperately needed a picker's hand to save it from falling to the ground, to be a prey to slugs. I didn't like the simile. I thought of her as an ivy plant that for years had run over the ground of school teaching and now desperately needed to climb into the air. Ivy looks best on the trunk of a green tree, but if there is no green tree around it makes do with a dismantled telephone pole. Whatever engineer Woodward was, he offered a modest altitude.

The next Sunday was one of the incredible bright warm days that may sometimes occur in Indian summer. Mr. van Bronk proposed a walk up to Riverside Park, to take a look at those arches on the grass. They were there indeed, ready to roll down to the viaduct approach. We walked to the edge and saw the row of concrete footings crossing the traffic lines of the Manhattan Valley. I had not realized what a tremendous job the viaduct builders had on their hands.

"It's a big job," I said. "There must have been a lot of graft in it."

"I don't think there was. You people up at Columbia don't know the natural history of graft. You think graft is everywhere. It isn't. It crops up under certain conditions.

"Suppose a big public improvement like extending a thoroughfare is before the Council. Every such improvement boosts the value of real estate somewhere and perhaps reduces the value somewhere else. There will be a lobby for it and a lobby against it. Both will try to drag in the Party. If the Party puts the project through the Council the real estate men who are going to enjoy a boom will shell out a little cash to the Party. That is known as graft. The real estate men keep most of the increased values for themselves. That is known as profit, and wins them great admiration.

"This viaduct isn't hurting any property values and

isn't boosting many real estate values. People on both sides of the Valley are happy to have the drive run all the way to the end of the island without going through the tangle of traffic in the Manhattan Valley. There are practically no people the Party can shake down.

"There was a point where bribery might have come in. The commissioners who regulate construction of public works had laid down the rule that all construction that will carry great weight must have a foundation resting on bed rock. The Manhattan Valley had been a chasm, produced by the great split in the earth's surface that made the Hudson channel. The Manhattan chasm may have been thousands of feet deep. In the course of ages it silted full and some of the silting produced a great stratum of clay, a very dense clay as heavy as rock. The engineers' borings struck the clay at about a hundred and fifty feet and went on another hundred feet without getting through the clay. It was of no use to bore farther. It might be several thousand feet to bed rock, and if they found it, it would be hot and brittle. The viaduct would have to let its foundation be supported by the clay. It was just as good a support as the trap rock usually prescribed for foundation bases.

"The engineers saw that any foundation for the approach to the viaduct would have to rest on the clay. They put the case before the construction inspector, who authorized them to go ahead. He could have got a fat bribe, but I don't think he did. He was a high-minded public-spirited man and I don't think anybody would have dared to offer him a bribe.

"But we've had enough of this viaduct. Let's go down into the Park and sit on a bench in the sun, looking out at the river. We won't be able to do that again before May."

As we walked to the steps he sang in a low voice a Barnard College ditty:

"Down by the Riverside
Side by side
She sighed, he sighed,
Down by the Riverside."

We found a bench where we could look out over the Hudson. The river was alive with little sail boats, making the most of what was probably the last warm day of the year.

"What do you think of this park?" van Bronk asked.

"It's wonderful. We Columbia students do almost all our walking here. Central Park is fine, and you can take a brisk little walk in Morningside. But here you have the river."

"Do you know to whom we owe this park?"

"No."

"Boss Tweed. What he found here was a kind of slum, shanties scattered all over the place, sometimes in groups, housing all sorts of dubious characters, smugglers, pickpockets, bootleggers. There were places no policeman dared to go alone. Boss Tweed had the city buy up the land for seventeen million dollars, big money in those days. The land couldn't be bought today for a hundred and seventy million.

"The good citizens raised an awful howl about extravagance and graft. There was graft. I've heard that the landowners got only thirteen million, the four million was distributed among the boys.

"Boss Tweed was greedy for money, but he wanted glory too. He had his park but it wasn't improved and nobody paid much attention to it. He dreamed of throwing a suspension bridge across the Hudson at 116th Street. Brooklyn Bridge was considered one of the seven wonders of the modern world. A bridge over the Hudson would stand out where the whole world could see it.

"Of course all the taxpayers and real estate men were

against it. Such a bridge would draw hundreds of thousands of people across the river to raise rents and the price of building lots for the benefit of New Jersey. But Boss Tweed didn't care much for the taxpayers and real estate men. They had few votes, and you never could count on them.

"If Tweed hadn't ruined himself by his reckless grabbing for money, we might have built that bridge. But a grand jury got hold of him and indicted him for bribery. He lost his nerve and skipped out to Spain. They yanked him back and put him in Sing Sing for a term he would never outlive.

"Well, that's enough of Tweed. You wouldn't think it of me, but I've been reading a book of history. History of Ancient Greece. By an English fellow who writes mighty well. Grode, I think."

"Grote," I corrected.

"Yes, Grote. Well I came across a big man, Periculs, I think his name was."

"Pericles."

"I was puzzled for a while about his office. He wasn't a king or a dictator. He wasn't a President or even a Chairman of the Assembly. Yet he ran Athens from the time he was thirty until he died in his seventies.

"What was he? Why, a boss."

"Yes, but with a colossal difference," I said.

"Sure. He put through the biggest public improvement project that had ever been done. It would be a mighty big project today.

"There was a hill alongside the city, the Ac—"

"Acropolis," I supplied.

"That hill was seven or eight hundred feet high and so steep on all sides even a goat couldn't climb it. In earlier times the city had jimmied out some sort of a road skirting around on a slope. It was good enough for a donkey cart, if you had a good donkey. The citizens climbed up there for refuge if the city was attacked.

"Well, Pericles cut a road up the side of the hill, a road you could drive up in a chariot, and that would take mule carts carrying stones weighing above a ton. He cut into the living rock, in some places for hundreds of feet. Without explosives. I've walked up that road. Our engineers couldn't do a better job.

"Then he leveled off the top of the hill and paved it with marble slabs. He put a wall around it to keep tourists in a jam from falling down the hill. Then he put up a temple to Athena, the—the—"

"The Parthenon," I supplied with conscious learning.

"It was a superb building; the finest man had ever laid eyes on. Solomon's temple was a soft drink joint in comparison. For a thousand years, according to Mr. Grote, tourists from all over the world, from India and the Sudan, from Spain and Morocco and even Britain went through the hardships of travel to visit the Parthenon. It is a ruin now, but still it seemed to me the most worthwhile sight in all Europe.

"Now, I wondered, where did Pericles get the money for that colossal project? From the taxpayers? They were tight-wads, as taxpayers are still.

"But there was a big pile of idle money in the Treasury. All the cities around the Aegean were desperately anxious to keep the Persians off salt water. Athens could do it. She had the strongest fleet in the Aegean and the best trained naval fighters. There was no reason why the other cities should build little fleets of their own. Better give the money to Athens, to build more ships.

"Athens knew that the Persians had given up the idea of becoming a sea power. The Athenian fleet was plenty strong enough to take care of the Persian's mercenary ships from Sidon and Tyre. More ships would mean training more naval crews, to sit around in the ports. And so the Athenians kept taking the money from the other cities but didn't build the ships. The money had become a big cumbersome pile. Boss Pericles grabbed it, for the Acropolis.

"No doubt high-minded citizens set up a howl. If Athens wasn't going to build the ships it ought to send the money back to the cities; Pericles had no time to listen to empty sounds.

"Then I began to ask Mr. Grote, where did Pericles get his political support? Were there enough enlightened householders and businessmen to back him? No. It was Labor that made Pericles secure.

"I had supposed that all workers in Athens were slaves. But Mr. Grote says not. All the crafts were manned by free citizens. The sculptors and painters, the carpenters and smiths and pottery workers were all free men. Slaves did the dirty work, the killing hard work, like getting marble out of the quarry and hauling it to the Acropolis. No slaves could cut a block square or lay it. The guilds of free artisans were strong enough to exclude slaves, even slaves who had been artisans before their capture.

"There were a lot of those free artisans. Grote doesn't say how many, but I figure from what he does say they must have been twelve or fifteen thousand. Mr. Grote says the total number of citizens who could vote in the Assembly—the only place men could vote—was twenty-seven thousand. Pericles could pack the Assembly with labor whenever he needed to do it.

"And there was something peculiar about Athenian labor. It didn't bite the hand that fed it.

"I got to thinking. What kind of people were those Athenians anyway? Pericles gives a picture of them, in his Funeral Oration. If the Athenians were as fine as he makes them out to be, they deserved a Pericles for their Boss Tweed. And when I think of our people, a bunch of would-be aristocrats that call themselves the Four

Hundred, householders that fight every improvement on principle—which means their pockets—businessmen who short-weight you, labor that goes back on you, I thought maybe we deserve a Boss Tweed for our Pericles."

"There is one point in which we match the Athenians," I said. "They never developed a more clever sophist than you."

The next Tuesday morning, I sat in my room, trying to write a seminar paper. The sound of wailing and sobbing came in over the transom of my door.

"Another Mrs. Melograno," I thought. I went softly down the stairs, opened the living room door and looked in. Why, it was Louisa Winthrop!

"Miss Winthrop," I said, "something terrible must have happened."

"Yes, it's all gone to pieces."

"What?"

"Everything."

I collected enough intelligible words from among her sobs to get a fair idea of what the trouble was. An inspector had come around Monday afternoon and had ordered the work on the viaduct stopped. The plan of swinging over the arches from the viaduct approach would not do. The approach rested not on bed rock but on clay. It could not support the enormous weight of an arch plus that of the apparatus for handling it. The arches would have to be built up down on the Manhattan Valley level and raised to their places.

This meant a huge increase in cost, and the contractor had made a close bid. The new procedure would ruin him. His contract had permitted him to draw city funds on a progress basis. He could throw up the contract without too heavy a loss. And that was what he proposed to do.

Louisa Winthrop's hero Woodward would be out of a job. And he was preparing to accept an offer of a job in British Honduras.

"I'm sure this can be straightened out," I said. "Is Mr. Woodward in his room? I want to see him."

"I'll get him," said Louisa. In a few minutes they appeared, Louisa still sobbing, Woodward as calm as a telephone post. He proceeded to tell me in technical language what Louisa had told me in sobbing English.

"Have you talked to Mr. van Bronk about this?"

"No, why should I talk to Mr. van Bronk?"

"Don't you know he is a power in the district? The Democratic Party leader?"

"No, is he?"

That stick! I thought. Not to know who his landlord was, and not to realize what van Bronk meant.

"He's a wizard in straightening out kinks like this. Let's go in and see him."

Apparently Woodward did not mean to stir, but Louisa seized his arm and made him come along.

Mr. van Bronk turned his chair toward us:

"My friends, what can I do for you?"

Woodward began a technological account.

"Just a minute, Mr. Woodward. Edgar, you tell me what's the matter in words of one syllable. You know, I'm pretty dumb."

I needed less than twenty "words of one syllable" to reach van Bronk's understanding of the situation.

"I see. That new inspector. I've heard of him. Mr. Woodward, can you get me your boss on the 'phone?"

Woodward sat immovably and mute, but Louisa almost yanked him out of his chair. He sat at the telephone, named a number and in a minute said, "Here he is."

Mr. van Bronk took the telephone. "Mr. Seymour? I'm Patrick van Bronk. I understand there is a little snag with the inspector. I want to see you. No, not here. Nor in your office. There's a disreputable-looking little joint on Amsterdam, just across from Columbia. The shanty with its shingles patched with tin can tin, and two old washboards nailed up for the window panes smashed at Hallowe'en. Yes, a saloon. You can't miss it. Nobody goes there this time of day. We'll meet in the back room in half an hour."

"He can't do anything about it," said Woodward gloomily, as we returned to the living room.

"Wait and see," I said, "and, Miss Winthrop, be easy. It's in the works."

Late in the afternoon Mr. van Bronk returned to the house. He sent his secretary to summon Woodward, Miss Winthrop and me to his office.

"It's all fixed up," he said. "I met Mr. Seymour and the inspector. I talked the matter over with the inspector, and he agreed he had made a mistake. I got a letter from him telling Mr. Seymour that further study of the engineering report convinced him that the foundation will carry the arches and the apparatus for swinging them. He hopes that the work will go ahead tomorrow morning.

"Mr. Seymour asked me to tell Mr. Woodward to be on hand early in the morning. He proposes to swing the two arches before noon."

Louisa nearly fainted. But Woodward preserved his superhuman impassivity.

After dinner, Mr. van Bronk invited me to come into his office.

"I feel you would like to know just how this affair was managed. After our conversation of yesterday, I'm sure we understand each other. I can talk with you about matters I usually don't talk about. And you will understand you can't tell the story I'm going to tell you for twenty-five years. Then if you tell it, nobody will believe it. They'll say you made it up."

"I'm not anxious to tell the story, even after twenty-five years. But I am anxious to hear it, right now."

"Well, I met Mr. Seymour, Woodward's boss, at that little joint on Amsterdam, across from Columbia. He looked as if he hadn't slept the night before, but he faced me hopefully. I didn't waste any time on preliminaries.

" 'Mr. Seymour, I know that inspector's doubt of the soundness of your foundation is bosh. I know it can bear any weight you can put on it. I can go to the Commissioners and get a new survey, which won't help the inspector's reputation. But that will take time, three months at least. I know another way which will let you go ahead with your operations tomorrow morning. It will cost a little money, a thousand dollars. Is it worth it to you?'

" 'It would be worth ten thousand to me!'

" 'Now I can't go into details about it. If you want me to do it, get me a thousand dollars in cash as quick as you can.'

" 'There's a branch of the Corn Exchange a few blocks from here,' Mr. Seymour said. 'I do a good deal of business there. I'll run over and get the thousand dollars.'

" 'And I'll stay here and get in touch with the inspector.'

"I had just got him and made an appointment for three in the afternoon, when Mr. Seymour returned with the money.

"I found the inspector just about the sort of man I had expected. You could see from the set of his jaw that he was after money, a lot of money. Anybody could figure out that it would be worth $5,000, maybe $10,000 to the contractor to get a go-ahead signal. And the inspector did not seem happy to find van Bronk mixed up in the business.

" 'I'm pleased to meet you,' I said. 'I've heard a good deal about you from one of the commissioners, an old pal of mine. I expect you to make a fine record. But I came down to talk with you about that Riverside Drive viaduct. I hear you have doubt about the approach foundation being strong enough to bear the weight of the arches and apparatus Mr. Seymour proposes to put on it.

" 'Now, I've gone pretty thoroughly into the engineers' reports on that foundation and I'm confident it will bear all the weight Mr. Seymour proposes to put on it. But to make sure we could strengthen it by a flying buttress put in the right place. That will cost $1,000.'

"He gulped. Only $1,000!

" 'Now, I have the thousand dollars right here.' I took the wad out of my pocket. 'Will you take charge of it and see that it is put in the right place?' I handed it to him. He took it with the best grace he could muster.

" 'I want to see the work go right ahead. May I trouble you to write a brief letter to Mr. Seymour telling of the revision of your views? Get me your stenographer; I'll dictate the letter for you to sign. I want to take it with me to Mr. Seymour.'

"The secretary appeared instantly. I dictated:

" 'Dear Mr. Seymour, On reviewing the reports of the engineers and geologists on the foundation of the approach to the viaduct you are constructing, I find that my doubts as to its bearing strength are baseless. I herewith withdraw my order of yesterday's date to suspend operations and urge you to proceed promptly with your great work. Signed, William Messvale.' "

"I got the letter into Mr. Seymour's hands, and he is calling up all his personnel, to be on hand tomorrow for the planting of the first arches.

"That's the story. You may say 'bribery' but you suspect by this time, a lot of construction in New York, though based on bed rock, is stiffened up a bit by bribery."

At dinner the next evening Woodward seemed a different man—slightly different. He nodded to all the guests—a new kind of courtesy, for him. There was good reason, I thought, for his glimmer of elation. Two of the arches had been swung out and were now standing majestically on their footings. The great work was actually marching. Wasn't that enough to make a dismantled telephone pole put forth a green leaf or two?

But that wasn't the reason, I soon found. After a few technical comments on the engineering feat—interpreted with fire by Louisa—he put on a semi-complacent face and said, impressively:

"The Boss gave me a raise. A fifty-per-cent raise. Because I had saved the day, by finding van Bronk and bringing him into the situation."

I caught Mr. van Bronk's eye. He winked. I glanced at Louisa. She was looking at me with round eyes, eyes a bit pathetic and appealing.

So I hadn't had anything to do with the matter, in Woodward's opinion. I was well pleased to be canceled out of the equation. I was happy with the end, the right of a great public work to proceed. I was not happy about the means—bribery. I had not anticipated that. I had supposed Mr. van Bronk's political power alone would turn the trick. It could have brought the inspector to his knees, but that might have cost a delay of three months, and the viaduct could not have been completed in contract time.

On the next Friday, Mr. van Bronk invited me to his office.

"Great news," he said. "Louisa has got her Archimedes by the scruff of the neck, and is swinging him out over the abyss of matrimony. She has the footings all prepared and will let him down on them Sunday afternoon. The wedding will be pulled off in the living room. I'm to give away the bride and you are to be best man."

"Best man! I don't know what the deuce a best man does."

"Got a dress suit?"

"Yes."

"And a white tie?"

"No."

"Well, I've got an extra white tie. You are to stand as stiff as the bridegroom, if you can. If there is anything more to do Louisa will push you around. She picked you and knows what to do with you."

I could not guess where the hostess had found such a wealth of white lilies to decorate the living room. She must have exhausted the stock of half a dozen green houses.

The guests filed in: the two philosophy students; three men from the engineering staff, strangely animate, for engineers; three school teachers, at first a bit chilled by Mrs. van Bronk's lofty courtesy but warmed up by van Bronk's bubbling good humor; Louisa's school principal, a man with weathered professional features veneered with suavity. The minister arrived; Louisa came in looking incredibly young and beautiful, Woodward stiffer than usual. I did my best to match his stiffness. Louisa gently pushed me into my place, and the proceedings began.

The minister was a bit long-winded but at last came to the point of pronouncing James Woodward and Louisa Winthrop man and wife. Woodward kissed Louisa and declared:

"The best man has got to kiss the bride."

I had grown up in a non-kissing family and non-kissing schools. I was not thrilled with the privilege being conferred on me. But I took two slow steps toward Louisa and she took three quick steps toward me.

"It was *you* who saved the day," she whispered as she offered her lips.

I meant to give her just a sparrow's peck kiss, but she gave me kiss enough for two. I felt my neck growing warm, and instantly my cheeks began to burn.

"Say folks," said the bridegroom, "the blushing bride ain't blushing, but the best man is blushing like a beet. Now what do you make of that?"

What they made of it was a roar of laughter which helped not at all to drive my blood back to where it belonged.

I was looking forward to a semester of leisure. For I had finished my courses and passed my examinations. I had written my doctoral thesis. It had been accepted by the Faculty and was in the printer's hands. In June I would become a full-fledged Ph.D., "registered and pasteurized," as van Bronk put it.

A letter from a Middle Western college came to my chief professor. There had been a death in the college faculty; the professor in the field where I was working. They needed an instructor, at once. My chief had given my name, and I received a registered letter telling me that I had been appointed instructor and would have to meet the classes in ten days.

At that time young scholars were looking out as anxiously for teaching positions as Robinson Crusoe looked out for sails. I packed my belongings, bade good-bye to my entertaining host van Bronk and my silently courteous landlady, shook Woodward's stiff, cold hand. Louisa kissed me again and I lived up to my expected part in the transaction. This time I did not blush. I was growing up.

When a Columbia Ph.D. leaves New York for exile

in the West, he promises himself that he will visit the city soon, and often. What are vacations for? He soon finds vacations, for a young scholar on the make, are too valuable to throw away on visits. There is a lot of work for him to do at home. If he does get away from home, he goes to one of the expanding universities to sit at the feet of the great scholars scattered through the country; men like Von Holst of Chicago, with his Teutonic slant on America, or Jacques Loeb in California, a biologist to be sure, but a man whose mind ranged freely and with clear insight over the whole terrain of human knowledge.

And so it was ten years before I found myself in New York, in the new Pennsylvania Station.

I had kept up a desultory correspondence with some of my friends of student days. One of them, the Neo-Hegelian philosophy student, had invited me to have lunch with him in Wall Street the day of my arrival.

He was employed in a brokerage house, and as I discovered at lunch, regarded a professor from the wilds of the West as an object of humorous pity. Why shouldn't he? He handled personally the account of a member of J. Pierpont Morgan's family.

While I was waiting for him in the lobby, a man came up from behind me.

"Hello, Edgar."

Van Bronk! Looking just the same, though perhaps a bit stouter.

"Tied up for lunch, Edgar? Yes? What are you doing this evening?"

"Nothing."

"Be here at four. My chauffeur will come by to pick us up, and we'll drive out to my igloo in Westchester. I can put you up for the night if you can stand the cold."

It was July, and very hot. Plainly van Bronk still had the habit of floating above the facts in his conversation.

I was there at four. Van Bronk soon appeared and we went out to find his car. It was the biggest and most cumbersome I had ever seen—a Rolls Royce. It was the most comfortable car I had ever sat in. The paving of the avenues was not yet perfect. But the car took the bumps in its stride and transmitted little of them to our comfortable seats.

"You may know," van Bronk said, "I'm off Tammany boss-ship for life. I'm president of a real estate concern. It's a much better graft—twice as lucrative. And now I am on the side of the angels. I can damn the bosses with the damndest. Of course if a boss tips me off on a good thing, I'm friendly with him, but I kick like a Texas steer when he comes around to shake me down. I'm still a Democrat but I'm all for President Taft. He knows that business is the life of America and does what he can for it.

"You're lucky that you got your education in Columbia while there was a little sense in the Faculty, under the layer of dust. Now they are running after that man Roosevelt like pigs after a wagon of corn. That man ought to be deported to the Cannibal Isles.

"One of your old professors has published a book pushing the idea of an income tax. Actually. An income tax would be the ruin of America. Why should a man work hard to grab money if the Government can stick its greedy fingers into his pocket?"

He looked as if he meant what he was saying. But there were points in his talk that indicated to me that he was the van Bronk I had known, saying dogmatically what he didn't believe at all.

"Mr. van Bronk, are you happier in real estate than you were as a Boss?"

"Well, now that's hard to say. In my years as Boss, I did an awful lot of things for little people, people who found themselves in conflict with laws they didn't under-

stand, laws that shouldn't have applied to them. Sometimes I had to skate on pretty thin legal ice. I may have
heard it crack but I never broke through. There wasn't
anything in it for me. I helped people for nothing. Now
I only help myself. And somehow I like best to think of
the times I helped people for nothing. I know that's
wrong, in this age of the almighty dollar."

We were traversing the country roads of Westchester,
turning sharp corners and more sharp corners. I was
reminded of the arithmetic problem of the frog in the
well, jumping up three feet and falling back two. But
we finally entered a rather steep road, rich in potholes
and thank-you-ma'ams which the Rolls Royce negotiated
without protest. Ahead was van Bronk's "igloo," a huge
red brick house on a commanding height. The car
stopped at the steps and Mr. van Bronk and I mounted
to the veranda, which looked like a quarter acre of blue-
painted floor.

"Let's sit here and wait for Mrs. van Bronk. She has
a job that brings her the independent income she needs
—and it doesn't come indirectly out of my pocket. She's
in the Bureau of Accounts. What she does there I don't
know, and I doubt that she knows. But she has a wonderful secretary who knows all about it. Every morning
she runs down in her little Packard and gets home about
this time. There she is now, coming up the road."

Her little Packard! It was a huge car wheezing like
a stranded whale over the bumps. It stopped at the
steps. She came up and gave me her warm hand.

After dinner Mr. van Bronk and I sat in the smoking
room, sipping coffee and Chartreuse.

"Mr. van Bronk, do you know what has become of
Louisa and her Archimedes?"

"Oh, yes. They are in Guatemala. She made him take
the job. He was awfully afraid of the fever, but I guess
she thought, a little fever might limber him up. It's an

English concern, and the English pay engineers about five times what we pay. The English engineer is considered a member of the aristocracy and has to be paid accordingly."

"And do you know what became of that inspector who tried to stop the work on the viaduct?"

"I got him fired. He was a crook. It took me four months to do it."

I had been hearing sounds upstairs, as if men were moving furniture. But I was not prepared for the surprise I had when I entered the room assigned to me for the night. My old room of 115th Street! Every piece of mahogany I had in that room was here, and no other furniture, placed exactly as they were placed then.

I sat in my Chippendale chair and rested my elbows on the Hepplewhite table. That kind Mrs. van Bronk had meant to make me feel at home. But the sudden resurgence of the past set my mind reviewing the intervening ten years, the things I had not done though I should have done them, the things I had done I should not have done. For the first time in my life I felt old. I was old, thirty-five.

In the morning the Rolls Royce threaded its way by stony country roads to the Albany Post Road, down the road to a little bridge, veering west to the Riverside Drive. In a quarter of an hour we were on the viaduct.

The car stopped on the familiar approach.

"One of these days," Mr. van Bronk said, "you may be in an awful jam here. Busses and autos trying to climb over the top of one another. There will be more weight on the approach than those arches and the contraption for handling them. But you can be easy about the foundation. As you know, it is stabilized by a thousand-dollar flying buttress, put in the right place."

ALVIN JOHNSON

Born in Nebraska in 1874, Alvin Johnson attended the University of Nebraska and Columbia University, where he received his Ph.D. degree in 1902. He has, in addition, received honorary doctorates from Nebraska, Brandeis, Yeshiva, Brussels, Algiers and Heidelberg, the New School for Social Research and Hebrew Union College. Mr. Johnson has taught economics at Columbia University, Nebraska, Texas, Chicago, Stanford and Cornell. From 1922 to 1944 he was president of the New School. From 1915 to 1925 he was an editor for *The New Republic* magazine. He also was associate editor for the *Encyclopedia of the Social Sciences* from 1928 through 1934. He has contributed articles to the *Yale Review*. Mr. Johnson has published a number of books on economics, including *Introduction to Economics*, 1907, and *Essays in Social Economics*, published by the New School in 1955; two novels, *The Professor and the Petticoat*, 1913, and *Spring Storm*, 1928; an autobiography, *Pioneer's Progress*, 1930; and a book of short stories and sketches, *John Stuyvesant, Ancestor, and Other Stories*, 1920. Mr. Johnson's previous short-story collection, *The Battle of the Wild Turkey and Other Tales*, was published in 1961. During World War II, as chairman of the Committee against Discrimination, Mr. Johnson drew up the bill that became New York's law against discrimination in employment and set up the enforcement agency, SCAD. He lives in New York City during the winter and in Nyack, New York, during the summer. Mr. Johnson's wife, Edith Henry Johnson, who died in 1961, tutored each of their seven children up to their college years.